K. M. Ryan

THE REUNION

WHAT IF
BOOK 1

K. M. RYAN

Paperback ISBN: 9798617464704
Hardback ISBN: 9798544097853

Cover design by Pink Ink Designs
Content proofread by Elisabeth Kauffman
Book design by Vellum
Author photo taken by Atlas Photography

Published by Misty River Publishing, LLC
Nine Mile Falls, WA

www.authorkmryan.com

To my husband Cameron and best friend Jeremy,
to without whom, this wouldn't have been possible.

ACKNOWLEDGMENTS

This book wouldn't have been possible without the help of so many.

To my husband Cameron for encouraging me to write daily and wrangling our toddler so I could do so on many occasions.—Who also encouraged me to take up writing full-time rather than it just being a hobby. To my best friend Jeremy, who read my book more than anyone else and encouraged me to continue when I wanted to give up.

To my mom for sending me articles about publishing ever since I expressed an interest in writing as a teenager. To my dad for giving me sound tax advice to make all of this possible. Despite us both being CPAs, sometimes a girl still needs her dad!

To my very first editor Elisabeth Kauffman, who helped me see the flaws in my manuscript and encouraged me to re-write it.

To my many, many friends, family, and beta readers who read through my book and made huge critiques that helped me re-write this book on numerous occasions: Kim Rogers, Kris Barnes, Jennifer Lyles, Jennie Jaquish, Pam Halliday, J.C., Sheri Bolen, Kerry Lee, Sonia Palermo, Jenna Britton, and Kimberly Miller.

CONTENT WARNING

Dear Reader,

This book contains content that could be sensitive for some read-ers. If you prefer not to know, please discontinue reading this section and continue on with the book.

The Reunion has a few instances of discussions of childhood sexual abuse involving one character. While it doesn't go into great detail, please make an informed decision if this book is right for you.

Thank you,

K. M. Ryan

1

Abigail stared at the flyer in her hand wondering why she was so stupid. The bold letters read "Modesto High School 10 Year Reunion." It should have read, "Come see all of the assholes you went to school with." But, alas, it did not.

"Fool," she muttered.

"Did you say something?"

She looked up at her Uber driver, who was staring at her through the rearview mirror, his expression a mixture of confusion and impatience as he watched her.

It was then that she realized they had arrived at the bar and he was waiting on her to get out. She shoved the flyer into her purse and thanked him before stepping out of the car onto the sidewalk.

The flashy fluorescent lights of the bar were blinding as the sun set behind her. The summer California air was warm around her, allowing her to wear her little white skirt and beaded teal tank top without needing a sweater. The stilettos on her feet caused her to wobble on the uneven sidewalk. She didn't know what she was thinking. Such an incredibly stupid idea. Who the hell wears stilettos anyway? They're so impractical. At that moment, she wished for a pair of flip flops. Almost reaching into her purse for them, she realized she didn't have them with her purely for that reason. She was going to be forced to wear these horribly uncomfortable shoes all night.

Standing in the doorway, she hesitated on entering. A table set up near the front door showed various classmates checking in, but she couldn't move her feet.

"Screw this."

She turned around and walked to the curb, looking around for an easy escape route.

Damn it! Why can't there be yellow cabs like there used to be?

Digging her phone out of her purse, her finger hovered over the Uber app when a text came through.

Are you there yet? You better be there!

Al, her best friend and her boss, had been nagging at her for months to attend this reunion. It was a lot of "But you could meet someone, Abi," "But people change," and "But you might really love seeing everyone."

She sighed and called him, holding the phone up to her ear, but attempting to stay out of sight from everyone in the bar.

"Tell me you did not leave already," he said. "If you did, you're fired."

She rolled her eyes. "You'd never fire your best friend."

"Watch me. There are plenty of skilled dental hygienists out there. Just because you're my best friend, I won't necessarily keep you employed."

"I'm rolling my eyes at you."

He laughed. "Girl, please tell me you haven't left yet."

She sighed loudly and ducked against the building, worried someone might see her. "I haven't gone in yet."

"What are you waiting for?"

"I'm not sure I want to do this, Al. It seems like such a waste of time."

"Abi, tell me this. Did you curl your hair?"

Her fingers instinctively went to her normally stick-straight, brown hair and felt for the shoulder-length locks she had meticulously curled. They were still intact. "Yes."

"Are you wearing that cute little white skirt?"

She looked down at herself. "Yes."

"Stilettos?"

"Yes, but they were an awful—"

He cut her off. "Then you're all set. Now sway that ass and march inside. Stay at least 30 minutes, and if you hate it, I'll never ask you to do anything ever again."

She hiked an eyebrow. "Ever again?"

"Never, ever again."

Pulling her lip between her teeth, she squinted her eyes out at the street, considering calling an Uber. But Al's proposition would be a great thing to hold over his head. Especially since she *knew* he would inevitably ask for something. Because there was no way she was going to enjoy her reunion. No. Possible. Way.

"Deal."

~

TAKING a deep breath before walking in, Abigail whispered, "Here goes nothing."

She made her way over to the now empty check-in table and smiled. "Hi, I'm Abigail Green."

The girl at the table glanced up, and then looked her up and down. Her name tag read, "Jessica Bench."

Abigail sighed. Seeing Jessica only reminded her of the time she slapped Abigail's books out of her hand in the hallway, scattering them across the floor with everyone laughing. No one bothered to help her pick them up. Somehow Jessica thought that made her cool. Apparently other people thought so too as she had an abundance of friends. Abigail thought everyone was only friends with Jessica out of fear of her humiliating them. But maybe not. After all, Abigail didn't have a bunch of friends and she was nice to everyone.

And then there was the time that Jessica stole her best friend...

"Well, hello Abigail. It's good to see you again." Her smile almost seemed genuine. They had art class together every year, so even though their high school was a decent size, Abigail couldn't completely avoid her. Abigail always tried to sit on opposite ends of the room from her, which wasn't usually a problem with Jessica being popular and having so many followers. Generally, there weren't seats open next to her, so Abigail lucked out in that sense.

"Hi, Jessica. How are you?"

She smiled again and handed Abigail some tickets and a name tag. "I'm doing well. Thanks for asking. Here's your name tag and two free drink tickets."

She thanked her, and tried to peek at the list to see if any names jumped out at her before walking over to the bar. She was slightly puzzled by the exchange, but Jessica didn't matter to her now, so she brushed it off.

Abigail's fingers tapped nervously on the bar as she looked around the room. The bar was on the smaller side, but large enough for their class. Several booths lined the walls with tables filling in the middle of the room. Various groups of people were seated at the tables eating appetizers or burgers. She considered ordering a meal, but knew she wouldn't have time to finish it. Not that she thought she could eat it anyway with the way her stomach was tied in knots. Trying to make small talk with people she barely knew was very difficult for someone who was somewhat introverted.

The floors were wood with various areas discolored, probably from the many drinks that had been spilled over the years. High school memorabilia covered the white walls, barely leaving space for anything else.

Ordering a margarita, she sat on a barstool observing the room again. There were probably a good fifty people there so far. Most of them she didn't recognize so she made an effort to snag a peek at their name tags without being so obvious. Several people approached her and made polite conversation. John, the captain of the football team, came over and chatted easily while he was ordering a drink. To Abigail, John represented the group of guys who stood off to the side rating the girls in the class by who was "worthy" to take to prom. He noticed her one day and she heard him rate her a two out of ten. At the time, the pain that came over her was insurmountable, but thinking about it now, it was petty. She wondered if he was judging her now, but his eyes said otherwise. When he walked away, she stared after him somewhat confused. Maybe Al was right. Maybe people had changed.

Overall, she was enjoying herself and starting to loosen up. Despite that, she kept her eyes on the time so she could duck out right after thirty minutes had passed with the intention of calling Al immediately to let him know he lost.

Only five minutes to go.

She stood up and ventured away from the bar to mingle closer to the door. Every person she had come across so far was actually cool. Like, cool enough that she would be friends with them, something she never thought possible.

But, alas, she had a bet to win. She peered at her watch. One minute. Tick tock, tick tock.

The second hand hit the twelve and she took a step toward the door when she saw him.

Logan Campbell.

The most beautiful man in their class and the man she had a crush on all through high school. No, she was in *love* with him all throughout high school. Of course he never paid her any attention. She wasn't popular. But, unlike most of the jocks in school, he was nice to everyone.

He was wearing a pair of dark jeans that hugged in all the right places. His dirty blonde hair was mussed and the white button-up shirt he was wearing reflected well against his tanned skin. He stood at around six feet tall and every inch of him was gorgeous.

Her heart immediately began to race. She needed a drink. She went to the bar, suddenly forgetting that she was about to leave so she could declare victory. Throwing her head back, she took a healthy gulp of her margarita to empty the glass. She definitely needed more alcohol in order to not make a complete fool of herself. She used her last free drink ticket to get another margarita and also ordered a shot of tequila. Patron, to be exact. She needed top shelf liquor tonight—no cheap shit.

"Make that two."

She turned around to find him standing behind her. Logan. The scent of his cologne washed over her and smelled musky. That was enough to make her want to turn and run away before she did something embarrassing. She bit her lip and tried to resist the urge to touch him as her back pressed up against the bar, her fingers gripping the edges. A faint smile crossed his face, and his beautiful green eyes watched her. His chiseled jaw and defined cheekbones made him look older. He was freshly shaven and had perfectly straight, white teeth.

"Hi Logan," she managed to say, putting her hand in something sticky. Shit.

"Abigail. It's good to see you." He paid the bartender for their shots and then handed her a napkin. She flushed and didn't even have a chance to protest him buying the drink.

"You can buy the next round."

She agreed to that, but only because it was too late for her to pay for her first shot and he wasn't about to accept cash.

"Shall we?" He gestured at the shots. She pulled off the napkin sticking to her fingers and slowly turned to face forward. They each picked up a glass and clinked them together. She licked the salt off the rim and took the shot fast, immediately biting into a slice of lime afterward, which the bartender had set on a plate in front of them. The bitter liquid glided down her throat and warmed her. She didn't normally take shots, and it had been several years since she had partied. She didn't know how it would affect her, but she immediately felt like it was dulling her senses. Most likely it was more of a placebo effect this early in the game, but what did she care? It was doing the job.

Logan ordered a scotch on the rocks when the bartender set her drink down. She picked it up and wasn't sure what to do. Did she stay and make conversation, or did she try to mingle with everyone else?

She fidgeted awkwardly wanting desperately to have an excuse to stay.

"So, what have you been up to?" he asked.

"Well," she laughed and tucked some hair behind her ear, suddenly glad she had taken the time to curl it. "I'm just sitting here drinking."

"No," he laughed. "I mean what have you been up to in life the last ten years? What do you do for a living?"

"Oh. I, uh, I'm a dental hygienist."

"Oh really? Do you enjoy it?"

She nodded. "Yes." She leaned back against the bar trying to relax again. Just when she had started to loosen up, this man threw her off her game. "I mean, honestly, I went to school for the job because of the awesome work hours."

He laughed loudly as his drink sloshed around in his cup. "I wish I could say the same thing. Well, I did the same thing a bit, but that hasn't worked in my favor. I'm a financial advisor. Ideally, I'd be working for myself and making my own hours, but I'm currently working for a firm who controls everything at the moment."

"So, why don't you quit and start your own practice?"

"That's a good question. I guess I just haven't had the balls to do it."

Her face turned red at his choice of words when her mind immediately went into the gutter. She imagined him pressed up against her, stripping down even with everyone around them, taking her right there on the bar. She turned away and took a sip of her drink to hide her face, attempting to clear her mind of her dirty thoughts.

"Abigail," he said.

Her face heated. *Shit*, she thought, *did he know what I was thinking*? "Call me Abi."

"Abi," he smiled and then gestured at the bar. "I think you leaned into that spilled drink."

If embarrassment could kill someone, she would be dead. Her face flushed as she pulled away from the sticky mess which was now on the back of her shirt.

Luckily, she didn't have to think of something to say because a few other people from their class came over to start up a conversation with them. Among them was a former friend of Abigail's—Kailynn, the friend Jessica stole.

Throughout high school and their childhood, the two were basically inseparable until senior year when Abigail heard Kailynn trashing her behind her back to Jessica and a group of her friends. Kailynn quickly became friends with them and dropped Abigail, not that Abigail would have stayed friends with her after that. One of the most hurtful experiences of her high school career was hearing her best friend talk about her lack of talent in painting, Abigail's favorite hobby. Abigail never claimed to be talented, but all throughout her childhood, she spent a great deal of time in art classes and was always told by her teachers she would go somewhere with it. She originally applied to colleges to get an art degree, but slowly switched to dental hygiene after a rumor went around school about her lack of talent. She was ashamed to say she never fully recovered from it.

"Abi, hi," Kailynn said.

Abigail stared at her and considered walking away, but decided to wait to see what she had to say. Plus, Logan was still beside her and she wasn't ready to walk away from him yet.

"Hi, Kailynn." Abigail immediately turned around and ordered another margarita, no longer embarrassed by the stain that was probably gracing her back. If she was going to have to deal with every mean person in her class, the alcohol was going to be necessary.

"Abi, I just wanted to say I'm sorry for everything that happened in high school."

She kept her back to Kailynn as she waited for her drink. That woman had thrown twelve years of friendship away to be popular. She never found out why, and while she was curious, she didn't really have a desire to ask at this point. Not here. Not with Logan so close by. She'd rather spend her time talking to him since she wasn't sure she'd ever see him again. And he had never done her wrong.

Kailynn stayed quiet while she waited for Abigail to turn around, and Abigail began to wonder if she had walked off. But when Abigail turned back around, Kailynn was still there.

"I know what I did was mean and petty, and you didn't deserve it."

She considered yelling at her and demanding answers, but this wasn't the time nor the place. She swallowed the lump that seemed to form in her throat. "Thank you for apologizing."

Kailynn looked relieved by the response. "Could we possibly get together sometime and catch up?"

Abigail considered saying no, but she wasn't sure she wanted to quite yet. She did want to know what happened, but at the same time, she wasn't sure she could let Kailynn back into her life after that much betrayal. Then again, it had to have taken a lot of courage on Kailynn's part to even approach Abigail, so what could it hurt? Al's words came back to her—people change.

"Sure." She could always change her mind later.

Kailynn looked elated as they exchanged phone numbers. She promised to call and then walked away.

Abigail turned back to the conversation that Logan was involved in. Shortly after, the reunion planners stood on the bar and asked everyone to grab a shot on the house to celebrate them all being there. She, of course, grabbed another shot of tequila as she didn't want to start mixing her liquors. Logan did the same. It took several minutes for everyone to get a shot, and watching the bartenders working so fast was amazing. Logan's eyes burned into her, but not wanting to make awkward eye contact and not knowing what to say, she kept her eyes on the bartenders. After fifteen minutes, everyone had a shot in hand, and they all toasted them in the air and drank together.

She swayed briefly as she set her empty shot glass on the counter. The liquor helped give her some liquid courage and she soon became more outgoing while chatting with a lot of the former football players at the bar. They laughed together and clinked their glasses while making ridiculous toasts.

≈

LOGAN WANDERED OFF TO CHAT, but kept a watchful eye in Abigail's direction. Once in a while he would catch her eye and he would smile at her. She always seemed to turn away abruptly, which he found amusing.

She's so adorable, he mused. Taking another sip of his second scotch he was slowly nursing, he worried she was going to get drunk too fast. He held back on his alcohol intake in case he needed to help her home, the thought of anything happening to her tearing at his heart. She always seemed unreachable in high school, but here she was, finally within reach.

In the past, he only had the courage to speak to her once, and it didn't go well. She kept to herself, but he knew she was a good person. She was always willing to help a classmate out, and he watched several times as she would tutor a student who didn't seem to understand a topic. Or when someone would fall in the hallway, she was the first to help pick up their belongings. When he finally worked up the courage to ask her to prom senior year, he never got the chance. His grandfather had passed away and his family was leaving town for the funeral which happened to be the same weekend as prom. He had always kicked himself for not asking her to any other formal in their four years of high school and prom had been his last chance.

By midnight, most of their classmates had left. She sat at the bar with a group of the few men remaining and asked to close out her tab. Logan strayed nearby so he could hear their conversation, hoping to find the opportunity to help her get home.

"No! Don't close it yet. Let's do another!" one of the guys shouted.

"I don't know, guys. I'm feeling pretty good at the moment." She swayed on her chair and gripped the bar top to keep from wobbling over. Logan's fingers itched to put a hand on her to steady her on the barstool, but he paused when she stopped swaying.

"Last one." They looked at her, and a few raised their eyebrows. He could only see her backside, but he imagined she was contemplating drinking another and silently hoped she'd say no. He wasn't quite sure how much she had had to drink at this point but worried another shot would be too much.

"All right, all right. One shot to close out the night!" They all shouted in excitement.

Logan hesitated on saying anything but decided it would be for the best. He appeared behind her as the bartender was pouring the shots.

"Logan! Do you want a shot? I still owe you one," Abigail said. He stared into the pools of her brown eyes, almost getting lost in the depth.

"No, I'm good," he said. He put a hand on her shoulder, and she shivered in response. Not quite sure if that was a good or bad thing, he whispered, "I don't think you should do this last one."

She smiled at him. "I'm totally good to do another one. Totally good." She drew out that last word, confirming his suspicions that she was drunk.

The bartender set the shots in front of them, and she picked hers up. "Don't do it, Abi. You're going to be so sick tomorrow," he whispered in her ear. Goosebumps peppered her slender neck, and he suddenly had to resist the urge to kiss it.

She turned and looked him in the eye with her long eyelashes casting a small shadow on her heart-shaped face. She was only a few inches from him, making it incredibly difficult for him to refrain from leaning forward and closing the gap. Her full pink lips looked so soft and inviting, but the smell of tequila on her breath kept him at bay.

Get a grip.

"I'm fine, Logan. I can handle it." Then she winked at him, which was not reassuring in the slightest.

Turning back around, she clinked glasses with the other guys, and they all shouted before downing the shot. The bartender set her tab in front of her, she signed for it, and then waved at everyone. "It's been fun, fellas."

"Abigail, you should join us for trivia next week!" one of the men crowded around her said enthusiastically.

"I might do that." She smiled. They all shouted bye and went back to drinking.

Logan watched her as she stood, wobbling slightly.

"Whoa," she said under her breath, but he heard it loud and clear.

Logan grabbed her arm to steady her, worry coursing through his veins. "Are you all right?"

She smiled and smoothed her skirt down over her small ass. It clung to her tiny waist, and he had to avert his eyes before he let everyone know exactly how he felt about her.

"I'm good." She turned to him. "It was good seeing you tonight." She stood there for a minute, and he wondered if she was waiting for him to hug her, but she walked away when he didn't say anything. She disappeared into the bathroom, slightly stumbling, but he wasn't sure if it was from the alcohol, the shoes, or a bit of both.

Leaning against the wall, he waited for her to come out of the bathroom. He shifted his stance a few times, trying to look casual. The last thing he wanted to do was scare her. He tried to picture the way she would see him when she came out, and he shifted again.

Don't look like such a fucking stalker.

She stepped out of the bathroom and wobbled a bit in front of him. His first instinct was to go to her side and grab onto her arm to steady her, but he hesitated. Would that come on too strong? He realized he hesitated too long when she put her hand on the wall to guide her while she walked. He mentally kicked himself. Another missed opportunity.

"Abi, how are you getting home?" he asked.

She gave him a puzzled look. "I'm taking an Uber."

He watched as she made her way through the bar and stepped outside, following closely behind her. Her head fell back and she closed her eyes. A slight smile pulled at his lips. The look on her face was the exact sentiment he felt after stepping out of the stuffy bar they had been cooped up in for several hours. The warm night air felt amazing despite the slight scent of alcohol wafting out the bar doors.

"Please let me help you get home." She started to lean, so he stepped closer and put a hand out to steady her.

She stared at him for a minute and the silence was agony. He just wanted her to agree so he could make sure she got home safely and to spend just a few more minutes with her.

"That might not be a bad idea. I'm slightly intoxicated." She swayed.

He put an arm around her waist to guide her to the curb as his heart did a happy dance. "I'm going to contact a car to grab us. We can head to your place first, and then I'll have it take me home afterward."

He pulled the app up on his phone as she recited her address. She swayed again, so he tightened his grip on her waist. Her shirt rode up slightly, revealing a thin strip of baby-soft skin. He resisted the urge to rub his fingers across it as the heat of her body warmed his fingers.

AT THAT MOMENT, Abigail was definitely glad Logan was standing there. She breathed in the smell of the cologne lingering on his clothes and noticed the strong grasp he had on her hip. His tight, toned muscles flexed through his shirt as she held onto him. This man was a beautiful specimen that she just wanted to...

She took a deep breath and closed her eyes. She seriously needed to calm down. He was just being a gentleman.

An Uber appeared a few minutes later. He helped her into the car and made small talk with the driver.

The driver nervously glanced back at her during the commute. She caught his expression and smiled. "Don't worry. If I feel the need to puke, I'll say something."

He didn't look so assured but didn't reply. If anything, he drove faster.

Logan furrowed his brows as he watched her lean her head against the window. "Are you doing all right?"

She closed her eyes and nodded. The space around her seemed to spin. She sat upright and tried to keep her eyes open. "Everything is spinning."

He looked at the map on his phone to see how far they were from her apartment and told her they were only a mile away. She would have just told him herself, but she couldn't exactly see anything outside. It was all one big blur and the buildings and houses flying by only seemed to make the spins worse.

"Hang in there."

"Hanging," she said. She took a deep breath and focused on the headrest of the seat in front of her. Focusing on her breathing seemed to help a little bit and at least took her mind off of her drunken state. She willed everything to stay settled in her stomach so she didn't retch all over this poor driver's car. Not to mention, she didn't want to leave that as a lasting impression with Logan.

When the driver pulled up to her apartment, Logan turned to her. "I would really like to walk you to your apartment."

She smiled slightly. There's no better time to be bold than when you can blame it on the alcohol. "Would you be interested in watching a movie with me? I don't want to go to sleep quite this drunk or I will regret it. And I always worry I will puke in my sleep and drown in my own vomit." She frowned at the words that came out of her mouth. Not quite what she was going for, but at least she was an honest drunk.

Smooth, Abi. Real smooth.

A hint of a smile played at his lips. "I would love to."

He tipped the driver and helped her out of the car. She pointed out the direction of her apartment and they slowly made their way across the parking lot. She swayed as she walked, and he kept an arm around her waist to help support her. Such a gentleman.

"Would you like some water?" she asked when they stepped inside.

Abigail's apartment was small, but large enough for her at only 800 square feet. Most importantly, it didn't feel confining. There was an open-concept kitchen near the front door overlooking the living room with a tiny space on the other side of the front door that she used as a dining room. A bathroom was down the hall along with a little bedroom with a decent sized closet. Another bedroom branched off to the left with the door shut.

She made her way to the kitchen. Grabbing the counter for balance, she took a deep breath, but it seemed to make the spinning worse. Logan was immediately beside her.

"Why don't I take care of that?"

She nodded. "I guess that last shot wasn't the best idea."

She pointed out the cabinet containing the cups. He grabbed two and filled them with ice water and brought them to the living room where she flopped on the couch, kicking off her stilettos.

He handed a cup to her after setting his down on the coffee table. "Drink up."

She shook her head. "I'm too full right now."

"Yeah, I don't care. Drink up."

She squinted at him to focus on his face. He was smiling. She couldn't help the smile that appeared on her face shortly after.

"All right. But only because you're so nice about it." The tone of her voice dropped slightly as she mocked him.

He laughed and tipped the cup up as she drank to make sure she drank it all. After the glass was empty, he went to the kitchen to fill it again.

She shook her head when he came back. "No more. I promise I will drink more in a half hour."

"I'm going to hold you to that." He set the cup next to his on the coffee table and looked over at her. "What movie do you want to watch?"

She haphazardly pointed at a black DVD case on the floor next to the DVD player. "You pick."

He got up and grabbed the case, bringing it back to the couch with him. She watched him flip through her meager collection and silently chose the ones she wanted to watch, trying to will him to choose the same.

"The DUFF?" he asked.

"That's a great movie. I approve." She held a thumbs up.

While he was putting the DVD into the player, she couldn't help but watch him. Those pants did wonders on his ass. She tilted her head as his muscles seemed to flex when he squatted in front of the TV and his pants pulled tight. When he turned around, she looked away quickly, hoping he hadn't seen her admiring him.

Nice, Abi, she thought.

He smirked when he sat down. He had caught her. Her cheeks flushed. She avoided looking at him again until her stomach growled.

She propped her feet up on the coffee table and lulled her head over in his direction, letting her body relax. "Do you want popcorn?"

"I can make it." He stood up, but she jumped up right after, swaying slightly.

"No, no. I make the best popcorn ever, and I'm going to do it," she insisted. She took a deep breath and gripped the arm of the couch with her hand. She shouldn't have had that last shot. Damn it.

"I don't think that's such a good idea," he said. The concern spread across his face as he grabbed her forearm to steady her.

"Yeah, I don't care."

Her quip made him smile and he reluctantly let go of her arm as he sat back down holding his hands up in defeat. Her hips swayed as she walked to the kitchen, and with the feeling of his eyes watching her, she chuckled to herself knowing full well that she was teasing him.

She prepped her Stir Crazy popper with coconut oil and popcorn kernels. While those were popping, she slipped into the bathroom. A pale face stared back at her in the mirror. Sighing, she reapplied her lip gloss and cleaned up the eye makeup that started to darken the skin below her eyes. She sniffed her underarms, and then reapplied her deodorant. Drinking alcohol always made her feel greasy.

She slipped back out of the bathroom when she heard the popcorn maker slowing down. Unplugging it, she was about to flip it over when he appeared behind her.

"Let me do that."

She put her hand to her heart and jumped back straight into his chest. He wrapped his arms around her waist to keep her from falling over and she flushed. His rock hard body was pressed up against hers, and she immediately wondered what it would feel like to be in bed with him. She bit her lip and took a deep breath, not making an attempt to move even though she really wanted to slide her ass against his groin. His hands moved across her stomach slowly until they rested on her hips. The trail of his fingers felt like a fire was being lit beneath her clothes and she was thankful she was facing away so he couldn't see her mouth drop open. She turned around, only a few inches from him, very well aware of their proximity.

"Do you always sneak up on people like that?" she breathed.

If she stood on her tip toes, she could easily close the gap between them and kiss him... Something she had always wondered about since she was a teenager.

His hands stayed at her hips as his fingers brushed the skin below her shirt. "I don't try to."

She flushed as she put her hands on his hips, unsure of what to do with them. His abs were sculpted beneath her thumbs and it took every ounce of effort in her not to trace them.

She looked up into his eyes as he started to lean in. Then, clearing his throat, he dropped his hands and stepped away. Behind her, he pulled the bowl and popcorn maker apart.

Disappointment spread through her like wildfire. She didn't try to mask it as her back was to him. Kissing this beautiful man would have been thrilling, but she realized he didn't feel the same way. It was wishful thinking. She turned around and clasped her fingers together. He looked away and busied himself by grabbing the bowl and salt, and then threw a small smile in her direction, which she tried her hardest to duplicate. They walked back to the living room and hit play on the movie.

Setting the bowl between them, he handed her the salt so she could season it to her liking. He then leaned forward and grabbed her glass of water and handed it to her.

She sighed loudly so he would know her displeasure at being forced to drink, eliciting a smile from him. She downed the glass which he immediately got up and refilled. When he walked back with it he set it down next to her.

"I'll bug you again in a half hour."

She rolled her eyes and then cracked a smile at him, so he would know she was giving him a hard time.

She appreciated his attempt to take care of her. And her body would definitely appreciate it tomorrow, but right now, the thought of drinking anything else just made her want to puke.

Eating the popcorn only succeeded in making her more hungry. She swiped her cell phone off the coffee table and looked up the number for the late-night pizza parlor nearby. "What kind of pizza do you like?"

He smiled and grabbed another handful of popcorn. "Pepperoni."

She placed the order for a medium pepperoni pizza and breadsticks and went back to watching the movie.

LOGAN WATCHED her out of his peripheral vision and longed to put his arms around her. Slowly scooting closer, he hoped she wouldn't notice. Doing the right thing and refraining from kissing her in the kitchen made him wonder if she thought he wasn't interested. He definitely wanted to make sure she knew he was interested, but didn't want to cross any boundaries in the process.

I definitely need to make sure she's sober first, he thought.

Soon the bowl of popcorn was the only thing that separated them. He was very well aware of their proximity and hoped to scoot a little bit closer. Her movement kept catching his attention, so he was watching her out of the corner of his eye to see what she was doing. As far as he could tell, she was watching him at times. He suppressed a smile.

At one point, their eyes locked. She smiled shyly and looked down, briefly breaking the contact, and when she looked back up, he was still watching her.

His fingers itched to touch her face. He reached a hand up to move a stray lock of curly, brown hair behind her ear and maintained eye contact. Cupping her cheek, her head tilted slightly into his touch. He leaned in, unable to resist the opportunity. Her lips felt soft, and an electrical current ran through his body. It was a simple kiss that lasted only a few seconds before he pulled a few inches back to gauge her reaction. He was worried he had gone too far, wondering if she wanted it like he did.

She leaned in toward him and he took that as a yes, she did want it, and inched closer, moving the popcorn bowl to the coffee table as their lips locked again. His hand circled her waist as the other slid into her hair, getting tangled in the soft curls. Her hands glided up his chest and around his neck, only making him want her more as their bodies molded together.

A knock at the door made them pull back.

Damn it, he thought. Pizza. He forgot about the pizza.

They separated as if they didn't know what they were doing. Her fingers touched her lips as she watched him for a second before she got up to answer the door.

He sat with his hands in his lap wringing his fingers together. Shit. He ran a hand through his hair and mentally kicked himself for kissing her while she's drunk.

Control yourself.

She came back to the living room with two plates and the pizza, throwing a small smile in his direction.

He ran his hands through his hair before grabbing the plate from her and taking a few slices from the box. They avoided eye contact while eating and watched the remainder of the movie in painful silence.

When the movie was over, she busied herself with putting the DVD away. He stood in front of the couch and watched her.

"I should probably get going." He glanced at his watch, seeing it was around 3 a.m. It had been around four hours since she had taken her last shot. Curious if she would ask him to stay, his hopes were shut down as soon as she replied.

"Thank you for getting me home safely. I really appreciate it." She turned around to face him, her fingers clenched at her sides.

"You seem to be a little more sober." Watching her, her pupils were no longer dilated and she seemed to be able to focus better. She no longer swayed and was walking straight.

She nodded. "I am."

He stepped past her and went to the door. She followed him but stayed a few steps back and his fingers itched to pull her to him, longing to feel her in his arms once more.

"Thanks for the pizza. It was really good seeing you tonight," Logan said.

"It was good seeing you, too."

He stepped outside and started to walk away as she leaned against the open door. He turned and smiled slightly, which she returned before he disappeared into the parking lot.

He pulled up the Uber app on his phone to get a ride and hesitated with his fingers over the button to call a car. She's sober. Running his hands through his hair repeatedly, he paced in the parking lot, closing the app. Seeing her tonight was a slap across the face of what he missed out on in high school. Leaving would be like missing out on another opportunity with her. He paced for a few more minutes and then made a decision.

LOGAN KNOCKED on her door and waited for her to answer. Taking a step back, he considered walking away again, but then planted his feet. No. He was going to do this. He didn't want to miss out on his chance with her again.

She pulled open the door and tilted her head, furrowing her eyebrows. "Hi."

"Hi. I just..." What did he want to say? He mentally kicked himself for not planning his speech out ahead of time. "I wanted to make sure you're okay."

She tucked a lock of hair behind her ear and scraped her toe across the floor. "I'm all right. Would you like to come back in?"

He nodded and she pulled the door open wider.

She fidgeted a little in front of him, tugging on the sleeves of the sweatshirt she was now wearing with a pair of shorts. Her arms crossed in front of her and she gazed past him.

He reached out and his fingers grazed her arm lightly. When her eyes met his, he took her hand in his and pulled her into his arms, suddenly feeling bold. Her arms hesitated before slinking around his neck. She felt so good with her body pressed to his that before he knew it, he was kissing her neck. His fingers slid to her hips and grazed the skin beneath her sweatshirt. She moaned and her arms slid down his arms to his chest and worked at the buttons on his shirt. He pulled her sweatshirt over her head to reveal a white lace bra and wondered briefly if her panties matched. Hooking his fingers in the waistband of her shorts, he tugged them off while his lips found hers.

The taste of tequila slapped him across the face. He let go of her and took a step back, breaking all contact.

What the fuck am I doing? There's no way she's sober.

"Did I...," she stopped speaking, but then started up again, the hurt clear on her face. "Did I do something wrong?"

"Of course not." He tentatively stepped toward her again, picking up her sweatshirt off the ground and handing it to her. "We can't do it like this. I don't want us to do this while you're drunk."

She shook her head, but pulled the sweatshirt over her head anyway before pulling her shorts back on. "I'm not drunk anymore."

"I would feel better if we were both completely sober with no lingering alcohol in our system." He wanted nothing more than to strip her clothes back off, but it was important that they only sleep together while sober, that much he knew.

Her arms crossed in front of her again like she was hiding herself. "Okay."

He sighed and pulled her into his chest again. "I've had so much fun with you tonight."

She relaxed against him and put her arms around his waist. "And I you."

"Do you want me to go?"

He hoped she would say no. He wasn't ready to leave yet, but it was getting late. Looking for signs that he was making her uncomfortable, he waited for her response. She pressed her face against his chest and shook her head.

"Are you tired?"

"If I say yes, are you going to leave?"

Smiling, he brought her back away from him so he could look into her eyes. "Not if you don't want me to."

"Stay the night?"

She took his hand and led him to her bedroom. He waited to see what she was going to do, unsure if he should strip to his boxers. The last thing he wanted to do was make her uncomfortable. She pulled her sweatshirt over her head and quickly replaced it with a tank top and crawled under the covers. Pulling off his button-up, he was left with his plain white undershirt and then dropped his pants, deciding his boxers were similar to shorts.

Sliding under the covers with her, he respectfully stayed on his own side. Looking over at her, she laid on her back, perfectly still, staring at the ceiling. A small laugh escaped him and she looked over.

"I'm sorry. You just seem really uncomfortable, and I don't know if there's something I should be doing right now to help you relax."

She smiled and relaxed slightly, turning on her side to face him. "I think I need more liquid courage."

He laughed and a small giggle escaped her. Reaching out, he tucked a few strands of hair behind her ear, exposing her slender neck. His fingers grazed it. Sliding closer, he tugged on her arm and she rolled onto her other side so he could tuck her back against his chest where she fit perfectly against him.

This is perfect, he thought.

2

The light filtering in through the curtains woke Abigail. She held her hand up against the sun directly on her eyes and groaned. Why the hell hadn't she closed the curtains? She moved to slide out of bed, but an arm around her waist stopped her. She glanced behind her.

Shit! Logan Campbell is in my bed! LOGAN CAMPBELL IS IN MY BED!

How the hell did she forget *that*! Lying perfectly still, she wondered how she was going to escape. Biting her lip, she lightly picked up his arm and slid away from him, gently setting his arm back down. He rolled onto his other side and then snored lightly.

She tiptoed to the curtains before pulling them shut to darken the room, and then snuck into the hallway, closing the door behind her. Doing a little dance, she bit her lip to refrain from squealing out loud and danced her way into the bathroom. Recounting the previous night's events, she remembered that they were about to get busy, but he stopped them because he was worried she had had too much to drink. At the time, she was a little disappointed, but now she was happy he had. While the alcohol would have given her the liquid courage she needed to let loose, she didn't want to wonder if he only wanted her because she was drunk.

What a good to honest guy, she thought. She liked that he was concerned about her wellbeing and making sure they wouldn't regret it. Her heart did a little flip flop in her chest.

She walked quietly back into the bedroom after freshening up and wondered how she was going to slip back into the bed without him waking. She lifted the covers and sat on the bed as softly as she could, but she may as well have jumped on it. Somehow moving him to get out of bed didn't wake him, but trying to get back in did. He rolled toward her and opened his eyes.

"Good morning," he whispered.

Lying on her side, she faced him and her mouth suddenly went dry. "Morning."

Him staying the night sounded amazing and all, but now that her head was clear, she wondered if that was such a good idea. She bit her lip and averted her eyes.

He moved closer to her and kissed her forehead, his lips lingering, and she was thankful she took the time to freshen up. She closed her eyes and enjoyed the feeling, all nervousness fleeing, the scent of his cologne still lingering around him.

He looked down at her and when their eyes met, they both laughed.

"Does this feel weird to you?" she asked.

"A little," he confessed. "I didn't anticipate ending up here."

Did that mean he anticipated ending up somewhere else? She frowned against the thought.

He tipped her chin so their eyes met. "I thought I'd be waking up in my own bed this morning."

He leaned in slowly toward her, and she closed her eyes just as their lips met. It started as a small kiss, but when she ran her hands through his hair, he deepened the kiss, his tongue grazing her lips.

Her body ached for his and her mind was shouting in glee that she couldn't believe any of this was happening. He pulled himself closer to her and his hands found her hips and massaged them lightly. His manhood pressed into her thigh and her craving for him increased tenfold. She tugged him closer to her and he pulled off her shorts.

Holy shit, is this really happening?!

Her fingers slipped into the waistband of his boxers and she almost purred at the taut muscles pressing against her fingers. Instead, she let out a low moan and yanked his boxers off of his hips, springing his member free.

His lips moved to her neck as a single finger rubbed her through her white, lace panties. Her hands fisted in his shirt. Pressing her face into his neck, a strangled moan escaped her mouth.

His finger slipped under the fabric, sliding along her folds. She didn't need to ask to know she was soaked. Her body begged for his.

He groaned against her neck. "You're so ready."

Her body pulsed against his finger. "Take me," she whispered. At that moment, she had no idea how she became so bold, but she needed him. Needed to feel him.

He pulled back and grabbed her panties, pulling them down her in one swift movement as he crawled off the bed. Momentarily, her heart sank. She wondered if he had suddenly changed his mind, but then saw him reaching into his pants pocket. Producing a condom, he crawled back onto the bed and rolled it down his shaft.

He aligned himself with her and looked into her eyes. "Do you want to?"

"Wait," she said. She yanked his shirt over his head and ran her hands down his chiseled chest. He pulled hers off and unfastened her bra, tossing it aside. His eyes gazed over her as he stroked his cock with hooded eyes.

She ran her hands over his chest once more as his hand cupped her breast, his thumb grazing her nipple. Her body instinctively arched into his hand, electricity shooting through her body.

"Now," she said.

"Now what?" His lips grazed her neck.

She moaned, knowing he knew what she wanted. "Fuck me."

He pulled her to him as he sank down, entering her hard. She gasped as he completely filled her, almost sending her into oblivion when he pulled back and entered her hard again.

She always wondered what sex would be like with him, and now that she was experiencing it, she wanted to enjoy every second. Her body completely relaxed as she let him take her, enjoying the feel of him entering her repeatedly, her limbs tingling in excitement. Her hips raised to meet his as they joined as one.

Her cries were quiet at first, but slowly grew louder as she entered the point of no return, her body contracting around him.

She was vaguely aware of a woman's voice, *her* voice, begging him to continue as her body continually climaxed. His fingers and mouth worked against her breasts, sending her body into overdrive. Licking, sucking, and nipping, he loved on her peaks. And she wasn't ready for it to end.

She screamed as her body clenched around his one more time, stars bursting behind her eyelids.

His voice came as a strangled groan as he pumped into her, releasing into the condom before collapsing next to her on the bed. They both panted as their heart rates slowed before he pulled her into his side and kissed her neck.

Oh my God, I just had sex with Logan! was all that seemed to be running through her head.

Fuck me, was it amazing.

Her lips lifted into a partial smile which she immediately tried to hide by coughing into her hand—allowing the perfect opportunity to cover her growing grin.

He propped up on an elbow facing her after a few minutes had passed. Her head lolled in his direction and she dropped her hand, daring a smile at him, so completely satisfied. His fingers brushed her bangs off of her forehead and a smile played at his lips.

The heat spread through her face and she knew she was bright red. Seriously. Out of all of the times to blush, it was right after they had sex. She turned her head away from him to try to hide it even though she was positive he already saw it. His fingers found her chin and he turned her head toward him. Leaning forward, he lightly kissed her lips.

They looked into each others eyes when he pulled away and started laughing.

"Well, this reunion was adventurous," she said.

"Yes, it was." He smiled as he intently stared into her eyes.

She blushed and looked away for a second before meeting his gaze head on. "Want to take a shower with me?" She bit her lip wondering if she had taken that too far. Yes, they just had sex. But taking a shower after is something someone usually does with someone they're dating, and they weren't dating.

He nodded, stood, and reached a hand down for her to take and pulled her up.

LOGAN FOLLOWED Abigail into the bathroom and watched as she turned on the shower. While the water was heating, she pulled an extra towel out of the hall closet and hung it up next to hers. When she began messing with her hair, Logan used the opportunity to dispose of the condom and wipe himself clean with toilet paper. He caught her eyes in the mirror as she was tying her hair in a large bun on the top of her head. She quickly looked away and reached into the shower to feel the temperature. When she stepped in, he followed behind her.

She lathered herself up and then handed him the bar of soap, turning away from him. He stared at her back while cleaning himself. Her skin tinged pink whenever she caught his eye and he had to smile. He didn't realize he could ever make someone so nervous. She moved out of the way so he could step under the stream of water, and he gladly did, the warm water enveloping him.

When he finished, he turned toward her. She stood at the back of the shower with her arms folded across her chest. When their eyes met, she shifted her gaze to the floor, and his heart started to thud.

Shit, he thought. The last thing he wanted was her to regret anything they did. It was too important to him for her to feel comfortable around him, for her to want to do things together, and for him to not take away her choice.

"What's wrong?"

She quickly met his eyes and looked away again, her face lighting up red. "Nothing."

Uh oh. He gripped her arms with one hand and pulled her to him. "What's wrong?"

His arms circled around her waist again, forcing her to uncross her arms. She wrapped her arms around him and leaned her head on his chest. "There's nothing wrong."

His head rested on top of hers, feeling her body sink into his, and he deduced that she was just nervous. He let out a silent sigh of relief.

The water poured over the both of them as they stood under the stream. Her hair soaked through as she leaned against him. His hand came up and tugged on the hair tie, letting her hair cascade around her. Taking a step back, he pulled them both further under the shower stream, letting her hair get completely soaked.

Water poured over his chest and she leaned back to wipe the water out of her eyes. He kept his arms around her and held her close to him as she scrubbed the makeup from the night before off of her face. He didn't mind. She was so beautiful without makeup he had to wonder why she bothered with it anyway. When she was done, she wiped her eyes one more time and opened them. She bit her lip.

Her lip pulling between her teeth was such a turn on. He imagined what else that mouth could do elsewhere. He groaned and his lips came down on hers again. He pushed her back against the cold shower wall and crushed his mouth against hers. His kisses came quickly as his hand ran down her side to her hip, not being able to get enough of her smooth skin. He gripped her hip gently but firmly and pushed himself up against her. He pulled his mouth back and looked into her eyes, asking the question again. She stared back up into his eyes and breathed heavily, not responding. His hand slid down to her center and a single finger slipped into her, warmth surrounding it as her liquid coated him. Her breath caught and her eyes rolled back slightly, tilting her head to expose the sweet flesh of her neck, his lips peppering it.

"Is this okay?" he breathed.

She moaned and gripped his shoulders, urging him to continue.

A second finger aligned with the first as he plunged deeper. "Is this okay?"

She bit her lip and circled her arms around his neck to hang on. Her legs gave way beneath her and he used his body to hold her up against the wall.

His thumb pressed her clit and his lips pressed to her ear. "You need to answer me. Is this okay?"

His thumb circled her clit again as he slowly pulled his fingers out of her. Her lack of response concerned him. Despite her seeming to enjoy it, he still worried he was pushing her too far. She gripped his shoulder and buried her face into it, stifling a moan.

"I'm sorry," he whispered and kissed her shoulder. He was definitely taking this further than she wanted, he decided.

She pulled back and looked into his eyes, her eyebrows merging.

"I should have asked without clouding your judgment like that."

He let go of her and stepped back. Her arms dropped to her sides, but not for long. She grabbed him and crushed her mouth against his. Taking his shaft into her hand, she pumped it a few times. "Is this okay?" she whispered against his lips.

He groaned and pushed his lips against hers, once again pushing her up against the wall.

She pulled her head back the best she could while being trapped. "You need to answer me," she whispered.

He kissed her again and picked her up, wrapping her legs around his waist. He paused in front of her. "You don't need permission," he breathed.

"Neither do you."

"I need a condom."

"Top drawer of the vanity."

Setting her down, he stepped out and quickly yanked the drawer open and had himself covered in no time. Picking her back up, he slammed into her as the water beat at his back. Her heat welcomed him, and he repeated the sweet assault he did in her bedroom. He pushed into her until they were both slick from sweat. They shuddered in unison and sagged against the wall, breathing heavily. Their foreheads touched as their bodies twitched.

AFTER THEIR SECOND ROUND, Logan cleaned up and stepped out to give Abigail some privacy to finish her shower—which she was more than grateful for. When she emerged, she heard sounds coming from the living room. She looked around and cursed at herself for not bringing a change of clothes into the bathroom with her. Popping her head into the hallway, she walked into her room with her towel clutched tightly around her. Not that it would have mattered if he had seen her in the towel; it's not like they hadn't just fucked twice. She laughed to herself while pulling on a pair of shorts and a tank top.

In the living room, she found Logan fully dressed and pulling on his shoes. She leaned against the wall with her arms crossed and watched him. His hair was messy from the shower since he didn't have any of his own belongings to fix it, but his clothes looked just as fresh as they had at the bar. He made everything look effortless.

When he finished tying his shoes, he stood up and turned to come back to the bedroom, but stopped short when he noticed her. A smiled played at his lips, causing her knees to go weak. He covered the distance between them and pulled her into his arms.

She wrapped her arms around his waist and laid her head on his chest, the clean smell of soap hitting her nose with a hint of cologne left on his clothes from the night before. She wasn't sure what was going to happen now. Do they go back to just being former classmates who didn't really know each other... even though they *really* knew each other now? Or do they go on talking regularly? Surely he didn't want a relationship with her. They pretty much skipped the date and went straight to the sex which screams one-night stand. She wasn't really sure what to say. Goodbye? See you later? They all seemed inappropriate for the situation.

"I had a great time with you." He laughed a little and a blush crept up his neck.

She couldn't help the smile that hinted at her lips. "I did, too. It was good getting to know you." She winked at him which only deepened his blush. She stifled her laugh with her hand, glad she had that effect on him.

He let go and took a step back while fidgeting. "Would it be possible to get your number?"

"Of course." Her heart not only fluttered, it danced.

They exchanged numbers, and then Logan walked to her door. "I will see you soon, I hope." He winked and was gone.

She stood still for a moment wondering if she would hear from him again. She figured she wouldn't. He was probably only asking for her number so it wouldn't seem like a one-night stand. Logan could get any girl he wanted, so why would he want her? A small smile crept onto her face when she realized he did come home with her last night. He chose to make sure she was safe. He could have taken any of those women home, but he didn't. Not to mention he was a complete gentleman. At no point in time did she feel pressured to sleep with him. Hell, she *wanted* to sleep with him.

She walked over to the mess they left on the coffee table the night before and halted. Her coffee table was clean. She frowned. She definitely knew she hadn't touched it last night. Going into the kitchen, she saw the pizza box folded into her trash can and the dishes rinsed and sitting in the sink.

He cleaned up for her. Her fingers found her lips as she covered them in astonishment. Grabbing her phone off the counter, she snapped a photo of the dishes in the sink and put it into a text message to Logan.

Thank you! That was very sweet of you!

A moment later her text notification pinged back. *It was my pleasure.*

She wasn't sure what else to say, so she left it at that and pushed the door to her spare room open. Her safe haven. Canvases leaned against the walls and every wall space was taken up by a piece of art. An easel sat in the middle of the room, a sheet lying beneath it to catch any splatters, and a box of paint sat on a shelf nearby. She pulled her apron off of a hook near the door and looped it over her head, tying it around her waist. A blank canvas sat in front of her as she bit her lip and chose her colors. Pastels. Filling her palette with paint, she held it in her left hand as her right worked across the white expanse of space with a paintbrush. Logan's face filled her head as her emotions spilled out in front of her.

Several hours later, she sat back and let out a sigh. A colorful masterpiece sat in front of her. A colorful masterpiece only for her eyes. A piece of her soul. An array of colors came across the canvas like a rainbow and her heart leapt. The painting was rather simple, but it meant much more to her as it depicted a bedroom, the sheets ruffled and only a few heads of hair made an appearance above the sheets, obviously showing a couple in love. She blushed. They weren't in love, not even close. But, it felt right.

She cleaned her brushes and hung her apron, closing the door behind her, feeling lighter.

3

At 5 a.m., Abigail's alarm blared. Shooting a hand out, she slapped at it until it shut off. She rubbed her eyes and dragged herself out of bed, glancing at her phone for any messages. There was one. She held her breath as she opened it, but was immediately deflated.

I'm guessing I won the bet.

She rolled her eyes, disappointed that the text waiting for her was from Al and not Logan.

You win this time. See you soon.

Damn. She shook her head at herself. *He's not required to text you, Abi. Get a grip.*

She quickly hopped in the shower to get ready for work, then applied her makeup and curled her hair, tying it up into a curly bun. Pulling her scrubs on, she ran out the door to her car, her mind straying to Logan.

Every morning on her way to work, she stopped at her favorite coffee stand. This morning she was especially looking forward to the caffeine after tossing and turning all night from not being able to take her mind off of Logan. All night she had obsessively checked her phone for any messages from him, but none came. It was stupid of her to think she would hear from him, but she couldn't help it. That was one of... no, the *best* time she had had in the sack. Was it so horrible she was hoping there would be a booty call waiting on her phone?

Al knew something was up as soon as she walked into the break room at the office, their morning gathering place before patients arrived. It may have been the smile plastered on her face that tipped him off, but he set his donut down and leaned forward.

"You met someone," he stated.

She nodded.

His eyes widened. "You slept with him."

She nodded again.

"Please tell me he's hot." He dropped his chin in his hand, a dreamy expression crossing his face. He was in his early thirties, had blonde hair that was starting to recede, and was a little on the plump side with rounded cheeks and a nose a little too big for his face. But it suited him.

She sighed and slumped into a chair. "So, so, *so* hot."

He stared at her and waved his hands. "So what's the problem?"

She pouted. "I think it was more of a one-night stand than anything." She scooted her chair in and picked at a donut from the box in front of her. Despite the fact that most dentists disliked sugar, Al always brought a box of donuts into the office at least twice a week. "I'm not sure I'll hear from him again."

He picked his donut back up and took a bite. "Was the sex good?"

She raised an eyebrow at him. "You remember when you told me about that guy you hooked up with... What's his name—" she thought for a second and then snapped her fingers—"Roberto! And you said it was the most amazing sex you ever had and you weren't sure that you would ever find better?"

"Mmm... Roberto..." He gazed off with the donut half raised to his mouth.

She snapped her fingers in front of his face. "Focus!"

"Oh sorry... I was just reminiscing. But yes, I remember."

"This was that times a thousand." She sighed and threw her head in her hands.

"Oh boy."

"Yeah, oh boy." She said while shoving the donut in her mouth.

Their secretary, Margi, popped her head in the break room and told them their patients were there. Al patted Abigail on the back as he walked by. "It'll all work out for the best."

Standing up, she drank the last of her coffee and threw the cup away before grabbing her first patient for the day.

ABIGAIL WALKED into her apartment and tossed her keys on the counter. Rolling her head from side to side, she massaged her shoulder. Something that she and Logan did during sex seriously tensed up her muscles. It was probably the rough sex on her bed or maybe even the shower. She blushed thinking about it. She didn't start feeling it until she was leaning over her first patient, and it only got worse as the day continued. After checking her phone for messages, she dropped it on the counter and vowed to not look at it again unless she heard it chime.

Walking to her bedroom, she stripped her scrubs off and threw on a tank top without a bra and a pair of her gray butt shorts, as she liked to call them due to the fact that they barely covered her butt.

Dropping on her couch, she flipped through the channels on the TV and settled on a 'Friends' marathon. Then, she continued to massage her shoulders one at a time.

A knock at her door pulled her from the marathon and she sauntered over. A glance through the peephole showed Logan standing on the other side. She sucked in her breath and leaned her back against the door.

Oh my gosh. He is here to see me.

She looked down at her attire, or the lack thereof, and glanced around for something to cover her a little more. Opening the coat closet, she grabbed a fleece jacket and quickly pulled it on. He wouldn't think that was strange. Nope. Wearing a fleece jacket in the middle of the summer when it was 90 degrees out. Not strange at all. She shook her head at how ridiculous she looked. It would have to do for now.

She took a deep breath and opened the door.

Boy was he beautiful. He stood before her wearing tan cargo shorts and a blue t-shirt that hugged in all the right places. His dirty blonde hair was mussed and he was holding Chinese takeout.

"Hi, I um..." He stuttered and looked her up and down. She pulled the jacket a little tighter around herself and blushed. He uncomfortably shifted, clearing his throat. "I should have called. I'm sorry."

She tried to smile to lighten the mood and pulled the door open wider. "No, it's okay. Come on in."

After shutting the front door, she crossed her arms over her chest. The shelf bra built into her tank top didn't offer her much support, and even though the jacket hid everything, she was going to have to take it off eventually.

He set the takeout on her kitchen table and turned around to face her. He stuffed his hands in his pockets and rocked back on his heels.

She rubbed the back of her neck with one of her hands while keeping her arms crossed in front of her. "Um... I'm going to go change." She started to walk away, but his arm swung out and caught her. He pulled her to him and wrapped his arms around her waist.

"You don't have to. I interrupted your evening and—" he swallowed and his voice lowered. "You look really sexy."

She felt the heat rising in her face and knew she was turning red. She looked down and set her arms on top of his, unsure of what she should do with them. "I really should change."

He let go of her. "You can if you would like, but it's really not necessary."

She watched him for a minute as he went into the kitchen and grabbed some plates and silverware. She debated quickly and ran back to her bedroom. Throwing the fleece off, she grabbed her bra and put it on under her tank top. It was uncomfortable, but she would have felt awkward without it. She decided to not change her shorts since he had already seen her in them.

When she came out he looked her up and down again. "You lost the fleece I see."

She smiled and tucked some stray hairs behind her ear. "I did."

As he pulled the different Chinese takeout containers out of the bag and laid them out across the table, he glanced at her. "I think I liked it better without the bra." And then he winked. Her face turned bright red as she crossed her arms once again over her chest.

He laughed and walked over to her, grabbing her hand. "Come sit down. I'm just giving you a hard time." He pulled her over to the table and they sat across from each other. "I hope you like Chinese."

They each dished up their plates.

"So, do you have any siblings?" Abigail asked. She tried to think back to high school. Usually she knew who had siblings and who didn't since their school wasn't huge by any means, but she was drawing a blank.

Logan nodded and finished the food in his mouth before wiping it with a napkin to speak. "I do. I have a brother and a sister, Trevor and Angie. They're twins and are quite a bit younger. They were a surprise for my parents. Apparently I was supposed to be an only child, and then poof." He gestured in the air as he said 'poof', his hands symbolizing a small explosion.

Abigail laughed. "I always wanted siblings. I thought it would have been fun to have someone else to experience life with. Don't get me wrong. I enjoyed all of the time I had with my parents and the attention I received, but I imagine having siblings is a little different."

"It is. I was seven when they came along. I spent a lot of time helping to care for them. It wasn't expected of me, but I liked to help my parents." He reached for the container of lo mein and added some to his plate. "Despite the age gap between us, I'm pretty close with them—my sister especially. She calls me for advice once in a while. I try to be the good big brother and help her out. They are both in college at the moment—studying business."

Pride came across his face as he spoke about his siblings. She could picture Logan sitting on the phone with his sister and doing the best he could to help her. It was an endearing thought. A small smile crossed her face.

"What? Am I rambling?"

She looked up to find him watching her. "Oh, no. I can tell you're very proud of them. And, I can see you sitting on the phone helping your sister. It's very sweet of you."

His face took on a red hue. "If I'm being honest, she has me wrapped around her finger." He looked over at her and blushed again. "Anyway, so you're pretty close to your parents?"

Abigail nodded. "I am. They are two of my best friends and favorite people in the world. They actually retired to Florida, so I don't get to see them very often."

"I'm sorry to hear that. What brought them to Florida?"

"They've both always wanted to live there. We almost moved there when I was younger, but both of them had good jobs in this area and they didn't want to uproot my life. They moved to a smaller retirement community, and they love it. I have yet to go down there to visit them. They moved a few years ago and generally come to me for the holidays."

"Maybe you'll make it down there to see them soon."

She smiled. "Maybe. They keep trying to talk me into moving over there."

"Have you considered it?"

"I have. But my life, friends, and job are all here. They want me to buy a house near them and work—" she paused. She was about to say work at craft fairs, but her painting wasn't something she mentioned to others. She quickly tried to cover it up. "Work as a dental hygienist. What I'm doing now."

He gave her a strange look, but then nodded. "I'm sure you could always find a job as a dental hygienist."

"Probably."

She shoveled food into her mouth to end the conversation. He seemed to take the cue and went on to tell her about the house he bought in an older part of town. He worked on it in his spare time fixing it up.

Not only was he smart and attractive, he was handy too, she noted.

When their conversation lulled, they ate in silence for a few minutes.

"You know, I almost didn't go to the reunion, but my friend Al talked me into it," she said.

"Why not?" He pulled an egg roll out of one of the takeout containers and offered one to her as well. She accepted it and dipped it into the soy sauce on her plate.

She shrugged. "I didn't really feel like I belonged there. People weren't nice in high school, and I didn't see a point in seeing everyone again. I mean, they didn't like me, and I didn't like them."

He studied her face and she pretended she didn't notice while picking at her egg roll.

"I liked you."

She smiled slightly at him, winked, and went back to studying her food. "You do now."

He reached out and grabbed her hand. "I did then, too."

She stared into those intense eyes for a few minutes in silence. Her eyes flitted back and forth while meeting his head-on as she tried to hold the contact. Finally, she coughed and withdrew her hand from his and rubbed her shoulder, breaking the eye contact. "Honestly, I didn't think anyone noticed me. I mean, I could have died and no one would have noticed."

"I would have," he whispered. His gaze was still on her and started to make her fidget. Meeting that look head on was so difficult that she stood up and started throwing the empty takeout containers away just to avoid it.

There's no way that was true. He never noticed me. I was invisible.

She heard him sigh as he finished the food on his plate. She didn't know what that sigh meant, but he almost sounded irritated. She furrowed her brows at him while watching the back of his head from the kitchen. She couldn't remember a time in high school when he ever gave her the time of day. Granted, she had never gone out of her way to talk to him, but he hadn't either. It seemed odd that he was now saying he noticed her. Especially when he was mister popular and had tons of people vying for his attention. She went back to the table to grab their empty plates to put them in the dishwasher. He boxed up the few remaining leftovers and put them back in the takeout bag. He didn't attempt to make eye contact this time.

After loading the dishwasher, she rubbed her shoulder again to release some of the tension and pain that had built up. Rolling her head back and forth seemed to help a little, but didn't quite do it for her. She looked up and noticed him watching her again. She dropped her hand.

"Do you want to watch a movie?" she asked. She wasn't sure if he was planning on leaving soon, but she was hoping to keep him around for a few more minutes since she didn't know when she would see him again.

"Sure, sounds fun."

She put the leftovers in the fridge and then followed him to the couch. She sat down in her usual spot and was curious to see if he would sit on the other side or more toward the middle by her. She hoped for the latter.

He sat down in the middle of the couch, not touching her, but closer than the other end. They discussed the movie choices available on the TV and ended up settling with a comedy. She wasn't planning on paying much attention, so it didn't really make a difference to her.

"Thank you for bringing dinner."

He smiled and rested his hand on her thigh, sending chills throughout her body. "You're welcome."

They sat in silence as he watched the movie. She sure wasn't watching the movie. She was too busy wondering why he had shown up tonight since he hadn't even attempted to get into her panties yet. Is it possible he didn't come for that? That would be a new one for her. That's usually what all guys wanted and the only thing they wanted. She furrowed her eyebrows against the thoughts.

A half hour into the movie, she couldn't refrain from rolling her shoulders to release some of the pain and leaned back to stare at the ceiling. Her muscles stretched with the movement that made the pain lessen. She brought her hand up to her shoulder to push on the sore spot again. There was something about massaging your own shoulders that only worked so well. She made a mental note to schedule a massage. She pulled her head up off of the cushion and went back to half-heartedly watching the movie.

Logan squeezed her thigh. "Are you all right?"

She smiled. "Yeah, I'm good."

She could see him watching her out of the corner of her eye. She didn't dare look at him because then he would question why she couldn't hold his gaze.

"Abi," he said. "Look at me."

She closed her eyes and took a deep breath before looking over at him. *Here comes the staring contest.*

"Are you in pain?"

Well that's not what she expected. She averted her gaze briefly before she met his eyes again. "I just have some sore muscles. I'm okay, though."

"From yesterday?"

She shrugged. "I'm fine." She gave him a reassuring smile and went back to watching the movie.

He patted her thigh. "Come here."

She furrowed her eyebrows at him. "What?"

He patted the spot on the floor between his legs. "Come sit."

She shook her head. "Logan, you really don't have to do that. I'm all right."

He tilted his head to the side and raised an eyebrow. "Do I really need to make you?"

She laughed. "What? You can't make—"

She was cut off by him leaning over and grabbing her. She squealed. He picked her up and sat her on the floor between his legs.

She marveled. "How in the world..."

He leaned down and pressed his lips to her ear. "I'm just that good, baby."

The blush rose up through her face, but luckily her back was to him. His breath grazed her, and goosebumps made a trail from her ear down to her arm.

His hands were immediately on her shoulders and feeling for any tense muscles. When he found one, he pressed his thumb into it, careful not to press too hard. She involuntarily groaned at his touch, and then slapped a hand over her mouth in embarrassment.

Way to go, freak.

She couldn't see his face, but knew he was silently enjoying it. He worked his hands up and down her back for several minutes as her knots diminished. Somehow, she kept herself from making anymore audible moans. Having his hands all over her made it a little difficult for her to relax at first, but as he worked his magic, she completely forgot about being self-conscious and enjoyed it. Slowly, he stopped applying pressure and lightly ran his hands along her shoulders and neck. Chills ran up and down her body at the sensual touch and she had to refrain from urging him to run those hands on different areas of her body. Her face heated, and her mind immediately dipped into dirty thoughts: his hands rubbing her through her panties, his lips on her nipples. She shifted beneath his hands and clenched her fingers into the carpet.

Slowly unclenching her fingers, she sighed and leaned against the couch. Logan's hands continued to glide along the tops of her shoulders and up the side of her neck. She tilted her head back to look up at him. He leaned forward and pressed his lips to hers. Her fingers immediately slid behind his head and played with the hair at the base of his neck. His hands slid down her sides and locked under her butt as he broke away and lifted her back onto the couch. She turned around and crawled onto his lap, straddling him.

She put her hands on either side of his face as she pressed a kiss to his lips, deepening it. His fingers grazed her butt underneath her shorts and slid forward lightly brushing her through her underwear. Her breath caught in her throat and she pulled out of the kiss briefly. She looked into those penetrating green eyes that were clouding over as his fingers slid under her panties.

Fuck, yes!

She slowly let out a breath and gripped his shoulders. Their eyes were still locked as his fingers circled her clit. She wiggled against his hand trying to urge them to explore, but his free hand gripped her waist to stop the movement.

"Logan," she breathed.

"Hmm?" One finger circled her clit and would slowly glide over it every so often while another was inserted just enough to tease her and pull back out.

She was going crazy. She wanted him right that second. "Please," she whispered.

"Please what?"

She bit her lip and put her hands in her hair, gripping, as he continued his assault. She was going to come all over his hand if he didn't stop his sweet torture.

"Fuck me. Now. I need you," she demanded. He drove her wild, and she didn't know how to express it in any other way than to demand he take her.

He removed his hands from her shorts and quickly pulled them off of her hips. Yanking her shirt over her head, he unclasped her bra in record time. He managed to slide his shorts off before she was even able to pull his shirt off.

Pulling a condom out of his wallet, he flung his shorts off to the side.

"Wait," she said.

He stopped and held his hands up. "I'm sorry."

She gave him a strange look. "No, I just want to put the condom on you."

He let out a breath and a smile came over his lips as he handed it over.

She tore the little foil packet open and and stared into his eyes, lightly biting her lip, and rolled the condom down his shaft, making sure to brush her fingers along the bare skin before it was sheathed. His breathing became shallow and his eyelids drooped.

Perfect.

He gripped her waist and, without hesitation, set her straight on his cock. She gasped.

With him sitting on the couch, she now had the control. His hands slid to her hips to try to start the rhythm he wanted, but she pulled them away from her. "No."

She put his hands above his head and gripped them with hers to trap them. The knowledge that he could break free whenever he wanted to made it more fun, and she was curious to see how long she could go on before he broke from her grasp to take control. She slowly moved up and down his shaft and watched his eyes darken. When she could see the frustration building on his face, she pulled up so just his tip was in her and made eye contact with him. She smiled slightly as she dropped back down fast, pleasure ripping through her body. He inhaled sharply.

She pulled up again and stared straight into his eyes as she continued this act, her body taking on a will of its own as she moved uncontrollably on him. His face contorted into frustration at the slow torture she was putting him through. She smiled and leaned in to kiss him, tasting lingering soy sauce on his lips. He kissed back and pulled his hands out of her grip and grabbed her waist. She was about to protest, but he silenced her with a deep kiss and thrust into her. The feeling was so good, all of her complaints fled. She broke the kiss and gripped his shoulders as he continued to drive into her. She screamed in ecstasy when they both came, her vision darkening around the edges.

With her heart hammering in her chest, she leaned against him on the couch as her body twitched. He was still inside her and neither of them made an attempt to move.

When her heart rate started to slow, she softly kissed his neck and slid her hands down to his waist. His throat rumbled.

Did she just find his soft spot? Curious, she slowly kissed his neck again and made a path up to his jaw. His fingers gripped her hips and the excitement caused her to continue.

He pulsed inside of her and slowly came alive again as she continued her path along his jawline.

"You need to stop," he whispered.

She smiled against his neck and flicked her tongue against it and then blew on the wet spot. His Adam's apple bobbed in response.

"Abigail, please stop." His voice came out strangled as his fingers tightened on her waist, halting her movement.

She watched his face as it looked pained, and she didn't dare move, not that she could anyway with the vise-like grip he had on her waist.

"Are you okay?"

"I just need a minute."

His eyes remained shut as his jaw worked, clenching and unclenching his teeth. She wondered if she should try to move off of him, but was worried she'd upset him. At the same time, she felt like she needed to give him space.

Watching his face, she tried to move, but was met with resistance. "I'm just trying to give you some space," she whispered.

His hands released her and she slid off of him quickly, taking several steps away. His hands moved to the couch cushions and clenched the fabric as his eyes remained closed.

Taking a deep breath, she grabbed her clothes and walked out of the room and into the bathroom, shutting the door behind her. That was beyond odd. She cleaned herself up, got dressed, and then remained in the bathroom for a few extra minutes trying to figure out what to do before she realized her hands were shaking. She shut the lid on the toilet and sat down, leaning forward to put her head in her hands.

LOGAN WORKED his jaw with his eyes clenched and fingers gripping at the couch cushion. The memories clawed at his eyes, blinding him and taking him back to the moment when he couldn't get her to stop. His fingers moving along the cushion reminded him he was in a different setting. This wasn't that cold room with the old carpet and rubber mats. This was a warm room with a fluffy couch.

And, he was no longer a child.

He pried open his eyes and looked around, taking in his surroundings. Then he remembered he was at Abigail's. She was no longer in the room with him. He was alone, naked on the couch, and he vaguely remembered her leaving.

Standing up, he grabbed his clothes and pulled them on after disposing the condom in the kitchen garbage. His hands still shook slightly from the memories, but he pushed them away. He would deal with those later, but right now, he needed to find Abigail.

It didn't take long to realize she was in the bathroom. He raised his hand to knock, but stopped short. What if she didn't want to see him? Should he just leave and call her later?

No. No. He couldn't leave it like this. Bracing himself, he knocked.

Several seconds passed with no sound and he considered knocking again when the door opened. She watched him with curious eyes.

"Hi," she said.

He mustered up the best smile he could. "Hey." She was wearing the same clothes she had been in earlier, but it seemed different now. She looked different. Her face was guarded, making it hard for him to read her. "Can we talk?"

She nodded and stepped out, looking toward the living room. He understood that look. It was one he had seen far too many times. It was the look of curiosity, wondering if it was the room that triggered him or if it was her. It wasn't the room, nor was it her exactly. It was her actions.

His hand slipped into hers and she looked back at him as he nodded a head briefly toward her bedroom.

She led him over to the bed and crawled on top, pulling her knees up to her chest, resting her back against the headboard. He climbed up next to her, his back also against the headboard, thinking it might be better to have a conversation if he wasn't directly facing her. Seeing pity from people he cared about wasn't something he exactly wanted to see again.

They sat in silence for a moment as she waited for him to speak.

He rubbed at his eyes, not sure where to begin. "I'm sorry." That seemed like as good a place to start as any.

"It's okay. I'm sorry I pushed you."

He took her hand in his and brought it to his mouth, pressing a kiss to her fingers. "You didn't do anything wrong."

"I hurt you."

He looked over at her, puzzlement all over his face. The pain in her eyes was candid and struck him in the chest. Turning toward her, he tugged her until she was leaning against him. "No, baby. No. You didn't hurt me."

The fact that she thought she caused him harm was laughable. She was perfect in every way, and he could never picture her hurting a fly, much less him.

"I just have a—" he paused, trying to find the right words before continuing "—complicated past. But there is nothing you did wrong and nothing you should have done differently. Okay?"

She nodded, but didn't say anything.

He wrapped his arms around her, instantly relaxing as her body heat spread over him. "Thank you for tonight. I really enjoyed spending time with you."

He knew he should have told her everything right then and there, but he wanted to be selfish and spare the looks for now. He wanted to tell her on his own terms and not because he freaked out in front of her. He wanted to take the control back and make the decisions. He wanted her without his tainted past getting in the way. So, for now, he was going to keep it to himself and tell her when he was ready.

Pressing a kiss to the top of her head, he pulled her closer. She was perfect.

4

A fter work, Abigail had a text waiting from Logan.

Come to my house?

She smiled. *On my way!*

He sent over his address and she got there in no time. The house was massive! A white victorian house with a large porch and beautiful towers on the upper story. The paint was old and chipping away, but he did say it was a fixer upper. The old paint made the house easier to find since there weren't too many on the block that looked unkempt.

She rang the doorbell and a tune played, reminding her of a carnival ride when she was a child. A silly song for such a perfect house.

The door opened, and he smiled as soon as he saw her and quickly pulled her into his arms. She sank against him. After everything that had happened the previous night, she had wondered if anything would be awkward between them. But with the way he was acting now, she completely relaxed and all worry vanished.

Grabbing her hand, he pulled her further into his house. "Let me give you a tour." They walked around as he showed her the different rooms. Her entire apartment could have easily fit in there five times over. The flooring was an old dark wood that was scuffed and needed to be refinished. There was furniture in several rooms which had sheets thrown over it to keep the dust off and several other rooms with no furniture. The kitchen alone was the size of her apartment and had a huge island in the middle. Logan told her he had already remodeled this area and she could tell. The floor had been refinished, so it was shiny. He had installed stainless steel appliances and white cabinets with glass doors to offset the dark granite counter tops.

Next, he showed her the master bedroom. He had already remodeled this room and the master bathroom attached with the same finished floor and the same granite countertops and white vanity. There was a giant jacuzzi tub and a stone walk-in shower next to it. Her mouth was agape the entire time at the beauty of the place.

Despite those beautiful areas, her favorite room in the whole place was the library. Although he hadn't fixed it up yet, she could see the beauty it possessed. She let go of his hand and walked around the room running her fingers along the massive bookshelves built into most of the walls. There was even an old ladder attached to the wall with wheels that would be used to grab books on the top shelves. She imagined what it would look like filled with books, and her paintings on the blank walls, an easel in the corner. She shook her head against the thought.

Along one wall were eight-foot windows that looked a little small on the twelve-foot walls. She went to the window and peeked out into the backyard. There was a little stream that ran through the yard with an old well and bench next to the water. She sighed at the beauty of it all. This place was perfect. It was airy and had wide open spaces that didn't make her feel confined.

She jumped when Logan's arms wrapped around her waist from behind and he laughed. "So I take it you like it?"

She turned in his arms so they were facing one another. "It's beautiful. Not to mention I am insanely jealous."

He smiled at her and she watched as he looked between her lips and eyes before he leaned in. She met him halfway and they kissed. His kiss seemed tentative at first as he hesitated on applying any pressure. She wound her fingers into his hair and pulled him down to let him know it was okay while she stood on her tippy toes to get closer. His fingers slid under her shirt and glided along the bare skin of her back, peppering her with goosebumps.

And then her stomach growled.

They pulled away and laughed. She put her fingers to her lips as the tingling started to fade. "I'm sorry. I've been busy all day and haven't eaten."

He grabbed her hand and smiled. "That makes two of us."

Logan took her into his kitchen and made them dinner after pouring them both a glass of red wine.

Watching the different muscles in his arms flex as he moved around the kitchen brought the heat to her face.

A man who can cook is the best kind of man. A sexy man... A man whom I would... She blushed at her thoughts and turned away from him so he wouldn't see it as she took a healthy gulp from her glass to distract herself. She didn't want to have to explain that.

"So do you enjoy cooking?" she asked.

He glanced back at her as he flipped vegetables in a wok. "I don't mind it. I figure if I have this large kitchen, I might as well use it."

"I'm not the greatest cook. I know how to make recipes and what-not, but coming up with something on my own is virtually impossible."

He laughed. "I like to experiment, but I've had several things go wrong."

"Oh yeah?"

He turned off the burners and started dishing up their plates. "One year, my siblings and I decided to try that phase that swept through the nation of deep frying a turkey."

She cocked an eyebrow.

"We lit the backyard on fire. Our parents weren't thrilled."

Abigail laughed out loud. "I can imagine they wouldn't be very happy."

"We weren't sure the grass would grow back, and it didn't. I ended up having to reseed it."

"How much grass did you destroy?"

He shrugged and a blush crept onto his face. "Oh, probably ten feet around the deep fryer. Luckily we did it outside and no one was hurt."

"How long ago was this?"

The blush turned crimson and he bit at his cheek as if he were thinking long and hard. "Oh, it was—" His voice came out muffled, and she couldn't make out what he said.

"I'm sorry, I couldn't hear you."

It came out muffled again when he turned his face into his shoulder.

"Come again?" At this point she realized he was embarrassed to tell her. "Let me guess," she said and tapped at her jaw as if she was thinking long and hard. "Last year?"

The grimace on his face gave him away, and she laughed loudly.

He pointed a spatula at her. "Watch it. Or I'll tickle you."

She rolled her eyes and only laughed harder. "Oh, heaven forbid you tickle me!" she exclaimed.

He dropped the spatula onto the counter and covered the distance between them in seconds before wiggling his fingers against her ribs. She squealed as he held her in place.

"Stop!"

"Or what?"

She squealed louder and tried to break free, laughing hysterically. "Or, or, or," she spit out between fits of laughter. "Or I'll never kiss you again!"

He immediately stepped back and held his hands up in surrender. "You drive a hard bargain."

He winked and grabbed their plates, setting one in front of her and then sitting next to her on the barstool.

She leaned over and pressed a kiss to his lips. "Thank you for making dinner."

They had the most delicious stir fry she had ever tasted. Part of her wondered if it was because she was so hungry, but the other part of her said that was impossible and he was just an amazing cook.

After dinner was over, she looked at the clock and saw that it was already 8 p.m. It was time for her to head home. He followed her eyes and then turned toward her.

"Abi, would you like to spend the night?"

Looking into his face was like looking into a hopeful kid's face when they were asking if they can have candy. She couldn't help but smile and nodded. She felt like she should have been nervous as they hadn't really seen each other much and had only spent the night together one other time, but she felt amazingly relaxed with him.

He led her up to his bedroom and handed her a pair of his pajama pants to change into. She was wearing a tank top under her scrub top so she didn't need to borrow a t-shirt from him. She threw on his pajama pants and piled her scrubs on the floor along with her bra.

They slipped under the sheets and he pulled her securely to his chest and kissed the top of her head. He was only wearing his boxer shorts, so she lay her hand flat on his chest and traced his abs with her finger. She had never been with a guy with such an amazing physique.

"Is this weird to you?" she asked.

He tilted his head down to look at her. "What do you mean?"

She turned her head up to look at him. "We went to high school together, never spoke except maybe a few times, and now look where we are."

He smiled. "It is a little if I think about it. I mean, I knew you when you still wore overalls."

She laughed and slapped his chest. "I loved those things. They were so comfortable."

He laughed and hugged her tighter to him. "It's a little strange. But we didn't really know each other back then, so I look at it as if we are just now meeting each other for the first time."

"Hmm... That's a good way to think of it." She continued tracing his abs as her mind wandered back to the previous night and she wondered what had happened to him to cause him to close off. She frowned against his chest. She should bring it up at some point so she could avoid triggering him in the future, but he didn't seem to want to discuss it.

"What is it?"

She looked up. He had been watching her. "It's nothing." She averted her eyes and he sighed.

"You're wondering about last night."

"We don't have to talk about it," she whispered. Secretly, she hoped they would since she was wildly curious. Not to mention that she felt like it was something she needed to know in case it happened again.

He drew in a breath as if he were trying to find the courage to speak. "When I was around six, I was sexually abused by a lady who watched me at the daycare my parents took me to. It continued for around four years. At the time, I didn't realize that it was wrong because I was so young when it started. By the time I was ten, I was starting to figure out it wasn't normal and asked my dad about it. That's when my parents found out, and, of course, the lady went to jail. She had apparently been abusing several kids, not just me."

Abigail listened in shock as he told his story, her heart breaking for the little boy who had to endure such a horrible experience and for the man in front of her still dealing with the trauma.

The silence passed between them for a few minutes as she processed.

"Your brother and sister?" she whispered, the color draining from her face. Not only would he go through it, but if his siblings did as well at such a young age, it would be even more horrifying. Especially for one family to deal with at once.

He shook his head. "No. Luckily since they're so much younger than me, they were in the infant room. Toward the end before she was caught, they had moved to the toddler room, but she didn't work in there. Thank God."

"Good. I can't imagine..." she drifted off.

He tugged her a little closer as if he was drawing comfort from her. "I spent several years in therapy, and I still go on occasion when I feel I need it." He paused. "It's not really something I want to tell people because I still feel a little stupid about all of it. You know, that I didn't know it was wrong. I feel like I should have known."

"No." She shook her head and sat up to face him. He sat up and leaned against the headboard. "You were just a kid."

He shook his head. "I know. And my therapist has told me that on numerous occasions. My parents have told me that millions of times. It's just a hard thing for me to wrap my head around. But now that I'm an adult and can look back on it, it just makes me wonder what I was thinking."

She grabbed his hands. "You were thinking that this nice, trustworthy adult was doing something to you and telling you it was okay, so it must be okay because adults don't lie."

He smiled a little and looked at her. "Why is it that what you just said made complete sense to me when my therapist has never been able to do that?"

She tilted her head. "Because I'm awesome, of course."

He pulled her to him and kissed her lightly on the lips. "You are awesome." He stared so intently into her eyes that she wanted to turn away, but something was drawing her in. It was like she finally understood him. How he always seemed to be observing her and how he always asked for permission before having sex. He didn't want to take that right away from anyone else. It all made sense.

She leaned forward and kissed him again while crawling onto his lap and straddling him. His hands slid up her back as he pulled her closer. His length hardened underneath her which made her wet in anticipation.

He held her tightly as he leaned forward and laid her on her back so her head was by the footboard. Pulling back, Logan looked into her eyes as he caressed her cheek. She nodded at him, letting him know it was okay as he pulled her shirt over her head.

He placed kisses along her neck and down her chest to her nipples. His tongue flicked out and licked one and then he blew on it. They puckered instantly in response, and she moaned, reaching for the waistband of his boxers. He batted her hand away and teased her other nipple. He continued his descent down her chest and her stomach to the waistband of the pajama pants. Untying them, he kissed her skin down the length of her legs as he pulled the pants and her underwear off.

He tossed them aside and watched her face as he slid his hand along her inner thigh. Her skin reddened with desire and prickled with goosebumps as she anticipated him touching her, but he never did. He continued to tease her as he slid his hands close up to her without ever touching her intimately.

"Logan..." She let out a deep breath. "Stop teasing me."

She reached for his boxer shorts again and this time he let her pull them off of his hips. He kicked them aside, quickly pulled on a condom, aligned himself right at her entrance, and then stopped. Looking into her eyes, he asked, "Are you ready?"

She nodded and raised her hips which caused him to barely sink in.

He took in a sharp breath as his sensitive tip hit her wet flesh. "I want to hear you say it, Abigail."

She slid her hands down to his butt and grabbed it, pulling him into her, saying the words she knew he wanted to hear. "Fuck me, Logan."

He slid into her, groaning as he filled her. Then, he pushed into her hard. Her body stretched and pulsed against him as he thrust into her. Her hips raised to match his rhythm, their bodies joining as one. As if he were releasing all of his frustration—all of his emotion from their conversation, he wildly pumped into her.

"You feel so incredible," he murmured against her.

She gripped at her hair, moaning in response.

He watched her until she saw his eyes starting to roll back when he was about to come. His ecstasy brought hers even faster and she screamed with her orgasm. He released and fell on top of her chest.

They both caught their breath without moving. He wrapped his arms around her back and hugged her to him with his head nestled into her neck. He didn't make any attempt to move as his member still sat inside of her.

She rocked her hips a little and watched his face to make sure she didn't trigger anything unpleasant. A smile slowly spread across his lips as he looked up at her. She bit her lip and continued to rock as she felt him come alive again. "Is this okay?"

"It's okay," he breathed out. He slowly started to rock with her hips and pressed a kiss to her lips and held it until they were both breathing heavily. They shuddered again with their climax and once again collapsed. Her body twitched against the orgasm and she suddenly felt very tired, yet completely satisfied.

He rolled off of her and pulled himself up onto his elbows to see her face. Raising his eyebrows, he asked, "Round three?"

Round three? Is he serious? Her body felt so exhausted after round two that she didn't think she would be able to do it. His hand slid along her stomach and down to her clit. She pulled away, inhaling sharply. "Way too sensitive for that."

He laughed. "I was joking anyway. You should have seen the look on your face. It was like a deer in headlights."

She rolled her eyes and punched his arm. "I'm going to get you back for that."

He pulled himself off of the bed and walked toward the bathroom laughing. "I guess we'll see." He stopped at the door and looked back at her, nodding his head toward the shower. "Come on."

She smiled and followed him.

5

Abigail woke up to her phone alarm blaring at 4:30 a.m. She had to set it extra early so she had time to go home and get ready for work. She rolled over to find Logan lying next to her, both of them stark naked, with only a thin sheet covering them. The memories from the previous night hit her at once. They had had sex, twice. And it was amazing.

She ran her hand down his arm to wake him. He didn't move, so she put a light kiss on his lips. He barely stirred.

She glanced down and saw that he had the typical morning wood that all men seemed to get. Biting her lip in contemplation, she pulled herself on top of him and rocked her hips against him. His eyes flew open.

"Good morning."

"It is a good morning," he said in a husky voice.

She started to climb off of him when he caught her hips. "Where do you think you're going?"

She smiled. "I need to get ready for work. I just wanted to wake you, 'cause you know, payback's a bitch." She winked at him and slid off.

He blew out a long whistle. "You're going to regret this decision."

She threw him a devilish smile as she walked away. "I guess we'll see."

Logan told her she could use his shower, so she tried to shower quickly at his house. He attempted to entice her to come to bed with him on several occasions, but she managed to turn him down every time telling herself she couldn't be late. He even climbed into the shower with her and rubbed his hands up and down her inner thighs, slightly grazing her along the way while kissing her neck. She had to stop shampooing her hair at one point when she almost slammed him up against the shower wall to do dirty things to him. She leaned against the shower wall with her eyes closed trying to steady her breathing as he kissed her shoulder, slipping a finger into her. She moaned and he smiled against her shoulder.

"Logan, I can't," she whined as her face flushed.

He rubbed along her clit and kissed her shoulder again. "But you're wet and so ready for me."

It took all of her willpower to pull away from him and finish rinsing the shampoo out of her hair. She dodged his prying fingers the best she could and she almost, *almost* caved. She let out a deep breath when she turned him down for the last time as her body ached for his.

He took a step back with his hands in the air. "All right, all right. I know when I'm not wanted."

He stepped out of the shower and waited for her with a towel. Wrapping it around her shoulders, he kissed her forehead and left the bathroom. It took her a few minutes to regain her composure and not go jump him right then and there, but glancing at the clock made her forget about him briefly. She was really cutting it close. She threw on her clothes from the day before and pecked him quickly on the lips before hopping in her car and driving home to grab a fresh change of clothes and makeup.

～

OF COURSE AL knew she had spent the night with Logan as soon as she walked through the door. Forget gaydar. This guy had sex-dar.

His brown eyes widened as soon as he saw her and he paused with a donut halfway to his mouth. "Oh my gosh."

She blushed. "How can you tell?"

"It's the way you walk. Plus the grin helps. Tell me all about it. I want details." He put his donut down and leaned forward in anticipation.

She told him she had gone to Logan's house and then everything that followed after that. A smile appeared on her face as she covered her mouth with her hand.

"Oh my God," Al said. "No wonder you're walking like you've been riding a horse all night."

Abigail choked on her donut. "Am not!"

He smirked. "Okay."

"I'm not!"

He didn't reply, only took a bite of his own donut. A few minutes of silence passed. Her body didn't hurt. She shifted in her seat to see if there was any pain she had ignored, and then stretched her legs out in front of her a bit.

She narrowed her eyes at him. "Are you being serious?"

"Oh my God, Abi. We're still on that? I was joking."

She breathed a sigh of relief.

"Or am I?"

She chucked a chunk of her donut at him which he easily dodged. "You're falling for him."

"No..." she said. She didn't fall for guys. It wasn't her thing. She had gotten her heart broken so many times in the past and had been cheated on by so many people that she had written relationships off for good. "This is just a friends-with-benefits type of situation."

He raised his eyebrows at her. "Girl, based on everything you have told me, it's definitely not a friends-with-benefits situation."

She leaned back in her chair and furrowed her eyebrows. What did Logan think they were? She assumed he thought they were friends with benefits as well, but normally when she had one of those types of relationships, they didn't bring food to each other or make each other dinner. It was more of a wham-bam-thank-you-ma'am type of meeting.

Her day at work was uneventful and as soon as her shift ended, she felt her phone buzz. It was Logan.

Won't be able to see you tonight. Working late since I took yesterday off.

Al leaned over her shoulder and read it. "Now he's telling you he can't see you tonight. Did you even have plans?"

She shook her head.

"Definitely not friends with benefits." He raised his eyebrows at her and walked away.

She quickly texted back. *I guess I can't finish what I started this morning.*

His reply was instant. *Tease.*

She smiled and went home to her empty apartment. She made herself dinner and sat down in front of the TV to catch up on some of her shows. She caught herself checking her phone repeatedly, but he didn't message her. She even jumped when she thought she heard someone knocking at the door.

Al was right. These were not casual feelings.

6

Abigail showed up at work the next morning and stared at Al in the break room, their normal gathering place. He immediately folded his newspaper and set it down. "You realized I'm right, huh?"

She nodded and flopped down on a chair. "What do I do?"

He laughed. "There's nothing to do. I mean, if you aren't happy, end it. If you are happy, continue what you're doing. I know you're anti-relationships, but what's it going to hurt?"

"I could get hurt." Her voice came out quietly.

"And you might not. You risk breaking your heart, but you'll be breaking your heart if you are happy and break up with him over the principle." He paused. "What if it works out?"

She laid her head on the table. "Why are you so smart?"

"I've been around the mountain a few times."

She could feel his eyes on her, so she propped her chin on her arm to look at him. "What?"

He shrugged. "In the last few days since you've been seeing him, you have been happier than I have ever seen you before."

A smile appeared before she could stop it. "I am pretty happy."

"So what's the problem? The title? Then don't call him your boyfriend. Go with the flow."

"I feel like that's easier said than done." She stood up and drank the rest of her coffee before tossing the cup in the trash.

What if it does work out? She shook her head, not wanting to entertain the idea at the moment. She had work to do.

THE DAY PASSED LIKE NORMAL. Nothing too exciting happened, and Abigail was about to get her last patient for the day, a new patient. She grabbed the files from Margi and stepped into the waiting area staring at the paperwork. Then, she noticed it. The name scribbled at the top.

Logan Campbell.

Her face turned red and she looked up wide-eyed to see him sitting in one of the waiting room chairs smiling brightly at her. "Um..." She looked over at Margi who gave her an odd look.

"His name is Logan, honey."

Logan laughed and stood up. "All ready for me?"

She cleared her throat and scratched the back of her neck. "Uh, yes. All ready." She brought him back to her patient room and closed the door behind him. "What are you doing here?"

"I'm in for a routine checkup." He leaned over and pecked her on the lips and then sat in the chair.

She stared at him baffled. "But... here?!"

"Sure. Why not?"

The glint in his eye and the Cheshire-Cat-like grin on his face gave away how much he was enjoying her bewilderment.

There wasn't really much she could do. She couldn't exactly refuse to clean his teeth, but at the same time she wouldn't want to do that anyway. It would have just been nice to know he was coming. But of course he didn't tell her. Why would he? He was enjoying this way too much.

She narrowed her eyes at him. "All right, well let's get started."

His smile grew as she lowered the back of his chair so he was lying down. She handed him the safety glasses which he promptly put on his face.

Jesus. Of course he looked sexy wearing those as well. She rolled her eyes.

"Why are you rolling your eyes at me, Ms. Green?"

She sighed loudly and stared at him. "Because I was just thinking... of course you have to look sexy wearing safety glasses as well. Do you ever not look sexy?" She slapped a hand over her mouth in disbelief that she actually said it out loud. She usually tried to rein in her thoughts, but it was proving difficult with Logan at times.

He laughed loudly and patted her leg. He kept his hand there as she asked him to open his mouth for her. Occasionally he would rub her thigh, but for the most part he kept it still. The heat from his hand on her leg made her nervous and made it hard for her to focus. She didn't want to ask him to move it because she thoroughly enjoyed him touching her.

She was working on his last few teeth when his hand slid slightly. She assumed it was because he shifted in the chair. She kept working away trying not to think much of it, but his hand slid again. This time she knew it was on purpose. She stopped for a minute and stared at him, raising an eyebrow. He smiled innocently and she went back to work on his teeth. Slowly his hand slid again and his fingers lightly brushed her crotch through her scrubs. She jolted.

"Logan," she whispered loudly in her best warning tone. "Stop it."

He smiled innocently. "What?"

"You know what."

"Okay, okay. I'll be good."

She was working on the last tooth when his hand slid again and he brushed her crotch a little harder. She jolted and dropped her scaler which landed straight on the bridge of his nose and then loudly clanked on the floor.

His face scrunched up and his hand pulled away as he touched his face. "Abi."

She stared, horrified at the small welt that started to form right before her. "Oh my gosh, Logan. I'm so sorry."

He sat up and looked in the mirror on her wall and frowned. Then he directed his frown in her direction.

She stared in astonishment. "Well! What did you think would happen?" She lowered her voice. "You just groped me in my office while I'm holding solid metal objects above your face."

"I was thinking that this was payback for the other morning!" he said, exasperated.

She smiled slightly. "Well, I guess this was my payback, too."

He laughed and lightly rubbed his nose. "No more getting back at each other. Deal?"

She nodded. "Deal." She leaned forward and kissed his nose. "All better."

He put his hand behind her neck and kissed her lightly, his face lingering near hers. "Yes, all better."

They stared into each other's eyes before she broke the contact and picked invisible lint off of her scrubs. "All right, you need to lay back down so I can finish or they're going to come walking in here and find us making out on the chair. And, I don't know about you, but I'd rather not explain that one."

He laughed and laid back down. She grabbed a new sanitized scaler so she could finish and then quickly polished his teeth.

"I'm going to go grab Dr. Cooper." She pointed at him. "No funny business while I'm gone."

He held his hands up in the air innocently.

She quickly left the room and found Al coming out of another room after seeing a different patient. "I'm ready for you."

He nodded. "I'll be right there."

She thought about telling him it was Logan in her room, but hesitated. She didn't want them to gang up on her, so she decided against it. She couldn't remember if she ever told Logan that Al was her best friend, so she decided to take her chances that they wouldn't know anything about each other and not put two and two together. She went back to the room where Logan was still waiting in his chair. She went over to her mirror and peeked in it. Her hair was a little crazy and her face was still a little flushed from Logan's groping, but she hoped that nothing would be noticeable to Al.

"You okay there, buttercup?"

She turned around and saw the solid welt on his nose along with a broad smile gracing his face. He had pulled the glasses off for now while waiting for Al and it looked worse when there weren't any ugly glasses on his face to distract from it. Al decided to walk in at that moment so she nodded.

"Dr. Cooper, everything looks great to me."

Al grabbed Logan's file and looked through it quickly. He reached a hand out to Logan to shake. "Hi Logan, my name is Alan Cooper. It's nice to meet you."

Logan shook his hand. "It's nice to meet you as well."

Al stared at Logan for a minute and then looked back at his chart. "Logan Campbell. Your name sounds familiar. Have we met before?"

She was standing behind Logan's chair so he wouldn't be able to see her unless he turned. She pursed her lips and narrowed her eyes at Al in hopes he would look over. She figured if he was about to figure it out, she should at least be the one to tell him, and she immediately regretted not telling him in the hallway. Things were about to get interesting.

Al glanced at her and gave her an odd look. She motioned at Logan and mouthed, "That's him."

Al raised an eyebrow and tried to fight a smile.

Logan turned around and looked at her, so she stopped gesturing and put her hands on her hips. He narrowed his eyes at her and then looked back at Al. "You're Abi's best friend, right?"

She sighed loudly and hung her head.

Al laughed. "Yes, I am. And you're Logan... Abi's 'friend'." He even had the gall to make air quotes. AIR QUOTES!

She slapped her hand to her forehead. "Al," she forced through clenched teeth. If she could have died from embarrassment, she would have. She shot Al a glare, and he laughed. Logan laughed alongside him, so she walked to the door and glared at both of them before stomping out.

"Abi, come back here," Logan called after her while laughing.

She ignored them both and dropped in a chair in the break room.

Now, I bet they are all laughing about me and telling stories. She heard the laughs from down the hall. She was happy that they were getting along, but hoped it wasn't all at her expense. After about five minutes she heard them saying bye to each other and then Al walked into the break room. She glared at him.

"Oh come on. You let me walk in there without knowing it was him. What did you expect? You didn't think we'd figure it out?"

She sighed. "I knew there was a chance, but I hoped you wouldn't. So what did you talk about? Were you making fun of me?"

He laughed and put his stuff away. "No. We just chatted and then I finished up his appointment."

"Did he leave?"

He shook his head. "He's waiting for you in the parking lot."

She hopped up and grabbed her purse. Al grabbed her arm when she walked by, so she stopped. "Abi, I like this one."

She smiled. "Me too."

Walking out into the parking lot, she found Logan leaning up against her car. He smiled at her and pulled her into his arms when she got closer. "Are you mad at me?" he whispered into her ear.

She did her best to put on an angry face. "Yes."

He looked down at her and laughed. "So I guess I need to make it up to you?"

She narrowed her eyes, not quite sure what he meant by that. But she took a gamble. "Yes."

Al walked out of the office to his car. He waved at them. "See you Monday, Abi. Nice meeting you, Logan."

"Bye, Al!" they replied in unison.

They both waved at him as he drove away. "Monday? You aren't working tomorrow?"

She shook her head. "We don't work Fridays."

"Do you want to go somewhere?"

She furrowed her eyebrows. "Like to a movie?"

He laughed. "You're cute. I mean like to Napa Valley."

She opened her car door and started putting her stuff inside, but stopped short. "What? Are you serious?"

"Yeah, I'm serious. Just the two of us and lots of wine." He wrapped his arms around her waist.

He wanted to go away on a trip with her? So soon? That was definitely more like a relationship, but it did sound fun. "Um, yeah, I guess."

He raised an eyebrow at her. "Wow. Don't sound so thrilled to spend time with me."

She laughed. "I just haven't been on vacation in a very long time. Especially not with—" Was she supposed to say boyfriend? Friend? She wasn't sure.

"Especially not with a friend?" he asked.

A friend. So he didn't think of them as anything more than friends. Which meant he definitely only thought of them as fuck buddies. It hurt her heart a little to hear him say that, but she wasn't about to say anything. At least she now knew where he stood. And she got her wish of not wanting another relationship. They were strictly sexual. Apparently. And she was surprisingly disappointed.

"I just haven't been on vacation with anyone but family."

"There's a first time for everything. So what do you say? A spontaneous trip with me?" His smile was contagious.

Her eyes searched his before she nodded. "Okay. Let's do it!"

Logan followed her home and waited for her to pack while he booked the hotel. The plan was to get up first thing in the morning and drive to Napa Valley, which was only a few hours away. While she packed, she asked him about the hotel and area as she'd never been there before. He gave her a generic run-down on weather and activities he wanted to do with her, but didn't elaborate much. When she tried to pack a bikini for a hotel pool, he insisted she didn't need one. She squeezed it into her bag anyway despite his protests. She wasn't about to go nude around other people. No way.

In the end, her bag was stuffed to the brim with a random assortment of clothes for nice events, lounging, and hiking. She had way more clothes than she could even think about wearing on a short weekend getaway, but it was better to be safe than sorry, she decided.

He wouldn't tell her where they were staying, but as long as it had four walls and a roof, she was happy. She didn't require anything fancy. She insisted they go Dutch on the hotel bill and gas, but he refused to let her pay, stating it was his idea.

They hopped in his car and went back to his house for the night and she watched him pack. He didn't grab much. Only a few changes of clothes, one fancy outfit which he insisted was for the "just in case" circumstances, some clothes for hiking, and swim trunks. She asked him why he was allowed to pack swim trunks when he tried to make her leave hers behind. He claimed he only did because she did. Likely story.

When everything was ready to go, they sat on his bed to watch TV which was mounted on the wall of his bedroom above a gas fireplace. His room really was perfect. When Logan got up at one point to go to the bathroom, she couldn't refrain from texting Al.

Going to Napa Valley with Logan. His idea.

The reply was immediate. *Definitely a relationship!*

He said we are 'friends.'

Logan walked back into the room so she set her phone aside. However, she forgot to silence it, so it went off a few minutes later with a text from Al. She flipped it over, so Logan wouldn't see the message pop up on the screen.

He gave her an odd look. "Who's that from?"

"Al," she replied.

He stared at her. "Aren't you going to read it?"

She shook her head. She knew if she picked it up to read it, Logan would be able to read it as well as her previous messages since they were sitting right next to each other. She quickly flipped the silence button on the side of the phone and set it back down.

"Is there something on there you don't want me to see?"

Seriously. Out of every guy, she had to be with the one who was so curious about everything. She rubbed her face with her hands. There was no point in lying about it. "Yes."

She could see him watching her again, so she decided to try to stare at him straight on. She turned and looked into his eyes.—Those soul searching eyes. His narrowed as he looked between hers. "What are you hiding from me?"

"It's nothing."

"It's not nothing if you're keeping it from me."

"Logan," she sighed. "I'm talking to my best friend about you. Those are my personal thoughts. They aren't something that you need to hear at the moment."

He stared at her for a few minutes longer and then turned away to continue watching the movie with a shrug. "Okay."

She watched him and he never pulled his eyes off of the TV. He knew she was watching him too. "Are you mad at me?"

He didn't look over, but shook his head.

"Are you upset?"

"Not really, no. I just find it odd that you're texting him about me when you're with me."

She pursed her lips. "I'm sorry. I was telling him that we're going to Napa and it evolved."

He nodded his head with a smile and patted her thigh. "I understand."

His attention focused back on the television. She watched him for a second before she focused back on the show as well. He trusted her. Most people would assume the worst and question everything. To say she was shocked would be an understatement.

"Are you bothered by me texting when I'm with you?" She was genuinely curious.

He shook his head. "No. Should I be?"

She furrowed her eyebrows. "I guess I'm just used to people being untrusting."

A slight smile appeared on his face. He turned toward her and grabbed her hands. "Abi, I trust that you aren't bashing me to Al, and I believe that you were talking to him about Napa and it evolved. I'm not assuming the worst, and I don't mind if you text your friends around me." He paused briefly, "Well, unless it's all the time. That would be a little annoying. But I know you won't do that."

In previous relationships, her boyfriends would usually get super mad whenever she used her phone around them, especially if she was texting. They all had a "you must be transparent" attitude. It was no wonder those relationships never worked out, but she assumed all men were that way.

"You've never been around a man who didn't mind?"

She snapped out of her thoughts and looked up at him. "I've just only ever been around men who expect you to have complete transparency about everything."

He tsked. "Everyone is allowed a little bit of privacy in a relationship. And if you can't trust someone, you shouldn't be with them."

Relationship? So this was a relationship? She bit her lip and looked over at him. No, he was referring to their friendship.

"I agree," she said.

They leaned back against the headboard and he pulled her closer to him where she laid her head against his shoulder. So this was what a trusting relationship was like.

But without the relationship aspect.

7

Logan woke to the sounds of the birds chirping and a slight bit of light coming in through the windows. It was still early and he didn't anticipate Abigail waking up for a few hours, so he tried to refrain from moving too much as to not wake her. He made his way into the bathroom to brush his teeth after slowly sliding out of bed. He quietly shut the door behind him.

After all of this time and he was thrilled to have Abigail at his side. After everything that happened the other night with his PTSD, he worried she wouldn't want to be with him. Telling anyone about his childhood was always hard for him, and he stressed about the judging look that he expected to come across her face. But she didn't judge him. She only cared for him. And because of her, he even started attending therapy again. He wanted to be the best man he could be for her.

Going on this small getaway was his way of seeing their compatibility. He already knew he wanted to spend every second with her despite them only being around each other for a week. He made a call into his office the night before and asked to use a vacation day. His boss begrudgingly said yes. Logan knew he was pushing it by asking, but figured it didn't hurt to try. If his boss had said no, he would have been sorely disappointed, but would have booked it another weekend. He was thankful he didn't have to.

He quietly padded back into the room and crawled into bed. Abigail stirred, so he stopped moving and waited for her to fall back asleep. She sighed and softly snored next to him.

He refrained from reaching a hand out to swipe the hair that fell across her forehead to avoid waking her. "I had the biggest crush on you in high school," he whispered. "One could even say I was in love."

She hummed and her eyes opened. He froze.

"I fell for you in high school. I loved you." She sighed, then she closed her eyes again and rolled over.

What just happened? Was she talking in her sleep? Did she actually hear me? He ran his hands over his hair repeatedly and stared at her for a bit longer. Her breathing was even as she softly snored.

Another hour passed before she moved again. Logan was now sitting in bed with a book, his stomach full of knots waiting to find out if she remembered anything he said.

She sat up and grabbed her neck, cringing. "Ouch."

He decided to act as if nothing happened to see what she'd say. "Morning, sleeping beauty." He tugged her over in front of him and started massaging her neck. "You were sleeping at an odd angle for a bit."

She sighed. "I fell asleep on your shoulder, didn't I?"

He nodded. "I did my best at moving you to a lying position. You sleep hard."

"Yeah, it can be a good thing sometimes."

The anticipation was killing him. He had to know if she heard him. "You also talk in your sleep," he whispered. He waited in painful silence as she sat perfectly still, her back stiffening.

"What did I say?"

He stopped massaging her shoulders as she looked back at him, worry etching her face. "Do you remember anything? You woke up at one point."

She shook her head.

He stared at her for a bit, contemplating on whether or not he should tell her what he said. On one hand, it would throw everything out on the table. On the other hand, he never intended for her to hear it. Not yet, anyway, for fear of scaring her off.

"Logan, what did I say?"

"You told me you fell for me in high school and that you loved me."

Silence deafened them as he waited for her to respond.

Yep, he decided. *I should have kept my mouth shut.*

She stared at him and slowly a deep red hue engulfed her face. Her gaze shifted down as she fidgeted in front of him. He took her hand and squeezed it.

"If it makes you feel any better, I had a crush on you in high school, too," he said.

She briefly looked up at him and gave him a smile before dropping her head again.

He frowned. "Abigail, look at me."

Slowly, she brought her face up to his and looked into his eyes. The last thing he wanted was for her to be upset or embarrassed by talking in her sleep. His eyes searched hers and then he leaned forward and kissed her. The same electricity that had been there since the first time they kissed ran through his body, but she cut the kiss short and got up, making her way to the bathroom. He got up and followed her, quickly grabbing her hand and pulling her back to him.

"Abi, what's wrong?"

"I don't want to talk about it." Her words came out short as a scowl graced her face.

When she attempted to walk away again, he gripped her hand firmly and pulled her back to him.

"Logan, does it really make a difference?" She looked him in the eyes and furrowed her eyebrows.

"Of course it does!" His eyes searched hers. "Tell me what's going on. Why are you upset?"

"I'm just upset I told you all of that. I could have told you numerous things and I wouldn't remember. And for all I know, I did.

And why? I don't know. I don't know why I said that to you. That was something that you definitely didn't need to know."

Perhaps it was for selfish reasons, but he really didn't want to tell her the truth. He didn't know that they were quite ready for that information, but for him, he was thrilled to know she felt that way about him at one point. He hoped she still felt the same way.

"Why does it matter? I'm flattered by it because I always had feelings for you in high school. I just didn't know how to talk to you." And that was the truth.

"No, you didn't."

He put a hand on her cheek. "I'm not lying to you."

She rubbed her face furiously, dismissing his comment. "Did I say anything else?"

"No. That was it."

She bit her lip and looked back up at him. "I'm sorry. I'm cranky and woke up on the wrong side of the bed and my neck is killing me."

"It's all right. We're all allowed to be cranky once in a while." He smiled tentatively at her, glad the situation was diffused for now.

Soon she was smiling back.

"You know what cures pain? Or at least temporarily takes your mind off of it?" He leaned in closer to her, a fire consuming his belly and making its way into his groin.

She slid her hand up his thigh and fingered his balls through his boxers. "I don't know. What?"

He growled as he felt the blood draining south. "You're getting close."

He pulled her clothes off and set her up on the vanity while he stripped his boxers off. Sliding her to the edge of the counter, he looked into her eyes. "Do you want to?" It took every ounce of effort in him not to enter her hard and fast right then, but he wanted to make sure she wanted it as much as he did. Nothing was more sexy than when a woman said yes.

"Yes, please."

He held onto her hips as she gripped the counter to hold her place as he rubbed his growing shaft against her sensitive flesh. Red spots splotched up her neck and up her face, and a soft groan escaped her lips, thickening his shaft. Pulling a condom on, he plunged into her. The feeling never got old. He loved every second of his cock inside of her, almost as if their bodies were made for each other.

His dick jerked inside of her as he came closer to his release. It would only be a few more minutes. As if almost violently, he slammed her onto him, trying to feel her deeper. Her moan of approval sent him over the edge, her body clenching around him in her release. He spewed into the condom as she arched her back into him sending him deeper into her.

He stayed pressed up against her while he caught his breath, his balls tingling. She leaned forward and kissed his neck. She ran a trail up to his earlobe and nipped at it. He inhaled sharply, trying to keep the negative memories at bay associated with his neck being kissed. It didn't take too much effort because she pulled away, all memories vanishing almost immediately.

"Are you ready to get in the shower?"

He nodded and picked her up, carrying her.

THE CAR RIDE was two hours long. Abigail checked her phone earlier to see what Al had texted her last night.

I'm calling the bluff. He likes you more than that.

I guess we'll see, she replied.

She tried to avoid texting Al anymore than that, but she couldn't help it at one point and sent him a quick text.

I told him I fell for him in high school.

What did he say?

I don't know. I told him in my sleep. This morning he said he had feelings for me back then, too.

And I'm sure he still does.

Their conversation ended and she put her phone back in her purse. Logan didn't say anything, but she caught him looking at her out of the corner of his eye and something about his body language said he was curious.

"I was talking to Al."

He nodded. "I figured."

"I told him that I told you I had fallen for you in high school, but I don't remember it since I was asleep."

He turned the radio down. "Does it really bother you that much?"

"It's not that I told you, Logan. It's that I wish I had told you when I remembered it because I don't want to freak you out, and I feel like that's more of a conversation to have when I can make sure I'm *not* freaking you out. It's just embarrassing."

More like mortifying, she added to herself.

"Why would something you felt in high school affect us now?" He glanced at her briefly before putting his eyes back on the road.

She didn't answer. She felt like it was super obvious that she was still crazy for the guy. If he didn't realize that, then he wasn't very observant. Not to mention she was terrified of scaring him away. She didn't want to lose him. Not now. Not after the progress they had made.

He set his hand on her leg and squeezed. "We can talk about something else."

Abigail shifted uncomfortably in her seat trying to think of another topic. Her mind drifted to Kailynn. "Can I get your opinion on something?"

"Of course. You know you can."

"Do you remember at the reunion how Kailynn came up to me?"

He only nodded in response.

"She and I had a huge falling out in high school." She went on to explain everything that happened. "And now she wants to meet up again."

He thought for a minute. "I remember those rumors circulating, but I thought they died out pretty quick."

She wasn't sure if they had. All she remembered was that they stung then, and they still stung now. It was never fun to hear something negative about you circulating, especially about something you were passionate about. "I'm not sure if I should meet with her."

"Honestly? That's up to you. But, if it were me, I would. What could it hurt? She may apologize and it could help heal some of the pain she put you through, or it won't. Either way, could it get worse?"

He had a point. It couldn't exactly get worse.

"Do you still paint?"

She startled out of her thoughts. "What?"

"Painting. Do you still do it?"

Shifting uncomfortably, she wasn't sure what to say. "Yes... sometimes."

"I'd really like to see your art sometime if you'll let me."

"I'll think about it," she whispered. "It's just really personal to me."

"I understand." He squeezed her knee, and with that, he changed the subject.

LOGAN AND ABIGAIL arrived at the hotel in the early afternoon. While he was checking in, she stood off to the side gaping at their surroundings. The swimming pool off of the main building was an infinity pool overlooking a vineyard. This particular hotel was special to him since it was one his family vacationed to for special occasions. Despite it being in wine country, there were plenty of activities for kids to enjoy.

And, boy, did they!

His family would hike around on the different trails, giving him a love of hiking and the beauty of the area. They spent hours at the pool and doing the different tours of the vineyards. Despite their young age and not being able to drink, Logan and his siblings still found the process of making wine fascinating. For several years Logan was convinced he would buy a winery. After some time, the dream faded, but he still loved visiting.

Abigail's gasp brought him back from his memories and he

watched her staring out over the view in front of the pool. You could see for miles. It was one thing he loved about the area. It was vast and beautiful.

Logan smiled and put his hand at the small of her back to lead her to a golf cart operated by the resort that would take them to their room. They hopped on and drove for a while, without seeing anyone along the way. The driving paths were separate from the walking paths, adding to the serenity of the place. The paths were paved and several smaller ones branched off of the main one.

The golf cart finally turned down a little path called "Lovers' Lane". Abigail raised an eyebrow and looked over at him, but he only smiled back.

The driver pulled up to the front door of a small cottage. He carried their bags and Logan tipped him before he drove off. Abigail walked inside and gasped once again. It was a small cottage not more than 1,000 square feet. It had a king-sized bed off to the left and large bathroom and small kitchen on the right. The bathroom had a jacuzzi tub, a double vanity, and a beautiful stone shower with full body sprayers.

Logan took her hand and led her out a back door onto their own private deck. There was an outdoor shower off to the right that was surrounded by lattice with vines and roses climbing up the sides. They had their own private hot tub off to the left and two lounge chairs nearby.

Aside from the amenities, the view from their room was astounding. Their cottage overlooked a large vineyard with mountains in the background. No other cottages could be seen around them as large trees filled any gaps on the sides of the small dwelling.

"Oh my gosh, Logan. This is so beautiful."

He walked over to her where she was leaning against the railing looking at the view. Wrapping his arms around her waist, he rested his chin on her shoulder.

She turned in his arms to face him. "I have to pay you for half."

He frowned at her. "That's not happening."

"But I'm benefiting from this weekend too."

"I don't care. This is my treat and was my idea. End of story."

She narrowed her eyes at him. "How about we compromise?"

He smiled. She was adorable when she wanted her way, but she wasn't going to win this one. "No."

"But you didn't hear my compromise." She pushed her bottom lip out in a pout, and he couldn't help leaning forward to kiss her.

"All right, I'm listening."

She leaned forward and flicked her tongue on his earlobe and then kissed a spot below his ear. "Mmm," she hummed into his ear. "How about in non-monetary ways?"

She placed a trail of kisses down his neck and his cock stiffened.

His hands tightened on her waist and his voice came out strained. He wanted nothing more than to take her back into their room, but now wasn't the time.

"I think we could make that work." She was certainly winning this one.

She gripped the bottom of his shirt and started pulling it up. He almost, *almost* let her, but grabbed her hands to stop the movement.

"As much as I would like to see where this goes, we have a reservation." At this point, he was about ready to cancel their reservation. He was hungry for something else.

"Fine. I will sex you up later." She winked playfully in his direction.

He groaned and his neck spiked red. He needed to get her to their waiting car before he changed his mind. He tugged her out the door.

"Can't wait," he whispered.

———————

8

L ogan had rented a car with a driver to take them between the different wineries for the weekend. They stopped at the restaurant at the first winery on the list to grab lunch. The restaurant paired wines with each of the three courses served and each was just as amazing as the previous. Being at this restaurant, Abigail realized how similar she and Logan were in their food choices. They ordered all of the same foods and both loved every bite.

They ended up buying a bottle of each of the three wines they tried for Logan's cellar. Loading into their reserved car, they headed to the next winery. They did a brief tour of the winery and walked among the grapevines while a vintner from the winery explained how they took care of them and kept them from freezing during cold spells. They gave Abigail and Logan grapes to try straight off the vine and even let them help mash grapes for the wines they were currently making with their wine press. Abigail was sorely disappointed to find out that the winery employees don't actually walk all over the grapes like she was led to believe in movies, but she still enjoyed using the wine press. They tried a few different types of wine at this winery as well and ended up purchasing several more bottles. After leaving the second winery, Abigail realized why Logan had rented a driver for the weekend. With wine tasting, you aren't supposed to swallow the wines, which is what the wineries were constantly reminding them, but they personally didn't spit the wine out. Where was the fun in that? They definitely were not able to drive after the second winery and they were still planning on hitting another.

Logan pulled Abigail to him in the car and kissed her temple as they pulled up to the third and last winery for the night. They went into a tasting room first and tried two different wines, and then they were led on a tour of the winery. They skipped the food pairing and tour of the vineyard, but wanted to see the storage of the wines in the cellar.

Walking down the stairs into the cellar underground, the damp, cold air hit Abigail's nose instantly. She took a deep breath and closed her eyes. The smell reminded her of her grandparents' house when she used to hang out in their basement with her cousins. There were wine barrels lining the walls in all directions with dates indicating when they were corked. They were led further into the cellar as more tour groups poured in behind them. Logan and Abigail were backed into a corner while the tour guide spoke as people continued to pour in.

Soon she realized how closed in they were and the only entrance was around 100 feet away, through several people. She closed her eyes and took a deep breath to try to calm her now racing heart. Sweat beaded on her forehead despite the cold air and she leaned against the wall for support as her breath started coming out in ragged spurts. Logan grabbed her hand and pulled her to him.

"Are you okay?" he whispered.

She shook her head and gripped his hand. "I need to get out of here."

He put his arm around her shoulders and started pushing through people, saying "Excuse me" the whole way. She kept her eyes closed and relied on Logan to lead her out of there. It felt like it took them forever, but they finally arrived at the steps. He squeezed her shoulders. "Open your eyes, we're going up."

She opened her eyes and let him lead her up the steps as her heart continued to pound. When they broke into the fresh air, she tried to take several deep breaths to calm her heart. Logan led her over to a bench under a tree and sat her down. He squatted in front of her and put his hands on either side of her face.

"You're super pale and clammy. Are you all right? Is it the wine?"

She shook her head and took another deep breath. "I'm okay. I'm just claustrophobic."

He swiped her hair out of her face, kissed her forehead, and sat next to her. His eyes never left her as she leaned forward and put her head in her hands, his hand rubbing her back soothingly. Her heart rate slowed to a normal pace, but she continued to sit there for a few minutes wondering what Logan was thinking and how he would react. She did, after all, just ruin their tour.

She sat up and leaned back. He took her hand and watched her until she looked at him. "Your color is coming back," he said, smiling.

She nodded and looked down briefly. "I'm sorry. You can go back into the cellar to finish the tour if you'd like. I don't mind waiting out here."

He shook his head. "You have nothing to be sorry for. I have done these tours before. I was doing them so you could see everything."

She rubbed her face. "Please, no more cellars."

"No more cellars. Consider it done." He smiled. "Are you okay to walk?"

She nodded as they stood up and made their way back to the main building following the marked path. He held her hand as they walked and continually threw concerned glances her way. "I'm fine, Logan."

"You should have told me you are claustrophobic. I would have never taken you into that cellar."

"I didn't think it would bother me since it was fairly large. And it didn't at first. Not until all of the people started coming in and we got backed into that corner."

He didn't say anything else as they walked through the building to their waiting car. The car ride was silent as they made their way back.

Is he mad at me? she thought. She couldn't tell. He didn't seem mad, but at the same time, he was silent which wasn't normal for him. She glanced at him and saw him staring out the window. She grabbed his hand which he continued to hold, but never looked at her. He was definitely upset.

When the driver pulled up in front of their room, they unloaded all of their wine bottles and Logan tipped him before he left.

They carried the bottles inside and deposited all of them into the kitchen in silence.

"Logan."

She watched as he slid all of the bottles onto the counter without making eye contact with her.

"Logan, please look at me."

He stopped what he was doing and looked over at her. He almost looked hurt.

"Are you upset with me?"

"Abi, why don't you trust me?"

She furrowed her eyebrows at him. "What does me having claustrophobia have to do with trusting you?"

"Abi," he sighed. Leaning against the counter, he crossed his arms over his chest. "You didn't tell me. Why didn't you tell me?"

"I guess the opportunity never presented itself. I didn't really think of it."

He nodded and walked to the back door and sat on a lounge chair. She followed him and stood in front of him. "Logan, I didn't do it to hurt you. It doesn't happen often and I didn't think it was that important."

He looked at her and she felt like a scolded dog by the look on his face. "Why would it not be important? It's something I should know about you, so I don't take you somewhere that can trigger you. Like, say, I don't know, into a wine cellar." His voice took a sarcastic turn and then he immediately shook his head and sighed. "I'm sorry. That was uncalled for. I just..." he said, pausing for a moment. "I told you about me."

That's what this was about. He felt like she should have told him everything about herself because he shared one of his darkest secrets. She felt terrible.

She sat on the side of the lounge chair next to him so she was facing him. Grabbing his hand, she leaned forward. "I'm so sorry I didn't tell you. I did not mean to hurt you. I honestly didn't think it was a big deal." They sat in silence. "How can I make it up to you?"

He looked over at her and squeezed her hand. "Please just be open with me. If there is anything I should know, tell me. Even if you think it's insignificant."

"Deal."

He pulled her so she was sitting on the edge of his chair and wrapped his arms around her waist. "Are you hungry?"

"A little."

Kissing her temple, he stood up and grabbed the room service menu and ordered a few plates of food. "All right, put on your swimsuit. How about we relax in the hot tub?"

She smiled. "I thought this was supposed to be a no swimsuit trip."

"I figured you wouldn't want to be naked when room service shows up. But you better believe that bikini is coming off as soon as they leave." He winked.

They changed into their swimsuits and eased themselves into their own private hot tub. The room service showed up a few minutes later. Logan had them set up in the kitchen and then came back to join her. He pulled her in front of him and slowly massaged her shoulders. Abigail sat in silence contemplating on finally answering his question about why it bothered her that he found out she had fallen for him in high school. She did just agree to be honest with him and she felt like she was going to be lying to him if she kept it a secret. And she certainly didn't need him to be upset with her again.

She spun around on him so they were facing each other, but pushed back so she was on the other end of the tub. He started to come to her, but she held up a hand. "I need to tell you something." He stopped. Concern spread across his face. "It's nothing bad... depending on how you look at it."

"What is it?" he asked.

She took a deep breath. "You asked me why it matters that I told you I fell for you in high school. It matters because I never got over it. I fell for you back then when I didn't even know you. And now that I know you, I have fallen even more." He started to come toward her again, but she held up her hand. "Hang on. You told me this was a friend trip, so I know you don't feel the same way, and it's okay. We can keep being friends with benefits or fuck buddies or whatever you think we are. That's fine. I just told you I would be honest, so that's what I'm trying to do."

He didn't move at first. He stayed where he was sitting, staring into the water. After a few minutes of silence, she turned around so she was facing the edge of the deck to look out over the view. It was so beautiful and peaceful. She didn't expect Logan to say anything. He was most likely going to pretend she didn't say anything and they were just going to go back to sleeping together. Or he was going to cut ties with her after this weekend, but either way, she was having a great time and would remember it forever.

Of course she hoped he would be okay with everything, but she felt like that was a shot in the dark.

She felt the water ripple and half expected him to climb out of the hot tub, but his hands came around her waist. "This morning while you were sleeping I told you I was falling for you. That was why you told me you fell for me in high school."

She couldn't believe it. She stared wide-eyed at the view before her. *He is falling for me?* She should have felt incredibly excited, but all she could feel was the disappointment. "Why didn't you tell me this morning?"

"Because I never meant for you to hear it."

She turned around. "I never meant for you to know that either. It was in my sleep, Logan! You should have told me this morning." She pushed away from him and stood to get out.

He grabbed her quickly before she could take a step. "Abi, let's talk."

She spun on him. "Logan, this being open thing goes two ways. You let me be upset this morning and here you didn't even tell me what provoked me to say it in my sleep in the first place." She moved to get out again, but he held her to him.

"Stop."

"Why should I? That's a double standard. It's not fair!" She took a step again, but he stood up also and wrapped an arm around her waist to keep her there.

"Abi, please stop. Just listen to me for a second."

She turned to face him and folded her arms across her chest, waiting for him to talk.

"You're right. It is a double standard. I was wrong, but I can't change not telling you." He put a hand to her cheek. "I'm sorry. I was worried if I told you, it would scare you away, and I didn't want that to happen. I wanted to see where this would lead. It was selfish, and I'm sorry." He gave her a hopeful look. "Can we please try to move past this?"

She continued to stand there and glare at him. They had both made mistakes with each other and most of the mistakes were minor. She sighed and dropped her arms, not wanting to ruin their weekend over something petty, and she would be lying if she said she didn't understand why he did it. "Fine, but we are getting everything out of the way right now."

He sat down in the water and tugged her down with him. "What do you mean?"

"For instance," she took a deep breath, "at the reunion, when I saw you, I went to the bar to take a shot of tequila so I wouldn't be so nervous around you in case you decided to talk to me."

He smiled. "And then I got to the bar and ordered with you so you didn't have time to loosen up."

"Yes, you did. You threw me off my game." She tucked some loose hair behind her ears. "Your turn."

"I went to the bar specifically because I saw you and didn't want to lose my nerve to talk to you, so I figured the sooner the better."

This time she couldn't avoid the smile on her face. Her heart grew ten times the size as her chest swelled. "I had a hard time keeping my eyes off of you the whole night."

"I had an even harder time."

"I thought you only wanted to come home with me to get lucky, but didn't actually care to be with me specifically."

"I only had eyes for you."

"I wanted you to come drink with me at the bar, so I had an excuse to talk to you all night."

"I wanted to protect you from the alcohol so I wouldn't have to worry about you all night long when you went home."

"It was incredibly difficult for me to ask you to come inside and watch a movie with me, but I used the alcohol as my courage." She moved closer to Logan in the hot tub.

"I was really hoping you would invite me in and would have probably made up an excuse to invite myself in if you hadn't."

She giggled at that.

"I obsessively checked my phone all day Sunday and Monday to see if you would contact me." She blushed and looked down.

"I had to physically stop myself from contacting you so you wouldn't think I was too eager to see you again." Logan reached out and pulled her to him. His fingers tipping up her chin. "But I was eager."

"I swore off ever dating men again since I have been hurt so many times," she whispered. She linked her arms around his neck.

He wrapped his arms around her and held her close, his face only a few inches away from hers. "I only went to the reunion in hopes of seeing you."

"You make me very nervous, but yet, I feel so calm at the same time."

He leaned in and kissed her lightly. "When you bite your lip, it drives me crazy."

She bit her lip and he growled, kissing her again. His hands slinked up her back and pulled on the ties of her swimsuit. Her top slid off between them. His fingers tangled in her hair as she reached down and stroked him through his swim trunks. He moaned against her lips as his fingers tightened in her hair. She pulled his swim trunks off and continued to stroke his shaft while pushing him up against the edge of the hot tub. "Sit on the edge."

He popped out of the hot tub so just his legs were dangling in the water. He pulled her to him, but she pushed his hands away. She slid forward so she was eye level with his erect member. Looking into his eyes, she took him into her mouth. The chlorinated water immediately assaulted her senses, but soon she was only tasting his saltiness.

He inhaled sharply and gripped her hair. Slowly pumping him, she ran her tongue up and down his length and swirled around his tip, sucking lightly and tasting his pre-cum. She took his balls in her hands and slowly rubbed them trying to be gentle with the smooth, sensitive skin. Her eyes were trained on his face.

His fingers tightened against her scalp, but he took care not to move her head to his will; although, she wouldn't have minded it. She wanted him to enjoy every minute.

He started breathing heavily and closed his eyes. She sucked a bit harder and pushed her mouth down until he hit the back of her throat. He quietly groaned as his body tensed and he released into her mouth.

Pulling away, she swam to the other end of the hot tub, watching him. He was leaning back and still had his eyes closed as he was recovering, his body slightly twitching from the release. To be able to wield that much control over him made her smile.

His eyes slowly opened and he slid back into the water. "You're the most amazing woman ever."

She smiled. "I told you I was going to pay you back in non-monetary form."

"If I had known you meant *that*, I would have skipped the wineries earlier today."

She laughed.

He waved her over to him and tugged on her swimsuit bottoms

until they slid off. He turned and lifted her onto the edge of the hot tub.

"Logan, you don't have to."

"I want to." He looked up at her. She frowned and he furrowed his eyebrows. "What's wrong?"

"Honestly? I don't really like it."

He raised an eyebrow. "What?"

She shrugged and slid back into the water. "I don't like it. It doesn't really do anything for me."

His hand slid down onto her sex as he slid a finger against her clit. "Does this feel good?"

She quivered. "Yes."

"It will feel even better if I use my mouth."

She bit her lip. "I don't know, Logan."

He grabbed her by the hips and slid her back onto the edge. "How about this? I will start, and if you don't like it, you can ask me to stop. I'll stop with no questions asked."

That seemed fair. And what would it hurt if he wanted to try? She nodded.

He pulled her hips to him as he leaned forward, firmly holding her thighs. His tongue felt warm against her and gentle as he caressed. His eyes focused on hers and he worked his way up and down her. She gasped as he plunged into her and came back out quickly to nip and tease her. She felt the warmth spread through her body as it ached to be with his. Her nipples hardened in anticipation and she gripped the side of the hot tub as his mouth worked on her most sensitive area.

Watching his mouth move against her was a turn on she didn't know was possible. She moaned and felt him smile, only increasing her arousal. His hands released the hold on her thighs and moved up to her chest, taking her nipples between his fingers. Her moan made him more eager as he picked up the pace, sucking, his tongue moving faster, thumbs rubbing over her buds. She tried to remind herself not to squeeze her thighs and crush his head, but all thoughts were fleeting at her impending orgasm.

She arched her back as the warmth grew, her hips moving against his mouth. His hands dropped to her waist and one of his fingers found her clit, only making her hips thrust in response. His strong arms attempted to hold her down by resuming a grip on her thighs.

Her face reddened and the release came all too soon, her body shaking with the orgasm. When she relaxed, Logan pulled her back into the water, her body still slightly twitching from the sensation.

"So it wasn't terrible?" he asked as she caught her breath.

"It wasn't terrible," she breathed. "It's never felt that way before." She nuzzled her face into his neck as they sat in the hot tub gazing out over the sun setting behind the mountains.

She thought back to the other men she had been with and wondered what it was that Logan did differently. Not just with sex, but with everything thus far. He obviously knew what he was doing, but it was more than that. It was chemistry. It was something she had never experienced.

She sighed against him, perfectly content until her stomach growled.

"I'm hungry," they both said at the same time and laughed. He got up, stepped out of the hot tub, and helped her out. They secured towels around themselves and went to the kitchen to check out the food room service had brought.

Logan had ordered an assortment of fruits, vegetables, meats, cheeses, and breads. The resort had also brought a bottle of wine from their own vineyard. They made themselves sandwiches and sat on the patio in their lawn chairs while they ate. Logan poured them both a glass of red wine. They enjoyed their conversation with each other as they spoke about their jobs and high school. Eventually they just laid on their patio chairs in comfortable silence looking up at the stars.

He reached over and tugged on the top of her towel so it fell down around her. She looked over at him and a smile crept onto her lips. Pulling his towel off, he pulled their lawn chairs together and leaned over to her. The moon lit one side of his face as he gazed into her eyes. Brushing her hair back with his hand, he cupped her cheek and met his lips with hers. Their tongues mingled while he slowly drew a trail down her chest with his finger. Goosebumps appeared along the trail as if he were dragging an ice cube across her skin. His finger circled her nipple, and she couldn't help her back from arching in response. He teased her until they slowly formed into solid peaks. He broke off their kiss and continued a wet trail of kisses down her neck and to her chest, taking her nipple into his mouth. Her face instantly flushed and she gripped his shoulder, her heart rate speeding up. She squirmed beneath him as he continued his trail to her other nipple. Not wanting it to feel left out, he continued the sweet assault. She bit her lip and closed her eyes as she arched her back again.

He pulled back and blew on her chest, which only caused her back to arch higher. She gazed at him, eyelids half closed. The crinkling of a wrapper told her she was about to feel him in more depth. He positioned himself on top of her and slowly slid inside. She inhaled as he filled her completely. With one hand supporting his weight, the other slid into her hair pulling her lips to his. They moved in unison with each other until both of their bodies tensed and relaxed again.

She wrapped her arms around his chest as he held her to him. This was the first time they had had sex where it felt like it meant something. She kissed his chest and laid her head against it. He leaned back briefly to kiss her forehead before resting his head on top of hers.

This moment was perfect. She finally felt like she was ready to be in a relationship again.

9

Logan rolled over and felt the bed next to him. It was empty. He sat up panicked and looked around. Maybe she had left. Maybe she decided she didn't want to be with a man with a screwed up childhood.

Various noises coming from the closed bathroom alleviated his thoughts. He didn't know why he had even had them in the first place. He hadn't been worried earlier, and after the previous night, he knew they were in a good place together.

He scrubbed his hand over his face as if he were wiping the memories of his troubled past away, wiping away the thoughts of Abigail leaving, wiping away anything negative.

He wanted nothing but good memories of this place with Abigail. He had never taken another woman here, but he also had never met another woman quite like her either. She was certainly one of a kind, and he didn't want to let her slip away.

The door opened, breaking him from his thoughts, and she poked her head out and smiled when she saw him sitting up against the backboard.

She's stunning.

The beautiful woman walked toward him with her hair down in

loose curls and makeup that perfectly enhanced her features. But she didn't need makeup. She was striking without it.

"Hey beautiful," he said, opening his arms for her to crawl into the bed with him. He loved the way she felt in his arms and still couldn't believe that they were together.

A blush worked its way up her neck. "I woke up like this." She winked.

"Well, it's a good thing you didn't take too much time getting ready because we are actually going on a hike today."

She pursed her lips together, the disappointment clear on her face.

"However, I did also have plans for us to take a wine train later this evening, but we could do that for lunch instead of dinner and maybe go on a hike afterward."

She smiled and pressed a kiss to his lips. "What should I wear?"

He suggested something fancy and hopped in the shower while she finished getting ready. He placed a call to the train to change their reservation which they were happy to do. When he finally stepped out of the bathroom several minutes later, she was wearing a black lace dress that hit her mid thigh with red high heels.

He suppressed a groan and stopped short as he wanted nothing more than to take her back to bed with him. He let out a low whistle and twirled his finger around signaling for her to spin. She laughed and did so as he looked her up and down.

"Damn, baby. You look incredible."

She blushed again and helped pull out his outfit as he styled his hair. When they were ready to go, he was dressed in black slacks and a maroon button up shirt.

They grabbed a light breakfast at the hotel restaurant before being picked up by their driver and taken to the train station. Logan kept her hand in his as they walked to their train. He wanted this to be their everyday life—holding her hand and keeping her by his side.

He shook his head against his thoughts. *Slow down there, buddy. Going a little too fast.*

"Are you okay?" she asked.

He smiled and tugged her against his side, kissing her temple. "Never better."

At the entrance to the rail car, he stood to the side and held out his hand motioning for her to go first. Nothing but the best for her. They boarded and were led to their seats in an elevated dome, the second story of the train car. The sides of the train were all glass allowing for panoramic views during the ride. Sitting at the table, menus were handed to them to place their orders for drinks and food to be served later on the ride.

She looked around in wonder at the old wooden tables, the wood paneling in the rail car, along with the blue and red carpet. Logan sat across from her and watched the amazement on her face. This was what he loved. He loved being able to bring her somewhere that would amaze her. She looked back at him and he reached his hands across the table to hold hers.

"You look beautiful."

She blushed. "You don't look so bad yourself."

A waiter came by and took their drink orders. They skimmed the menu and ended up each ordering the beef tenderloin for lunch. When the train pulled out of the station, her eyes were glued to the windows. She stared in awe at all of the vineyards passing them by. The grapes seemed to go for miles, and the mountains in the background made it picturesque.

When they were in their car heading back to the hotel, she leaned back and took a deep breath. "I'm so full, I could explode."

Logan laughed. "You know, you didn't have to finish everything on your plate."

This girl was like a garbage truck. She just kept on shoveling it in and he had no idea where it all went. She could put him to shame.

She pshawed. "To hell I didn't. My mother taught me not to waste food. Not to mention it was soooo good and food is my porn."

He laughed and blushed at her statement, sending his mind reeling into the gutter. "I'm glad to know the way to my baby's heart is through food."

Her face lit up as she laughed alongside him. He interlaced his fingers with hers as they sat in comfortable silence the rest of the ride back.

$$\sim$$

"OF COURSE IT'S ALL UPHILL," Abigail muttered. Because, really, where's the fun in it being easy?

When they arrived back at the hotel, they immediately changed into hiking clothes. Abigail threw her hair up and pulled on a pair of capri yoga pants, a sports bra, a loose tank top, and some old tennis shoes. Logan wore a pair of loose basketball shorts, a t-shirt, and some hiking shoes.

The resort had hiking trails going off in several directions and Logan said he had chosen that particular trail because of the view. He mentioned it was one his family used to hike regularly when he was a kid. She thought for sure it wouldn't be that difficult if he did it as a child.

Better be a damn good view.

She was out of breath after the first quarter mile and it was a two-mile hike just to get there, not to mention another two miles back. She never realized how out of shape she was until she was trying to walk up a rocky trail at Logan's pace.

By the time they hit the first half mile mark she told Logan she needed a break. She was dripping with sweat and her makeup was running everywhere. She regretted not scrubbing it off before they left.

Logan, of course, hadn't even broken a sweat since he was perfect at exercise, too. *I hate him*, she thought, trying to avoid glaring at him.

She leaned against a tree to try to catch her breath. He handed her a water bottle which he pulled out of a small backpack he had thrown on at the last minute. She looked at him as she took a drink and he had a bright smile on his face.

Her eyes narrowed. "What?"

"Nothing," he said. He looked around as if something had caught his eye, but she only narrowed her eyes more.

"What, Logan?"

He chuckled. "You're just so cute."

"Why?" Several gulps of cold water slid down her throat, quenching some of her thirst.

"You can't just be cute?" He put a hand to his chest in feigned innocence.

"No."

He laughed. "You're in terrible shape for being so thin."

Did he really just say that to me? Of course, she knew it was true. She *was* in terrible shape. And he was right—she was very thin, especially for rarely exercising. But she was blown away that he was so comfortable saying it to her. She continued to stare at him. He stopped laughing when he realized he may have upset her. She refrained from smiling when he started to squirm.

"Is that something you really want to say to the woman who holds all the power?" She handed him the water bottle which he deposited into his backpack.

He raised an eyebrow. "Explain."

She started walking up the trail and he followed her. Silence ensued. It would definitely be more fun for him to make himself nervous thinking about what she could have meant. He asked her a few times what she meant, but she only smiled at him. He looked awfully curious.

She tried her hardest to hide how exhausted she was and refrained from making it obvious she was breathing heavily. Blisters were forming on her feet from sweating, but she didn't want to take a break since she knew he would only laugh at her again. It's not that it bothered her, she just wanted to show him she could work hard and keep up with him. Overall, it was probably a stupid idea.

When they hit the one mile mark he asked her if she wanted to stop and she told him she was fine, so they trekked on. She really, *really* should have stopped though, but her pride got the best of her. Not to mention, she wanted to get the damn hike over with.

At the mile and a half mark, Logan grabbed her arm. "Abi, let's take a break."

"I'm fine," she said. She started walking again, but he pulled her over to a rock off the path.

"Sit down." He sat down and pulled out their water bottles and handed one to her. She grudgingly sat down next to him and took a drink out of it, but was glad that he suggested sitting and not her. He watched her as she took a drink and she avoided making eye contact so he wouldn't see how exhausted she was. Her heart thudded in her chest and her stomach churned. The heat in her cheeks seemed to intensify at the embarrassment she felt for how out of shape she was. She hoped the heat would mask the red of her face as sweat poured off of her. She told herself she was going to get a gym membership after all of this, especially if Logan and she ended up spending a lot of time together. She knew he was going to want to do some outdoor activities and her body just wasn't in the right condition for it. She had proven that much.

She took a deep breath and looked away from Logan so she could let it out without him realizing just how burnt out she was. Her lungs felt like they were being crushed and were tightening up as the air felt restricted. Her feet were on fire and were definitely covered in blisters. The question wasn't if they were, it was how many and how big?

Overall, she was a hot mess.

"Do you want to turn around?"

Her heart continued to pound so hard, she was afraid it would spring right out of her chest. She was at the point where if she continued this exertion, she knew she was going to be sick, but she didn't want to tell him they should go back because he would pick on her. She could finish this hike, and they were almost there.

"Abi?"

She realized she hadn't answered him, so she shook her head, but never made eye contact. "I'm fine."

His eyes were burning a hole in the back of her head. She could feel it. "All right, we're going to play a little game."

She looked back at him, her curiosity piqued. "What?"

"We're going to play a game called 'Truth'. With this game, we are going to tell each other the truth about everything."

"We did that last night, Logan."

"I know, but we're going to continue it."

She sighed. She knew he was trying to get her to tell him she was worn out.

"I'll go first," he said. "Truth: I'm worried you're going to pass out."

Well, might as well dive straight in.

"Truth: I'm worried I'm going to puke on you."

He scooted a few inches back and she couldn't refrain from laughing.

"Truth: There's a waterfall back in the trees with a little pool beneath it. I was hoping we could swim in it together."

"Truth: My body is going to hate you tomorrow."

He smiled. "Do you want to finish the hike or head back?"

Her body screamed for them to turn back, but they were almost there, and she wanted to show him she could do it. "Let's finish."

They continued to hike up the steep hill and her feet regretted the decision. It was getting to be painful to walk as she could feel her heels and toes rubbing inside her shoes since her socks were soaked through with sweat, but they were almost there, and she wasn't about to turn back now.

Almost there, she repeated to herself.

After the last grueling half mile, they made it to the top. If Logan was right about anything, it was this: the view was absolutely breathtaking. They were high enough up to glimpse the ocean in one direction and the vineyards and mountains in another direction. She stared in awe and wished she had her cell phone or a camera with her to take a picture, but a mental image would have to suffice. She tried to memorize every detail in hopes that her acrylics could capture it on canvas later.

Logan grabbed her hand and led her off the path to a small waterfall and pool. He set the backpack down and pulled off his shoes, socks, and t-shirt before wading into the water in his shorts. He looked back at her. "It's very cold since it's mountain runoff, but it'll cool you down."

She pulled her shirt off, but left her sports bra and yoga capris on. She yanked off her shoes and socks as well and stared down at her feet. She had blisters on the sides of her big toes the size of a nickel. The backs of her heels were also covered in a cluster of small blisters. She dreaded having to put the shoes back on to make the final trek down the hill.

She stepped into the ice cold water which immediately soothed her feet. Slowly making her way to Logan, she worked herself into the water. The only thing that kept her moving was telling herself her clothes would keep her cool on the hike down and it would be nice to rinse the sweat off. When she reached him, he wrapped his arms around her and they slowly sank until they were neck deep in the water. She wrapped her legs around his waist and her arms around his neck as he held onto her.

"Truth," he whispered. "I wouldn't change this vacation for anything."

Her heart fluttered, but she was so miserable, she didn't have anything sweet to say back. "Truth: I'm not a fan of hiking."

He laughed. "I can see that." He pressed a kiss to her lips as they floated around in the water. "Thank you for coming with me anyway."

A moment of silence passed. "Can I ask you something?" she whispered.

"Of course you can. Anything."

"Why did you seek me out at the bar?" She was referring to the reunion. When he had told her he saw her at the bar and didn't want to lose the nerve to talk to her, she wondered why. Why would he want to talk to her? The question had been burning in her mind all day.

"Because I had a crush on you in high school."

On her? Why? She voiced these questions aloud and stared at him blankly. He had already told her that in his bedroom a few days prior, but she didn't actually believe it. It made no sense. Then, he said it a second time. "You were so popular in high school. You could have picked from any girl in our class. Why me?"

He smiled. "First of all, I wasn't popular."

Her eyes widened. They continued to wade around the pool of water. "Yes, you were! You were an athlete. AKA popular."

"Not all athletes are popular. And I especially wasn't. I kept to myself. I didn't go to the parties or hang out with the guys on the team. It wasn't my thing. I was a bit of a loner."

She thought back to high school, and, while she remembered watching him occasionally in the hallway, she guessed she never did see him surrounded by a bunch of people. She must have assumed he was popular based on his association with the football team. She stereotyped him, she realized.

Wow. I wasn't very observant, she scolded herself.

"I guess I never noticed," she said quietly.

"Most didn't," he said. He wrapped his arms tighter around her. "And I had a crush on you because during sophomore year of high school I remember a time when Justin, you know, the clumsy kid with glasses? Well, anyway, Justin had tripped and his books went flying everywhere. Everyone in close vicinity started laughing, but didn't make an attempt to help him up. I was about to walk over to help him, but you immediately dropped to the ground and helped him gather all of his papers. You handed everything back to him, asked him if he was okay, and then told him to have a good day." He smiled. "His face had brightened so much just from that little gesture. I felt like I could see how good of a heart you had in that moment. It made me fall for you."

She remembered that moment like it was yesterday. Her heart had gone out to Justin because she had done something similar to that her freshman year in high school. Someone had helped her up and it meant so much to her that she felt the need to pay it forward. All of the students laughing at Justin just killed her. The pure embarrassment on his face was heart-wrenching, and it was a feeling she had been all too familiar with.

"I hurt for him because I did something similar freshman year and someone helped me up."

"I know," he said.

She looked at him and tilted her head. "You know? Oh man. I took my spill in front of you?"

He shook his head. "No. Well, actually, yes you did, but I'm the one who helped you."

He stopped walking around the little pool of icy water and held her closer.

"You... what?" She searched her memory for that moment. To remember who it was that helped her, but for some reason, Logan's face never came to mind. She squinted, hoping the memory would come back to her. "I don't remember..."

He smiled. "Well, considering it was only like the second day of school and there were so many new faces, I wouldn't expect you to remember."

"But you remember," she whispered.

"I do," he said. "Because I thought you were one of the most beautiful girls I had ever seen."

She splashed him with water and giggled, her body shaking against his. "No, you didn't."

Logan smiled. "I did."

Despite the chilly water, she could feel the heat seeping into her face and just knew it was bright red. "I'm such a jerk for not remembering you."

"Maybe," he winked.

She splashed him again and laughed.

"No," he continued. "You probably don't remember me because I looked completely different freshman year. I had glasses and braces."

"No, you didn't!"

He nodded and laughed alongside her. "I did! I looked like a complete nerd. Check the yearbook!"

Their bodies shook against each other from laughter. She leaned her forehead against his and hugged him tightly to her. "Well, I appreciate you helping me back then. It meant a lot."

He kissed her forehead. "Anything for you," he said softly.

After a few minutes, they were both chilly and crawled on top of some rocks to sunbathe and dry off their feet before putting on their shoes. Logan hadn't seen her feet yet, and she was trying her hardest to hide it from him until they got back to their room; otherwise, he would probably try to carry her or something crazy. It was hell pulling her shoes back on, and she worried she was going to pop a blister. Somehow, she managed to do it without saying a bunch of curse words, and pretty soon they were walking down the trail, even more uncomfortable than she was on the hike up.

Being miserable walking up is nothing like being miserable walking down. There was a *whole* new muscle group that was rarely used that was needed to keep from sliding down a hill. If she ever felt like dying, this would have been it. When they had made it a mile, Logan pulled her off to the side for a water break. She sat on a nearby rock and put her head in her hands, trying to force air into her lungs. She could feel the blood draining from her face as her heart pumped at a ridiculous rate, and she was nauseated. At this point, she wasn't going to try to hide how miserable she was from Logan. He would find out at one point or another when she threw up.

He put a hand on her back and rubbed. "Are you doing all right?"

She shook her head.

"Are you going to be sick?"

She nodded. She wasn't sure if she would actually puke, but if this wave of nausea didn't pass, she would be puking in front of Logan.

He squatted in front of her and handed her a water bottle. She shook her head at it and took a deep breath. "You need to drink. It will help."

She sat up and grabbed the water bottle from him and his eyes widened.

"Abi, you should have told me you were feeling sick. We would have taken a break earlier." His hand touched her cheek and based on the concern on his face, she knew she was probably sheet white.

"You would have made fun of me." She took a deep breath and drank from the water bottle.

Guilt washed over his face. "No, I wouldn't have. I was giving you a hard time, but I didn't mean for you to take it to heart."

She shrugged. Forcing herself to drink over half of the bottle made her feel slightly better as her color slowly returned and the nausea diminished. He sat down next to her and rubbed her back as he watched her. "I'm sorry."

She didn't say anything, unsure of what to say.

They had to have been sitting there for at least twenty minutes as their bodies cooled down and her heart rate returned to normal. She knew he was feeling guilty, and she felt slightly guilty for being responsible for it, but at the same time she didn't. She knew the reason she wasn't asking to take a break was because she was trying to prove herself to him, which was partially because he was picking on her during their first break.

"Why do you enjoy this?" There was nothing about this hike that explained what made him enjoy it. Yes, the view and water at the top were amazing, but you weren't always rewarded with something beautiful in the end. So, why bother?

A smile touched his lips. "It's good exercise."

"It's painful exercise." She sighed and took another drink from the bottle before handing it back to him to throw in his pack.

"It's not supposed to be painful. You just haven't worked up to this level."

She didn't know how he did it, but she was pretty sure her feet would never be able to work up to this level. They were destroyed and she knew she would feel it for at least the next week. Not worth it.

"I'm sorry for taking you on this hike, Abi. I didn't think you would have this hard of a time with it. I should have chosen an easier one." The puppy dog eyes and the guilt that seemed to wash over his face every time he looked at her told her he was sincerely sorry. She couldn't be mad. She was just miserable.

"I know how you can make it up to me." A sly smile slid across her lips.

He laughed. "Uh oh. Is this where you hold all the power?"

She nodded and stood up. She looked around, but who was she kidding? They were the only crazy fools on this trail as they hadn't seen a single person since they left hotel grounds, but just in case, she pulled Logan further into the woods.

He gave her a strange look. "Where are we going?"

She laughed. "Not far." She pulled him into a heavily wooded area and then pressed him against a tree. She planted her lips on his and slid her hand down to his shorts. Pretty soon he knew where she was going with it and slid his hands to her hips. Her hands tucked inside his shorts as she pulled them down. He smiled against her lips as he tugged her capris down to her ankles. They were loose enough to pull over her shoes and soon they were both naked from the waist down, aside from their shoes, and their clothes were in a pile on the forest floor.

She briefly worried she smelled and wanted to do a sniff check, but there was no way to do it discreetly.

"In the woods? You do hold the power," he whispered.

She forgot any lingering worries and winked at him, propping her leg up on the tree, and poising herself above him.

"Wait," he said. "I didn't bring a condom. I didn't think we'd be doing this on our hike."

She dropped her leg and watched him. The condom hadn't even crossed her mind, but she didn't feel like they actually needed it.

"Well," she said hesitantly, wondering if she should continue. "I was tested after my last relationship and I'm in the clear. I'm also on birth control."

His hand came up to her cheek and caressed it. "I'm clear too. Are you sure you're okay going bare? I haven't done that before."

It only took her a second to think before she was nodding. She trusted him. In her heart, she knew he would tell her if there was a reason for them to wear a condom. And she wanted to feel him, skin on skin. "I'm okay with it if you are."

He nodded in return, so she propped her leg back up on the tree. Looking into his eyes, she slowly sank down onto him. He inhaled sharply and she bit her lip as she exhaled. Sex without a latex barrier was much more intense. Her nerve endings were screaming for more as they moved together, after finding their rhythm.

The light scent of sweat filled the air around them, but it wasn't a turn off. She found that she craved it. It was intoxicating in itself, and it only made her want him more. All exhaustion was fleeting as her body ached for his to come closer.

Logan's lips found hers as he pumped. As he continued his assault, the leaves rustled in a light wind that sent shivers across her bare chest, turning her nipples into peaks. The sound of a twig snapping sent her heart racing with thoughts of being caught, only increasing her arousal. She considered stopping but was enjoying him too much. Let them be caught—she didn't care.

Turning them around, he pressed her up against the tree and wrapped her legs around his waist as he continued to pump, only picking up the pace. The tree at her back was incredibly uncomfortable when the bark bit into her shoulder, but the pleasure drowned out the pain. She arched her back as they both climaxed and a shooting pain went through her shoulders.

"Ouch, ouch, ouch," she gripped his shoulders and leaned forward, her body twitching from her orgasm, but the pain in her shoulder overriding it.

"Ouch? Didn't you get yours? Did I hurt you? Was I being too rough?" He pulled back and put a hand on her cheek, breathing heavily, his dick still pulsing inside of her.

"The sex was great, but this wasn't." She pointed at her back and turned her head to see the damage as she dropped her feet to the forest floor, moving away from him. She couldn't see much aside from some bark sticking to her clothes and arms.

Logan turned her around and was silent. She tried to look back at him, but she couldn't see what he was seeing.

"What, Logan? Just wipe the bark away. It's just a few cuts, right?"

He turned her back toward him and frowned. "Just so we're clear, this was your idea, not mine."

She rolled her eyes. "I know." He handed her the capris to put back on as he pulled his shorts on. She yanked them on quickly, and her shoulders throbbed from the movement. She still felt the bark sticking to her. She reached back to start wiping the bark, but Logan caught her hand. "Logan, it hurts. Wipe it off."

He shook his head. "It's not that simple."

"Tell me what's going on."

"You have like," he bit his lip and his face looked pained, "one inch splinters in your shoulders."

Holy shit! Her eyes widened as she tried again to look at the backs of her shoulders. The tips of bark she saw were actually imbedded into her back. "Well, take them out!" she shouted.

He grabbed her hands. "Abi, calm down. It'll be okay."

Now that she knew they were splinters, the pain seemed to feel different. It definitely wasn't pain from scratches. She could feel a foreign object in her skin. "Pull them out!"

"I can't," he said.

Well if he wouldn't, she would. She pulled her hand out of his and reach for her shoulder again. He snatched her fingers.

"Let's wait until we get back to the room. If we pull them, they will just break in your skin and it will be harder to get the little pieces out. It will be easier to know which ones still have pieces left if we do it all at the same time."

He did have a point, but walking back a mile with bark stuck in her shoulder was not her idea of a good time. But, honestly, *none* of this was a good time. "Fine, let's get back." Her grumpy meter had just hiked up another ten decibels.

They made their way back to the trail and grabbed Logan's pack, then began their descent down again. The pain in her shoulder distracted her from the pain in her feet, so she barely noticed the blisters as they worked their way back down the trail. This was the worst hike ever. After this experience, she didn't care to ever try it again.

She sighed. *And today started out so well.*

～

LOGAN GLANCED over at Abigail partway down the hill and took hold of her hand. She looked miserable. The pieces of bark sticking out of her shoulder looked so incredibly painful that he couldn't help but cringe at the sight. The sweat between their hands was slick, so when she pulled her hand away shortly after to wipe her hair off of her face, he didn't take it personally, nor did he try to grab her hand again when she dropped hers to the side without attempting to reach for him. They just needed to get back and he would make everything better.

They made it back to their room in record time. She was breathing heavily beside him and he suspected she was having a harder time than she was letting on. He pulled off his shoes and socks, then went into the bathroom to grab the complimentary sewing kit. He washed the needle with soap as she grabbed her tweezers out of her makeup bag. She pulled off her shoes and socks while he used the restroom, and when he came out, she quickly stood up acting like a deer in headlights. Her eyes were wide and she fidgeted.

Poor girl, he thought. *She must be really hurting.*

He pulled two of the dining room chairs out and flipped one around. "Sit," he said. She sat down with her chest facing the back of the chair and hugged the back to her. He pulled the other chair as close as possible so he was nearly straddling her hips. The sexual nature in which they were sitting wasn't lost on him, but he pushed the idea out of his head as he stared at her angry back.

"Are you ready?"

She nodded and took a deep breath. He grabbed the tip of the bark with the tweezers and slowly pulled watching for all signs that he was hurting her. She seemed tense, but didn't make any noises as he released it from her back. He set the first chunk on the table and an audible sigh escaped her lips.

Maybe this would be easier than he thought.

The first piece was probably three inches long and had a sharp point on the end that had imbedded itself into her. He told her that one came out clean and she nodded along, still not saying a word. The hope of it being easy was shattered when he pulled on the next piece. The chunk broke in half, still leaving the bottom half embedded in her back just under the skin with no visible piece to grab with the tweezers. He cursed. He slid the needle off of the table and she gripped the back of her chair. He winced.

"Tell me if it hurts. I'm going to try my hardest not to hurt you." He hoped his assurance would help, but knew it probably wouldn't. It was hard knowing someone was about to dig a needle into your skin and didn't know how much pressure to apply. He recalled a time when he got a splinter as a child and the anticipation from the needle was always the worst when his mom would try to dig it out. And this was much, much worse.

She held perfectly still as he dug the needle into her skin, trying to take care not to poke her more than he needed to. He stopped poking with the needle as soon as he thought some applied pressure around it would take it out. After what felt like an eternity, it came free.

"Aha, bastard." He pat her side. "How are you doing, beautiful?"

She shrugged nonchalantly, but he knew she was just trying to be brave. There was no way this wasn't hurting. "About as good as I can be doing."

"It's a good thing you didn't take your shirt off, or this could have been a lot worse." He laughed briefly with his poor attempt at a joke, but when she stayed silent, he sobered up and grabbed the tweezers again.

The process went on numerous times as he pulled six different splinters out of the backs of her shoulders, where only two came out clean. By the time he finished with the last, she was slightly shaking. He tried his hardest to give her encouraging words, but knew that it really wasn't going to help all that much.

When he said he was done, she sighed in relief. Leaning her head against the chair, she took a deep breath. Logan hugged her back to him and kissed her wounded shoulder.

"You did amazing, sweetheart."

She didn't respond, but he didn't expect her to. Taking her hand, he led her to the shower so he could scrub the wounds.

"Are you hungry?" he asked. She nodded as he soaped her back. "Should we just do room service tonight?" She nodded again.

She wasn't saying much of anything and hadn't in a while, but he didn't necessarily expect her to. She had just been through a lot and with as angry as her skin was, he knew she must be hurting pretty bad. They stood under the shower sprayers to rinse before stepping out. Logan wrapped a towel around her and slowly kissed her lips. She sighed into him.

When he pulled back he pushed her hair out of her face. "I'm sorry about today."

"It's not your fault. I didn't know hiking was this miserable. I have never done it before."

"It's not normally miserable, sweetie. I will take you on an easier hike and you will see."

She cringed.

He smiled at her expression. "How about I order us some food and you can slip into the hot tub to soak your muscles."

She nodded and he kissed her forehead and left to order room service. When he walked out on the deck shortly after, she was soaking in the hot tub with her eyes closed. She looked so peaceful. Logan slipped in beside her. He set down two glasses of wine on the edge of the tub, and then rested a hand on her leg.

"Does the water feel good?"

She nodded.

He reached for her foot and took it in his hand to rub it for her. Nothing felt better than a good foot rub after a long hike. But she halted him and immediately sat up, pulling away, her eyes snapping open.

"What's wrong?" he asked. "I was just going to rub your feet so they feel a little better."

"Nothing," she said a little too quickly.

He narrowed his eyes at her.

"Logan," she sighed, "can't you just let me mope in peace?"

"No, I can't. Why are you acting so weird? I get that the hike was not your thing and that you don't like strenuous exercise like that, and then of course the incident with the tree didn't help, but you're acting like that was the most horrible experience of your life. I'm trying to help you out by massaging your feet so they don't hurt so bad, but you act as if I'm trying to hurt you." He threw his hands up dramatically. "Frankly, I don't get it."

He knew he was being ridiculous, but he was just trying to be nice. She was absolutely miserable, and he just wanted to make her feel better, but she wasn't making it easy on him.

She rubbed her eyes. "Logan, it's not that I don't like exercise. That's not the problem. I just don't like exercise where I'm so damaged, I'm going to be hurting for a week or two."

He looked at her strangely. "Your back wasn't a result of the hike, and if your muscles take a week or two to heal from exercise, you should probably go to a doctor. That's not normal."

"I'm not talking about my muscles." She shook her head. "I'm talking about blisters. I mean, you said that I could 'work up' to that level of hiking, but my feet will never get used to that. Never. And I don't care to ever try again."

"Blisters?" He put a hand to his forehead. Suddenly it all made sense: the way she was walking, how she looked like a deer in head-lights when she took her shoes off, how she was just downright miserable the entire time. He was so stupid. So, so stupid. It was a rookie mistake that he should have been looking for. "Baby, blisters only happen if you have crappy shoes or overdo it. That's not supposed to happen every time you hike. If it does, you probably need new shoes or socks."

She stared at him funny. "So you're telling me, that if I were wearing different shoes or socks, THIS," she pulled one of her feet out of the water, "wouldn't have happened?"

He grabbed her ankle to steady her foot and his mouth dropped open. "Holy shit." He studied the quarter-sized blister on the side of her big toe, plus several large ones on her heel, with a bunch of other little ones scattered between her smaller toes. He let her foot go and motioned for her to show him her other one. She pulled it out of the water so he could inspect it. He let go of that foot and she let it sink back under the water. He went back to her side, put an arm around her, and kissed the side of her head. "You're a trooper. You know that?"

She shrugged.

"Now I understand why you hated it so much. No, that's not normal. If you had told me you were getting blisters, we would have turned around." He pulled her closer to him. "I feel like this is my fault. I should have suspected that based on how cranky you were."

"I wasn't cranky."

He laughed. "Yes, you were, but you definitely had a reason to be." They sat in silence for a few minutes. "That hike beat the shit out of you."

A knock sounded on the door signaling the room service had arrived. Logan hopped out of the water quickly to let the staff in to arrange their food, letting Abigail take her time. She seated herself at the table, bringing their glasses of wine with her, and he sat across from her. They immediately began eating, which lifted her spirits immensely.

"I'm throwing your tennis shoes away and we're getting you some new ones."

She looked at him briefly as she shoved a forkful of mashed potatoes in her mouth. "Fine by me. Those shoes can suck it."

He laughed. "Would you be willing to try hiking again if we get you some proper hiking shoes?"

"Only after my feet heal and my trauma from the tree goes away." She winked at him, and then paused with another forkful of mashed potatoes poised in front of her mouth. "And we don't have anymore sex in the woods."

He smiled. "Fair enough."

They finished eating and then soaked in the hot tub to enjoy some more relaxation time. When she told him her muscles felt immensely better, they finally crawled under the covers to sleep. She quickly fell asleep against Logan's chest. He kissed the top of her head and pulled her closer against him. This was one woman he never wanted to let go.

10

A knock on the door woke up Abigail. Logan got up quickly and answered it. He spoke softly with the person on the other end and then the door shut. He came around the corner pushing a room service cart. She smiled and pushed herself into a sitting position.

"I'm sorry, I was trying to let you sleep longer." He left the cart and sat down next to her, placing a kiss on her forehead. "How did you sleep?"

"Like a rock."

He had already showered and was wearing a pair of cargo shorts and a polo shirt. "I ordered us room service since I figured you wouldn't want to walk much today."

Stepping out of bed was incredibly difficult as she dreaded the shooting pain that was expected to fly through her feet. Never to disappoint, pins and needles seemed to shoot everywhere as she stood. She cringed slightly and hobbled over to the table where Logan was pulling all of the food off of the cart. The dull ache in her legs was trumped by the pain in her feet.

"How are your feet?"

"Sore," she sighed. "It's going to be a flip-flop kind of week."

Logan had ordered pancakes, French toast, waffles, bacon, sausage, eggs, oatmeal, bagels and fresh fruit. She stared wide-eyed. "Planning on feeding an army?"

He smiled. "Food makes my baby happy. I heard it may be her porn."

She laughed and put a little bit of everything on her plate. Logan raised an eyebrow at her. "Don't judge me. If it's here to eat, I'm going to eat it."

When they finally finished breakfast, they packed their bags to head home. She took one last shower in the beautiful hotel room to take advantage of the full body sprayers. She was sad the weekend was coming to an end since it had been so much fun to spend the time with Logan. But at the same time, it was nice to be able to go home to relax, so she could put her feet up to ease the pain. Logan tossed her tennis shoes in the trash can before she could put them in her bag. She wasn't planning on taking them home when she realized just how beat up they were and especially after how easily they destroyed her feet within a few hours, but he wanted to make sure she never wore them again. She didn't complain. She made a mental note to buy new tennis shoes since those were her only pair aside from her work shoes.

Logan kept a hand on her leg for just about the whole drive. She linked her fingers with his and smiled out the window. Her heart felt full after the weekend, but she also couldn't help but feel nervous. Logan was a wonderful person, but she was worried he wasn't falling for her like she was for him. He may have said he was falling for her, but that didn't mean he would get there as fast as she did. She was already crazy about him and had been for so many years. She could only hope he felt the same way. All of the signs were there. He had called her baby or *his* baby on numerous occasions. He held her hand, and he was so concerned about her when she had her claustrophobia attack and when she was feeling sick on the hike. And he took care of her after the hike. She didn't want a relationship initially, but now she did.

She did with Logan.

She looked over at him while he drove. They hadn't said much to each other as he was focusing on the road. His eyebrows seemed to merge and he looked like he was deep in thought. Frown lines started to appear around his mouth, so she squeezed his hand. His expression immediately cleared and he looked over at her with a smile on his face.

"Are you all right?"

"Yeah, I'm good," he said. He squeezed her fingers and focused back on the road.

She continued to watch him. Something seemed off. "Logan, what's wrong?"

"Nothing is wrong."

He didn't look at her this time. "Logan," she said.

He waited a minute, probably waiting to see if she would say anything else. When she didn't, he looked at her briefly. "Yes, Abigail?"

"What are you thinking about?"

"Just work stuff. Nothing to be concerned about." He didn't look at her again.

She frowned. There was obviously more to it than that, and his lack of eye contact was the give away. She dropped the subject since she didn't like being pushed for answers, so instead, she switched back to their game in hopes he would tell her.

"Truth: My favorite part of the weekend was getting to spend time with you."

He smiled. "Truth: My favorite part of this weekend was getting to know you better."

"Is that a good thing or a bad thing?" She laughed. She assumed if it was his favorite part, then it must have been a good thing.

He squeezed her fingers again. "Good, of course."

The rest of the drive was in comfortable silence. Once in a while she would look over at Logan, and that concentrated look with frown lines would appear. Since he didn't want to tell her what was going on, she didn't push it, but it still made her wonder. She hoped he would honor their truth agreement and tell her eventually, which was why she didn't want to push him. She would squeeze his hand every so often when he would get that look and it would all of sudden vanish, like she was bringing him back to reality. Whatever he was thinking about, it worried her. The fact that she was able to spend the whole weekend with him and never once saw that look, and now after they were on their way home and it was appearing frequently, led her to believe it had to do with them... or her. She sighed and put her thumbnail in her mouth and chewed on it.

Maybe it is just his work.

When Logan finally pulled up to her apartment building, she had chewed off nearly all of her fingernails. He pulled into a parking spot and hopped out of the car with her. Grabbing her bag, he carried it to her apartment as she hobbled behind. He set her bag on the floor by the front door and pulled her to him after she let them inside. He hugged her tightly and kissed her forehead.

"I'm going to head home and work on my house before the day is over," he said into her hair.

The disappointment that spread through her was obvious, but since he couldn't see her face, she didn't have to hide it. She did her best to put a smile on, bummed he wasn't planning on staying for a while. She grasped at a few straws to spend a little more time with him. "Would you like some help?"

"No, it's okay. You should rest your feet." He pulled back and went to the door. "I had fun, Abi."

"Me too," she said. He smiled and left.

She stared at the door. *What the hell just happened?*

He didn't even kiss her goodbye aside from on her forehead.

Was it my breath? She put her hand in front of her face and breathed out, doing her best to smell it. It didn't smell bad to her.

There was definitely something wrong. He had just spent most of the car ride frowning and now he left rather abruptly. Part of her wondered if she would hear from him again.

Pushing those thoughts aside, she grabbed her bag, carried it to her room, and emptied it into her laundry basket. Her laundry pile had started to overflow since she hadn't really touched any of it since before the reunion. Today was going to be a laundry and cleaning day.

Carrying everything to the laundry room in the next building, she threw all of her clothes in the same load, not wanting to spend the time on several different colored loads. She waited for her load to finish in the washing machine as she texted Al.

I'm back. He told me he was falling for me.

His response was immediate. *I knew it!*

I had such an amazing time, but then something weird happened. He was frowning the whole drive home and didn't say much. He said it was work, but then he dropped me off, kissed my forehead, and left. Is that bad? He was acting so strange.

I don't know. It may have just been work like he said. Give me more details tomorrow.

She sighed and pulled her legs up to her chest and stared at the washer until it finished. Moving her clothes to the dryer, she considered texting Logan, but didn't want to sound clingy, so she refrained. Her heart ached to talk to him, and she started to wish she had pressed him to tell her what was wrong in the car. Lost in her thoughts, she stared at the dryer for an hour until it signaled it was done. She put all of her laundry away and fell into doing chores to distract herself until bedtime. Her apartment was spotless by the time she crawled into bed.

LOGAN DROVE BACK to his house chewing on his thumbnail. While Abigail was sleeping, he had received a concerning text from a co-worker that they were about to lose a very large client. He was in charge of keeping that client on with the company. If the client decided to leave, someone would lose their job, and he worried it would be him. On the other side, if he could keep the client on, he would receive a major bonus and would be trusted in the future with several larger clients. It could potentially work in his favor, but the pressure he was going to be under was insurmountable.

He pulled into his driveway and grabbed his duffel bag out of his car, wandering into his house. Sighing and looking around, he wondered where he should continue with the remodel. He was ready to start a new room since all of his previous projects had been finished.

The library, he thought. *Abi loves the library.*

He walked into the room and looked around, debating on what to start on first. Deciding the floors would be the best since he needed to strip them, he gathered all of his supplies and started working. When Abigail had offered to help him today, he was tempted to take her up on it, but he knew he wouldn't be good company. Mulling over his work problems would keep his mind fairly occupied and the physical work on the house would keep his body occupied. He didn't want her to worry that she had done something wrong by his lack of conversation. And this was a problem he needed to figure out on his own. Plus, her poor feet needed a break.

He stripped the floors and sanded them. Afterward, he spent time wiping everything down to minimize the amount of dust in the space, since most of it had just been created by the floors. His goal was to finish this room for Abigail. He wanted her to love this space, a space that could possibly be hers one day. He smirked. He was certainly getting ahead of himself.

His phone buzzing interrupted the music he had been streaming. He glanced at the caller ID and saw his sister's name pop up. Forgetting about work temporarily, a smile lit his face.

"Hey Angie! How's my favorite sister?"

Her laugh on the other end of the line immediately brightened his mood. "Stressed out with my damn finance class."

He could remember those days. Working on finance projects that some of the teachers gave seemed nearly impossible at the time. Now they were his daily job. He could easily do them in his sleep, so he always told his siblings if they needed help to call him.

"Do you need help?"

She sighed. "Not at the moment. I just wanted to take a break for a bit. What are you up to?"

He glanced around at the mess of the room which was still half covered in dust. He tossed the dirty rag in a bucket of water and went to his kitchen to grab a beer. Popping the top, he took a long drag. "Stripping the floors of my library."

"Do you ever have any fun, or do you just work all weekend and then work even more on your house?"

"I enjoy working on my house. But, yes, I do have fun. Actually, I just got back from spending the weekend in Napa."

"In Napa? Damn, you should have invited me! I would have kept you company."

He stayed silent, wondering how to tell her he wasn't alone. It didn't take her long to figure that out.

"You didn't need me to keep you company, did you? Who is she? What's her name?"

He could almost picture his sister sitting down and tucking her legs under her, leaning forward to hear the gossip.

He laughed. "Her name is Abi. We actually went to high school together."

"Abi? Why does that name sound familiar?"

Logan smiled. His sister had the best memory of anyone he knew. "She's the one I wanted to ask to prom senior year."

"Oh." Her voice drifted off before she spoke softly. "And then grandpa died."

He nodded even though she couldn't see him. He didn't have to say anything since she immediately began talking again.

"Give me the deets."

"She's amazing."

"Aaaaand?"

"Aaaaand what?" he drawled out, imitating her.

"Logan! Do you see a future with her?"

"Jesus, Angie. I've only been seeing her for a week."

"Point being?"

He scrubbed his face and took another long drink of his beer. Then, he let out a sigh. "Honestly? I think I do."

She squealed, and he pulled the phone away from his ear.

"Oh my God! I'm so happy for you! It's about time you get back in the game."

He rolled his eyes. It had only been a year since his last relationship, which had lasted a few years. Eventually he and his girlfriend had decided they weren't right for each other and ended it. He didn't think taking a year off from dating was that extreme. And it wasn't that he was trying to take a year off, he just hadn't met anyone worth dating.

Until Abigail.

WALKING INTO WORK, Abigail looked forward to talking with Al about everything. He was just as eager to see her as he immediately pulled her into the break room and pressed for details. She told him everything that had happened while they were there and described Logan's reactions to each situation. The smile that lit her face during the story never faltered, even as she described their terrible hike and everything that followed. When she was done, Al just stared at her.

She stared back at him and waited. He didn't say anything. Finally she threw her hands up. "Al!"

He let out a low whistle. "You have it bad."

The heat filled her face and she knew she was turning red, so she looked down to hide it. "So, I kind of have a crush..."

He interrupted immediately. "Kind of?" His eyebrow raised.

"All right, all right. So I am a little crazy for him!" She looked up at Al and sighed, jutting out her lower lip. "What do I do?"

Coming around the table, he sat next to her and patted her on the back while laughing. "Oh girl, I am so happy for you."

"Do I call him?" She gave him the most pathetic look she could.

A small smile crept onto his face. "I think he's just as crazy for you and probably confused about it. Send him a text or call him tonight if you don't hear from him."

"You don't think that's too forward?" she asked, hoping he would say no.

He shook his head. "Based on everything you told me, I definitely think he feels the same way as you. As for his behavior in the car, I don't know. He was probably just thinking about work. I wouldn't worry too much about it. Besides, he gave you his wood in the woods, and then took care of you after. That's some serious prince shit right there."

Abigail laughed and blushed thinking about Logan inside of her unsheathed. Clearing her throat, she looked away and took a bite out of a donut before her mind wandered into dangerous territory right before she had to meet a patient.

Al had seriously lifted her spirits so the rest of her shift she was able to take her mind off of Logan and pay attention to her patients. She had hoped to have a message from Logan waiting on her phone when she left work, but she didn't, which left her to wonder if she should message him. While thinking about it, a message came through from an unknown number.

Hey Abi, it's Kailynn. Would you be up for dinner tonight?

Abigail stared at her phone and considered saying no in hopes of seeing Logan, but immediately brushed that thought aside. After all, it was Logan who encouraged her to talk to Kailynn.

She shot back a reply saying yes and asked where they should meet before driving home to change out of her scrubs.

During her drive home from work, she chewed on her lip pondering if she should still text Logan.

What harm would it do if I messaged him? He may be happy to hear from me, or he may choose to ignore it, or he may think I'm being too pushy. She frowned.

Walking into her apartment, she dropped her purse and phone on the kitchen table and changed. A text from Kailynn had come through almost immediately with dinner plans, so Abigail went straight back to her car after freshening up.

She arrived at the diner that Kailynn picked. It was an old high school hangout of theirs, which had old fashioned sodas and burgers. Abigail twirled her straw around her glass, watching the soda swirl, her chin in her hand. Kailynn would be there any minute, and

Abigail wasn't sure if she was quite ready for this conversation. But, at the same time, she was. She wanted answers and it would take her mind off of Logan for a little while.

Logan's encouragement to make up with Kailynn was the reason Abigail finally agreed. She didn't want to harbor any ill will toward her former best friend, so even if they didn't become friends again, at least they could clear the air.

Her phone seemed to be taunting her as she waited for Kailynn, so she grabbed it and opened up a text message to Logan. Pursing her lips, she sighed and set her phone aside. "Don't do it," she whispered to herself.

She stared at her phone still sitting there taunting her. She bit her lip and snatched it up really quick, sending a message before she could change her mind.

How was your day?

The phone sat silent and she stared at it for a few minutes before she rolled her eyes at herself and flipped it over. She needed to stop caring so much. This was pathetic.

Abigail's thoughts were interrupted when Kailynn dropped in the seat across from her.

"Thank you for coming to see me."

Abigail sat up straight and plastered a smile on her face. "You're welcome."

They sat in awkward silence for a minute before Kailynn pushed some hair behind her ear and laughed nervously.

"I'm sorry for everything I put you through senior year. You didn't deserve it."

Abigail skimmed the menu and then pushed it away from her when she settled on what she wanted. "Why did you ditch me for Jessica?"

"For popularity." She shifted uncomfortably in her chair. "I know that's a poor excuse. It's no excuse, really. I wanted so desperately to be popular that I gave up the one honest, good person in my life."

Abigail averted her eyes, unsure of how to respond. "You really hurt me when you all started the rumor about me being a terrible painter."

She nodded. "I know. I regret it every day, but I knew you wouldn't let it hold you back. You were amazingly talented and I always told you that growing up. I knew you wouldn't believe it."

That was funny, since she *did* believe it. She met her gaze head on. "You crushed me."

"You didn't actually believe that rumor, right?"

Abigail only stared at her before the waitress walked up, taking both of their orders, and then disappeared again. "I guess you didn't know me as well as you thought you did."

"Abi, I was one of your biggest cheerleaders growing up. I knew you doubted yourself, but by the time we were applying for college junior year, you were confident in your art. And the art schools you were applying to, they all wanted you."

Abigail took a sip of her drink and wondered why some petty rumor could stop her from her dream. But, she knew why. It was because her best friend was the one who started it. The person who had always been so honest with her about her work was the one telling everyone how horrible it was. By the end of it, she didn't know if Kailynn had been lying to her all along. She began doubting whether or not her parents were giving honest opinions or if they were just telling her her work was good because they felt obligated. She hadn't known what to believe. So, she had given up. As stupid as she now realized that was, she had given up.

"I'm so sorry." Kailynn's eyes welled with tears as she realized she completely shattered Abigail, completely destroyed her best friend for popularity.

"You know," Abigail said. "It's okay. I ended up with a good career as a dental hygienist. It's safe and it's a guaranteed paycheck. I'm probably doing better now than I ever would have been as an artist anyway."

"What? You gave up painting?"

"No. I still do it for fun, but no one ever sees it."

Kailynn leaned against the table. "I feel horrible. You are so talented and you're hiding it away. That's awful! Everyone needs to see your work."

Abigail only laughed, the thought of that a serious joke to her. No one cared to see her work, except maybe her parents. Well, and Al, since he had been bugging her ever since he found out she was a painter. Afraid he'd hate them, she had yet to let him in on that world.

"I'm serious, Abi!"

"Okay."

Kailynn glared, a look Abigail knew all too well growing up.

Here it goes...

"Let's make a bet!"

She couldn't help but laugh at Kailynn's predictability.

"About?"

"You let five people see your work, and if their reviews aren't all positive, then I'll back off and never say anything about art again."

Abigail raised an eyebrow. "And if they do like it?"

"You have to try to sell your paintings."

Their food arrived and Abigail sat back, eyeing Kailynn as she put a fry in her mouth. What did she have to lose? On one hand, her worst fears of not being talented would come true. But, on the other, her work was already just sitting in a dark room collecting dust without anyone seeing it. Would it really be that big of a deal if she finally showed it to people? If she received a negative review, she wouldn't lose anything by it except maybe a little pride.

"Okay. Deal."

They reached across the table and shook on it, then fell into a comfortable silence as they ate their food. Abigail's mind swirled around who she would show her work to. Al was a given and maybe Margi, but who else?

Her mind immediately went to Logan and she hesitated. Her heart picked up its pace. Could she show Logan? Could she open herself up to criticism from him?

As if Kailynn were reading her mind, she asked, "Do you know who you're going to show your art to?"

Wondering if she should mention Logan to Kailynn, she hesitated. Kailynn knew Abigail had had a huge crush on him, and she was almost surprised that that rumor hadn't gotten around after Kailynn became Jessica's friend. But, surprisingly, it had stayed under wraps.

"Well, I'm going to show it to my boss, who is also my best friend. He's been asking me to see my work for a few years now, but I've never found the courage. Then, possibly my secretary. And, maybe... Logan."

She lifted her eyes to Kailynn's to gauge her reaction.

"I was wondering if you two were seeing each other."

Abigail couldn't keep the surprise out of her voice. "Why do you say that?"

"Oh, please. At the reunion, you two were throwing each other some serious looks, and then I saw you both leave together."

Abigail blushed as her mind went to the morning after the reunion. "Yeah, that was an interesting night."

Kailynn stared at her and waited as the silence passed between them. "Please tell me you aren't going to leave it like that. I want details!"

Abigail laughed. "Well, I had had a lot to drink, so nothing happened that night. But we are seeing each other now."

Kailynn covered her mouth with her hands. "Oh my gosh, Abi. I'm so happy for you. I always wondered if he would get the courage to ask you out."

"What do you mean?"

"Because of high school. He had a huge crush on you."

Abigail gaped. "How do you know that?"

"When the rumor about your art circulated, he squashed it."

Abigail was dumbfounded. She thought back to when the rumor was circulating. She remembered being in a hallway one day crying while classes were still in session. Logan had appeared out of nowhere and asked if she was okay. She was mortified that he had seen her cry and she ran off to a bathroom to hide. It wasn't one of her finer moments, but she didn't want the boy she was crazy about to see her so weak.

Within a week the rumors had died out.

"How did he do that?" Abigail whispered.

"Honestly? I'm not entirely sure. He pulled Jessica aside one day and after that, she decided to stop talking about you. She never brought you up again."

Abigail's heart fluttered and she wanted to text Logan again and tell him she missed him, but refrained. She needed to bring it up in person.

Kailynn was nearly done with her food before Abigail realized she had zoned out for several minutes with her plate still full.

She shook her head. "Enough about me, what have you been up to over the last several years?"

Kailynn went on to tell her how she went into the clothing business with her long-time boyfriend. He handled the website and business side of things, while she designed the clothes. It had always been Kailynn's dream and Abigail couldn't help but feel a little jealous that Kailynn went for what she wanted and got it. Abigail's heart sank as the feeling of failure settled into her gut. Then, a renewed sense of strength shot through her. She was still young. She could still achieve her dreams. And the first thing she needed to do was show off her work.

They parted ways on good terms. Abigail dropped into her car and started her commute home. Her phone chimed and a message from Logan came through.

It's still going. Still at work.

I'm sorry to hear that. I hope you get to go home soon!

Her mind immediately went back to her conversation with Kailynn, no longer concerned about waiting on Logan to write. A fire was lit inside of her to try to pursue her dreams. A fire that had been dampened over time that was now growing with newfound hope.

Pulling into her parking lot, she marched straight into her studio and sat at the easel.

The images from the hike flew through her head, so she pulled out her paints and tied the apron around her waist. Before she knew it, it was midnight and the view of the mountains and vineyards was drying in front of her with a slight view of the ocean on one side.

She stepped away from the canvas and viewed her work. A smile graced her lips. The image was exactly as she remembered it. And this was definitely one of the best pieces she had done. She snapped a picture of it and immediately texted it to her parents. Cringing, she glanced at the clock. It was nearing one in the morning which meant it was nearly four in the morning in Florida where her parents lived.

Sorry! I hope I didn't wake you!

A reply never came through, so she sighed in relief and slipped into bed. She knew she would pay for the late night in the morning, but she didn't care. Her heart was full.

LOGAN GLANCED at the clock and saw 10 p.m. displayed on the face. *Damn it*, he sighed. He had meant to call Abigail, but knew it was now too late. She was usually in bed early. He considered sending her a text, but decided against it in fear of waking her. He would call her the next day.

Logan and his co-workers had spent most of the evening listening to their boss, Paul Leonard, yelling at and firing another one of their colleagues. Apparently their colleague was the reason they had risked losing their biggest client. He had ignored several of their requests to invest in specific funds.

After his co-worker was fired, Logan's boss called him in and told him to do whatever it took to keep that client on board. Logan spent the evening trying to think of a way to make them happy.

The company he worked for was unique. They had a team of advisors working with the clients. They didn't work on a commission basis, but rather a bonus basis if they kept the clients happy. Roughly ten advisors worked in his office, several of which were in entry-level positions. Logan had been with the company long enough that he was deciding whether or not to branch out on his own. There weren't many more spots to climb the ladder. He was on the highest rung available to employees at the time unless a partner position opened up, which was a very rare occurrence, and not something he necessarily wanted.

He took a deep breath and stared at his computer screen. He had way too much riding on this and this client risked making or breaking his career.

A voice interrupting the silence startled him out of his thoughts. His co-worker Kevin stood in his doorway.

"Dude, why are you still here?"

Logan sighed and leaned back. "Working on the Voss file."

Kevin let out a low whistle. "I don't envy you, man."

Kevin had been with the company almost as long as Logan had. He was sitting on the same rung of the ladder as Logan, but, unlike Logan, he was content with his position.

Logan ran a hand over his face. "I know. I'm getting a bit sick of this shit."

Kevin dropped himself in a seat across from Logan's desk. "Thinking about jumping ship?"

"I won't lie. The thought has crossed my mind."

"Word in the office is that several people are thinking so after that meeting."

This caught Logan's attention. He leaned forward in his chair. He generally didn't involve himself in the office gossip and tried to keep to himself, so it wasn't unusual for him to not hear about anything going on. But Kevin always kept Logan caught up on anything super juicy.

"Really?"

"Yeah, man. Apparently Sandra was crying in the bathroom today. Kylie saw her and asked what was wrong, and I guess the pressure is just getting to her."

Kylie was the office gossip. If anything was happening to anyone, she knew about it, and she spread it. That was one of the reasons Logan tried to avoid getting involved. If he stayed away from everyone, his business would remain his business.

"Kylie even said that she's getting worried she'll lose her job. But I kind of think she's just saying that for attention."

Logan nodded along. Kylie definitely enjoyed having the attention on herself, so he wouldn't put it past her. He did feel bad for Sandra though. As far as he knew, she was a decent worker. She was only an intern. Generally this was a business where you needed thick skin, but he had heard the opposite from others in his field. He began to wonder if it was only the company they were involved in that was that way. It was unfortunate that Paul could possibly turn people off of working in the industry, just another reason Logan filed in his "start my own firm" file. If he were ever fortunate to be able to start his own company, he surely wouldn't treat his employees poorly. He had always understood that if employees were treated well, they would work harder for their company. But this company was by far the opposite. Being the first and only financial company Logan had worked for right out of college, he didn't have anything to compare it to, aside from working oddball retail jobs throughout college to help pay his loans. And he was certainly treated better working at those minimum wage jobs than he was in this profession.

He ran his hand along his hair and packed up his briefcase before grabbing his jacket and walking out the door. He had some thinking to do and his bed was calling him, but he didn't ignore the fact that he wished it were Abigail's bed he was crawling into.

ABIGAIL WOKE up the next morning without any messages waiting for her. Rubbing her eyes, she told herself she was pathetic. She definitely had it bad. She couldn't remember the last time she stared at a phone willing it to ring or notify her she had a text message. It had to have been in high school. It was almost embarrassing at how eager she was to hear from him.

When her phone rang while she was driving to work, she answered it eagerly, expecting to hear Logan's voice ring through.

"Hi, honey!"

Abigail smiled. "Hi, Mom."

Abigail's mom, Anita, was always a perk to Abigail's day. Abigail loved hearing her voice. As if it were some sort of magical power she possessed, Anita was able to bring a smile to Abigail's face whenever she talked to her.

"I know you must be getting close to work, but I just wanted to tell you that the painting you sent us during the night is so beautiful!"

"Aw thanks, Mom."

"Your dad thinks so too. But, honey, don't you think you should be going to bed at a decent time? You must be exhausted!"

Abigail laughed. Her mom, always the worrier. If her parents hadn't moved to Florida, Abigail would half expect her mom to be waiting at her apartment door when she got home to bring her dinner and make sure she went to bed early.

Her dad's voice rang out in the background. "Anita, let the girl do what she wants. She's an adult."

"George, I'm going to make sure Abi is getting enough sleep. I don't want her getting sick."

Abigail laughed. It was times like these she wished she lived closer to them. At the same time, she enjoyed having the space. She loved her parents dearly, but having them hover over her was a bit much. She only wish she lived a few hours away from them instead of across the country.

"Mom, I'm getting enough sleep. Don't worry. I don't normally stay up that late. I'm just getting to work, so I'm going to let you go. Tell Dad hi for me. I love you both!"

"We love you too, honey."

Abigail laughed and made her way into the break room. Al asked about her evening as soon as she walked in and she told him about her visit with Kailynn, but left out the part where she suggested Abigail show her art to several people. She knew if she told Al, he would be all over her to show him her work, and she wasn't quite ready for that pressure.

Then, she told him Logan had worked late, and she hadn't heard from him otherwise. He frowned. Although he didn't say it, she could tell he was thinking that maybe they had both misjudged Logan's feelings for her. She was still elated that Logan had looked out for her in high school, but that didn't hold any bearing to his current actions.

After work, Al asked her if she wanted to go to dinner with him, which she suspected was to take her mind off of Logan. She happily accepted as they hadn't spent time together outside of work in months. They both went home to change and then he picked her up. She wore a red, fitted, lace dress with cap sleeves, and white wedges that had a single strap to avoid putting any pressure on the blisters on her feet. Her hair was pinned up in a curly bun. Al was wearing black slacks and a blue button up shirt. His blonde hair was slicked back.

"You look sexy," she said when he knocked on her door.

He winked at her. "Right back at ya, beautiful."

He held a hand out to allow her to walk in front of him, but she hesitated. Now would be the perfect time to show Al her art.

"Are you coming?" He stared at her expectantly, arm still poised for her to come outside.

"Um." She glanced down the hall toward her studio and then looked back at him. "I'm wondering if I should show you my art."

His eyes widened and he immediately stepped into the apartment, shutting the door behind him. "Of course you should! I want to see!"

She laughed at his eagerness and motioned for him to follow her. She could almost hear him skipping behind her in excitement, even though he was walking normally. She led him over to her spare room and paused in front of the door, turning around to face him with the door at her back. Her hands started shaking, so she clasped them together in front of her.

"Maybe we shouldn't do this."

"Are you kidding me? I'm so excited!"

She cast her gaze down. "I'm just worried you won't like them."

"Honey, first of all, that's impossible. Second, I've been wanting to see your artistic side for years. YEARS! You cannot take this away from me!" He stamped a foot for good measure. "You just held out a piece of meat. You cannot take it back! I will fight to the death!"

She laughed at his dramatics and moved her hand to the knob. "Okay. Well, since you asked so nicely." But she pause before pushing the door open. "I need you to be completely honest. I don't want to go listing these for sale if they aren't good. I trust you wouldn't let me embarrass myself like that."

"You're going to list them for sale?!" His voice raised an octave.

She arched an eyebrow at him in response.

He rolled his eyes. "We are going to discuss this at dinner. You're being so dramatic. Just open the damn door."

She pushed the door open and closed her eyes as Al stepped inside.

Here goes nothing.

The silence dragged on as she waited, so she finally cracked her eyes. He was standing in front of a stack of her paintings that were leaning against the wall. The particular piece he was looking at was probably four canvases deep and it depicted a beach sunset. She had taken a picture of the sunset when she was a teenager and on summer vacation in Hawaii with her parents. In the painting, she had tried to match the colors exactly, but was always slightly disappointed that they didn't quite capture the sunset the way she saw it. The painting, however, wouldn't be compared to the photo by anyone. But she still never felt like it was worthy of being hung in someone's home.

He lifted it out of the stack and held it at arm's length in front of him. It was on the smaller side, only being a 10x14, so Al could easily view the whole thing at a short distance. He turned to face her, the art still in his hand and her heart sank. Of all of the paintings, he had to choose one she wasn't nearly as proud of. She prepared herself for the bad review.

"Abi," he started.

"Yes?"

"This is perhaps the most beautiful painting I have ever seen."

Her head snapped up at him, looking for any hint of a joke on his face. "You're kidding me."

"Why would I be kidding? The colors are radiant. They seriously pop. You captured it so beautifully, and I can picture this exact sunset as if I were seeing it myself."

She stared at him, waiting for the punchline.

"I'm saying you are incredibly talented. Every painting in here," he waved his hands around him to indicate the stacks of paintings against the walls, "is beautiful."

Relief flooded through her. She didn't realize she had wound herself up as tight as she had, but his praise slowly released the tension she was holding and tears suddenly pricked at her eyes. "Really?"

"Really." He took a step toward her, still holding the beach scene. "I can't believe you've never tried selling these before. And, now, I'm your biggest fan. You're going to sell these. I'm going to see to it."

She laughed as the tears spilled over. He pulled her to him in a side hug.

"And, I want to be your first customer. I'm buying this and hanging it in the office."

She wiped at her face as she pulled back. "You don't have to buy it. You can just have it."

He gave her a look saying "oh please", and negotiated back and forth with her on a price. She insisted several times he could just have it, but he wouldn't take no for an answer. Eventually they settled on a price, and then went to his car to head to dinner. Abigail felt amazingly lighter.

LOGAN GLANCED at the clock and saw it was nearing the time Abigail was about to get off of work. He grabbed his coat and headed toward the doors with the intention of showing up and surprising her with a nice night out to dinner, but Paul stopped him before he could leave.

"Logan, I need you to take Mrs. Voss out to dinner. Schmooze her," he said.

Logan nodded. "I will call her tomorrow and take her out."

"No, you need to take her tonight. We've been working on her to stay with us, and I really think you could win her over if you just use your charm on her and assure her that we will do whatever it takes to keep her around."

"Mr. Leonard, I had plans to take..." he stopped when Paul raised an eyebrow. That eyebrow raise usually meant he was walking on thin ice and needed to shut up. "Yes, sir."

"I knew I could count on you." He clapped him on the shoulder as he walked by.

Logan sighed and walked back to his office to put in a call to Mrs. Voss.

ABIGAIL AND AL pulled up at an expensive, fancy restaurant in the area, and Al held out his arm to escort her to their table. She gladly accepted it. She was grateful for her friendship with Al. He had already saved her from staring at her phone all night, plus his vote of confidence in her paintings was a serious high. They sat at their table and looked over the menu as their waiter approached them. She felt like she was about to burst with excitement.

"Hello, my name is Brian, and I'll be waiting on you tonight." He started filling their water glasses from the pitcher he was holding. "Date night?" He was around five feet, nine inches tall with darker skin and had boyish dimples that made him look like he was in his late twenties; although, he was probably older. He looked between them and there was a little flicker in his eye as she saw him quickly look Al up and down. She hid her smile behind her hand.

"Yes, but it's a friend date," she said, enunciating 'friend' a little more than necessary. Al kicked her under the table.

He flashed them both a smile and said he would be back to take their orders shortly. She pressed her lips together and looked over at Al as he walked away. A blush crept up Al's neck as he pretended to stare at his menu. She reached over and slapped his arm. "He's cute!"

Al shrugged.

"Oh my gosh, don't even pretend you don't think he's cute." She stared at him in disbelief. She might have thought Al didn't find their waiter attractive if a little smile hadn't crept on his face.

"Don't make a scene, Abi," he whispered, keeping his eyes on the menu.

She rolled her eyes and figured out what she wanted to eat. When Al finally set his menu down she raised her eyebrows at him twice in a suggestive way. He sipped his water to try to hide his smile as their waiter came back to take their order. She told him what she wanted and then Brian turned to Al.

"And for you, sir?"

As Al told Brian his order, Brian's gaydar seemed to go on high alert. He raised his eyebrows, an appreciative smile coming over his face. Abigail bit her lip to keep from laughing as he walked away after winking at Al.

"Shut up," Al whispered.

"You should slip him your number!" She tore off a corner of her cocktail napkin and pulled a pen out of her purse, writing Al's number on it. Al reached over and snatched it from her. She pouted. "Oh come on! You should go out with him. If anything, you might have a little fun." She waggled her eyebrows at him suggestively again and he rolled his eyes.

"Let's change the subject, please," he said.

She could tell he was secretly enjoying it as his eyes followed the waiter around the room, but she didn't bring it up again. Al and Abigail laughed at the suggestive remarks and advances Brian made to Al every time he came over, and she told herself she was going to give it her best effort to slide Al's number to him before they left. Their food was amazing and Brian gave them a dessert on the house for "forgetting" to bring them their drinks. Of course, nothing was forgotten, but they didn't complain.

"We should come here more often," she whispered and Al turned red.

She told Al she was going to go to the bathroom and slipped by the hostess booth to grab a business card off of the podium. She wrote Al's number on the card and planned on giving it to Brian the next opportunity that presented itself. As she walked back to their table, she veered off to the side where Brian was clearing another table.

"Brian, his name is Al. Give him a call." She winked and the smile that grew on his face made him look like a kid in a candy store. She couldn't help but laugh at his expression, when she suddenly caught the eye of the man at the table next to where they were standing.

She would know those eyes anywhere. Logan.

Her eyebrows merged together and the smile fell off of her face, her high now turning into a low. All she could tell of the person he was with was that she was a slender brunette wearing a slimming black dress. The jealousy that slapped her across the face was blinding, but not as horrible as the pain that shot through her chest. His eyes flickered with recognition as he saw her, but she didn't wait to see what he would do. She turned and went back to her table where Al was taking care of the tab.

"Let's go," she said and grabbed his arm.

"Hang on, I'm not done." He was scribbling his number across the top of the receipt.

"That's not necessary, I already gave it to him. Let's go, please."

He sighed. "Abi." When he looked up and saw her expression, concern lines etched across his face. "What's wrong?"

"He's here with another woman. Can we please leave?" She looked around and saw Logan watching them from his table. She quickly turned away and looked back at Al. "Please."

"Of course." He stood up and said thank you to Brian as they passed him. They, unfortunately, had to walk by Logan's table to get to the front door. He didn't say anything, and she didn't attempt to look at him. Al put his hand on her back and led her to the door. She tried to refrain from looking back, but couldn't. She caught Logan's eye just as they slipped out. He looked like he wanted to come after her. But, he didn't.

And that spoke volumes.

11

Abigail wrung her fingers together while Al drove her back to her apartment. Al looked at her frequently and patted her leg with his hand. "I'm sorry, Abi. Do you want to talk about it?"

"I fell for him, Al," she whispered. Her heart felt like it had cracked in half. "I don't know what I did."

He shook his head. "You didn't do anything."

"We had such a great weekend together. Or at least I thought we did." Her voice broke and she covered her mouth with her hands as tears brimmed her eyes.

He squeezed her leg. "He's probably just one of those guys who never settles down and doesn't know a good thing when it bites him in the ass."

She sniffled and nodded. "Maybe that's it." She didn't actually believe it, but it made her feel better thinking it could be a possible reason.

They didn't say anything else until he pulled up in front of her apartment building. "I will walk you to the door."

She shook her head. "No, I'll be fine."

His eyebrows knit together as his eyes roamed over her face. "Are you sure?"

Nodding, she said, "I'm fine. I'll see you tomorrow. Thanks for dinner."

He gave her hand a squeeze. "Anytime sweetie. Call me if you need me."

He waited until she was out of sight before he drove away. She sighed and walked into her apartment, dropping her purse on the table. She fought her tears, telling herself she wouldn't cry over Logan. She took several deep breaths until her tears vanished. Even though it had only been a week and a half since they hooked up, it felt like it had been much longer. Her heart hurt as she thought back to the pretty woman he was with. He was playing the field. She shook her head and kicked off her shoes as her cell phone rang. Digging it out of her purse, she saw "Logan" flash across the screen.

"Now you want to talk to me." She hit the decline button. "No thanks."

Dropping the phone on the table, she went into the kitchen to grab a glass of water when her phone rang again. She dropped her head back as she walked back over to her phone, and once again, "Logan" flashed across the screen. Again, she hit the decline button. This time she waited. She wondered if he would call a third time, but figured he got the picture when a text came through from him.

That wasn't what you thought it was. Please answer the phone.

A minute later the phone rang. She stared at it and debated. He could have contacted her the last couple of days and didn't bother, but now she caught him dating another woman and he all of a sudden wants to talk to her? No thanks. She didn't want to be a fall back. She definitely deserved better than that. This time she didn't bother to decline the call; she just let it ring through to voicemail.

She sat down at the table with her glass of water and stared at the phone. After waiting five minutes in silence she stood up and went into the bathroom. Staring into the mirror, her chocolate brown eyes looked dead and sad. It was still early, but she was definitely going to bed. A knock at her door pulled her out of her thoughts. Her eyebrows furrowed as she wondered if Al had come back to check on her.

Looking through the peephole, she saw Logan standing on the other side. She leaned her forehead against the door and sighed, considering whether or not to open it. Her phone rang at that moment and she grabbed it to see he was calling. She hit decline and watched through the peephole as he put a hand against the door jamb leaning forward.

"I know you're home, Abi. I can hear the phone ringing. Please answer the door," he said loudly.

She closed her eyes and he knocked again. Not wanting him to disturb her neighbors, she pulled the door open only about a foot and looked at him. He was wearing a navy blue suit with a white button up shirt. He had pulled his tie off and loosened the neck of his shirt which was no longer tucked in. His dirty blonde hair was perfectly spiked with gel, and he still looked like a million bucks.

Damn him. Leaning her hip against the wall, she crossed her arms and stared at the ground.

"Can I come in?" he asked.

She debated this. If she let him in, she knew he could convince her of anything and she would have a hard time refusing him. But at the same time, if she made him stay outside, all of their drama would be on display for her neighbors to hear which she didn't want either. She sighed and pulled the door open wider and closed it behind him. She turned around and leaned against the door, folding her arms across her chest and briefly looked up at him before casting her gaze downward.

"Abi, that wasn't what you thought it was. She's a client. I'm not dating her and I have no interest in her."

She bit her lip and didn't say anything. A client? She wasn't sure she believed him. She cleared her throat. "You don't owe me an explanation."

"Yes, I do." He stepped closer to her and put a hand on her arms. "You're upset, and I don't want to see you upset."

Her arms tingled where his hand rested. They were still crossed in front of her and she was having a hard time paying attention to what he was saying with him standing so close. She stepped away and walked into her bathroom before he could so easily break her resolve. Logan followed behind her. He watched her from the door as she tugged the bobby pins out of her hair.

"Abi," he said.

She ignored him and continued pulling them out until her hair cascaded down around her.

"Abi, look at me."

She put her hands on the edge of the counter and sighed, looking over at him. He was leaning against her door jamb watching her with his hands stuffed in his pockets. He looked like he was about to walk into a GQ photo shoot.

"She's a client. Nothing more."

"Okay," she said and looked back into the mirror.

"You don't believe me." He didn't ask. He stated it. "Don't you think if I was dating her I would be with her right now? I wouldn't have called you four times and come over here. That wouldn't make sense."

She didn't say anything, but she closed her eyes. He was right. It didn't make sense. She wanted to ask him questions, but didn't want to sound like a jealous girlfriend. As far as she knew, they weren't really dating. They were just friends with benefits who liked each other a little more.

He took a step forward and grabbed her hand, pulling her to him. "Abigail, please believe me. I'm not into cougars."

She furrowed her eyebrows and looked at him strangely. *What's he talking about?*

His eyebrows shot up. "You never looked at her, did you?" When she didn't respond, he continued, "she's in her fifties, and, by the way, has five kids. One of who is our age."

She is in her fifties? A laugh escaped her lips which she tried to hide. She did only see the other woman from behind. She just assumed she was young. Relief flooded her chest. Her small laugh turned into a loud laugh as she thought of how ridiculous she must have looked getting jealous over a fifty-year-old. He started laughing beside her and soon she was leaning into him laughing against his chest.

When their laughs subsided he pulled back and looked down at her. "So are we okay now?"

She nodded and dropped her head, suddenly feeling very embarrassed about her behavior. Any other girl probably would have reacted the same way she had, but she felt a little silly that she didn't realize the lady was older and he was probably there on a business meeting. But why hadn't he told her he had a business meeting tonight? Why hadn't she heard from him at all?

Logan's hand found her chin as he lifted her face up to his. "What's wrong?"

"Nothing," she said.

He raised an eyebrow. "Are you still upset with me?"

She shook her head. His eyes searched hers and she wanted badly to close them, but knew he would just press her for answers. That gaze of his seemed to intensify so she pulled back from him and dropped her eyes. She couldn't handle his soul-searching gaze right now. Walking to the living room, she dropped on the couch and he followed right behind her. He pulled his jacket off and laid it on the back of one of her dining room chairs before joining her on the couch. He sat down facing her and gave her a questioning look.

"Abi, talk to me."

She looked straight ahead and closed her eyes. She wanted to ask him about why he hadn't called her the last few days and why he was acting weird in the car ride home from Napa Valley, but she was afraid of freaking him out. She didn't know what to say. He wanted her to be honest with him, but frankly, it was hard.

Logan grabbed her hand and tugged it, until she turned to face him. His hand came up to her cheek. "Are you still upset?"

She opened her eyes and looked straight into his. "No, I'm not."

"Why are you acting weird?"

"I'm not," she whispered. She knew she was, just like he did. She hoped he would drop it just like she did in the car for him, but he was too curious of a person and she knew he wasn't going to let it go.

He watched her and sighed. "Abi, please don't play any games with me. I'm not good at guessing."

Her eyebrows raised. Games? She pulled back from him and frowned. "I'm not playing games, Logan. Is it a crime for me to keep my thoughts to myself once in a while?"

He reached for her again, but she scooted back. Dropping his hands into his lap, he watched her. "I just want you to be honest with me. What's on your mind?"

Her emotions seemed to erupt from her as all of her worries and frustrations from the last few days tumbled out. "What's on my mind? You really want to know? I'm wondering where you've been the last few days. I haven't heard from you and when I sent you a message, all you said was that you were working late. I don't know what I did to upset you or why you've been avoiding me. And then I see you tonight with another woman. Which, at the time I didn't know was a client, so of course I was upset.

"In the car on the drive home on Sunday, you were silent and had such a pensive look on your face, which I automatically assumed was about me, because, let's be honest, I'm insecure. I asked you if you were all right, and I *knew* something was wrong, but you wouldn't talk to me. So I gave you your space. I've only been crazy about you since I was fifteen, so when you go MIA I sit here and dissect everything I've done, wondering what I could have done to upset you.

"And here I am, trying my hardest to keep my mouth shut, but you keep asking questions. And I don't feel comfortable asking *you* questions because I'm afraid of scaring you away. Talking to you is incredibly difficult because I don't know what we are or where we stand." She took a deep breath and her eyes widened as her brain caught up with everything her mouth just spit out. She put a hand over her gaping mouth as she watched him in astonishment.

He seemed stunned. Leaning back slightly, his eyes were wider than normal as he took everything in.

She had definitely scared him. She stood up and stepped backwards as he stood up as well. Then she turned and ran to her bedroom, hoping he would just leave and let her drown in her own embarrassment.

She laid on her bed and put her face in her pillow like she used to do when she was a teenager and was upset. She wasn't upset right now, more embarrassed, and putting her head in her pillow at least hid her face from the world. Her bed shifted as he crawled up next to her and put a hand on her back. His hand slid to her shoulder and he tugged her until she was lying on her side facing him. He lay in a similar position facing her.

The heat spread across her face and she closed her eyes. His hand came to her cheek and he leaned forward pressing his lips to hers. When he pulled back, she opened her eyes. "I'm sorry. I shouldn't have..." she started. He cut her off as he pressed another kiss to her lips. "Logan..." Again he cut her off. "I'm sorry..." He deepened the kiss as he leaned forward and moved her onto her back. She sighed against his lips as her attempt to talk to him failed. He leaned over her and put one of his knees between her legs to hold his weight, careful not to trap her.

He let up and propped himself over her. "Never," he kissed her, "apologize," he kissed her again, "for telling me," another kiss, "what's on," and again, "your mind." He placed another kiss on her lips but lingered this time. His fingers slid through her hair as his eyes roamed over her face. "It's not that I didn't want to talk to you the last few days, Abi. I've been very busy with work and trying to keep a client with the company. My boss expects me to keep this client happy and I'm afraid I'll lose my job if I don't. I was planning on asking you to dinner tonight, but just as I was leaving, my boss grabbed me and said I needed to take the client you saw to dinner. I couldn't say no."

Her fingers fiddled with the bottom of his shirt as she stared at his chest. He caught them between his hands. "I have a hard time with relationships and for some reason, it's even harder with you. I don't know what to say, and I don't want to disappoint you. And while I'm realizing that you would prefer me to say something over nothing," he laughed, "I didn't know that before, so I will try to be better about contacting you. No matter what time it is."

He brought her hand to his lips. Their fingers intertwined as he kissed the back of her hand.

Her eyes met his as she whispered, "Truth: You look very sexy tonight."

He smiled. "Truth: I had a hard time not grabbing you and doing naughty things as soon as I saw you in the restaurant."

She blushed and bit her lip. He dipped his head to hers again and kissed her. Her fingers found his buttons as she slowly undid his shirt and slipped it over his shoulders. Grabbing his undershirt, she pulled it over his head as they broke away briefly and he fiddled with the zipper on the back of her dress.

Zip. The sound sent goosebumps down her body, her body trembling with excitement.

She lifted off of the bed momentarily for him to slide it off of her, and then reached for his pants. Soon they were both lying naked on her bed. His hand roamed down her sides and teased the side of her breasts, sending chills down her body again, before gripping her hip.

His eyes roamed over hers before she reached up and pulled his face down to hers. His hands continued their exploration. She took his hard-on into her palm, rubbing up and down to excite him. He kissed her harder and his fingers slipped into her. Her breath caught as he worked her up and down bringing her onto the brink of an orgasm and then withdrawing.

All thoughts of not hearing from him were fleeting. This was where she wanted to be. This was how she wanted to spend her evening—with him. She didn't want him to be with anyone but her.

She raised her hips toward his retreating hand and moaned in protest, but his shaft was quick to replace it. He thrust into her and stared into her eyes as she matched his rhythm. Her hands gripped his ass as she pulled him hard into her until he couldn't get any closer. Pleasure ripped through her body as he continued the hard thrusts she wanted, hitting her in all the right places.

He was deliciously hers.

The heat began to build in her chest and rose through her neck and up to her face as she reached her climax. She arched her back and moaned as he thrust harder and released into her at the same time. Slowing his pace, he dropped next to her on the bed to catch his breath.

Her body ached to be with his again. She was dreading him leaving. She needed him to stay, to be with her for the rest of the night. She needed him here.

She slipped her hand down to his and intertwined their fingers. Rolling onto his side, he pulled her up against him and kissed the back of her neck.

"This ended up being a good night," he said.

"Stay," she whispered.

He nodded and they fell asleep wrapped in each other's arms, not a care in the world.

12

Logan awoke to a stream of sunlight pouring in through the parted curtains on the window. Staring at Abigail, he swiftly swiped some hair off of her forehead and leaned down to kiss it. It was still early and he knew her alarm wasn't set to go off for another hour, so he looked around for a piece of paper. Walking into the hallway, he opened the door to the spare room and stopped just inside the doorway. Piece upon piece of art hung on the walls and several canvases were stacked up against the walls, each one a different masterpiece.

His mouth agape, he took a tentative step into the room and looked at every piece surrounding him, memorizing every detail. So much talent was bundled up into that beautiful woman. He was blown away he never knew she was so skilled. He recalled his conversation with her about Kailynn and the rumors that circulated in high school about her being a terrible painter. He never knew her talent, but he had put an end to the rumors by charming Jessica. It wasn't hard since she always flirted with him heavily. And it was his experience that when Jessica attacked someone, it was because she was jealous. He could see now that she was clearly jealous of Abigail's talent. Painting was definitely Abigail's calling.

Shit. She said this was personal.

He turned to leave to avoid invading her privacy when a canvas lying on the easel in the middle of the room caught his eye. The painting consisted of an array of beautiful colors making up mountains, vineyards, and the ocean. He recognized it as the view from the hike and a small smile made its way onto his lips. It completely transported him back as if he were standing on the top of the mountain staring at it in person. He reached out to touch the canvas, but thought better of it and dropped his hand. He would never forgive himself if he ruined such a beautiful piece.

He immediately pictured that painting hanging in his library. It would fit perfectly between a few of the bookshelves on one of the empty walls.

Glancing at his watch, he realized he had spent over a half hour in her studio and quickly looked for a piece of paper, his original mission. He scribbled a note and set it next to her phone where he knew she'd see it and left.

～

ABIGAIL WOKE up alone in bed. A note sat on her nightstand next to her phone where the alarm was blaring. Shutting the alarm off, she grabbed the paper and read the scrawled words: "Needed to get to work extra early this morning. Dinner tonight?"

She smiled and shot him a quick text.

I would love to.

Good morning, beautiful. I will pick you up at 6.

Sending back a smiley face, she dropped her phone on her nightstand and went through her morning routine. She walked into work with a beaming smile on her face which caused Al to stare at her blankly. She quickly told him everything that happened the previous night to catch him up.

"So she was a client?"

She nodded and grabbed a donut from the ever-present box lying on the table.

"And you believe him?"

She faltered and looked up at Al. "Should I not?"

He shrugged. "I don't know. I just don't want to see you get hurt."

"What's going on? You were rooting for him originally." She picked at her donut and watched as he fidgeted. Should she believe that Logan was lying to her? He seemed sincere when they were talking and it was true that she never did see the lady's face, so she could have been any age and she would never have known. Logan didn't know that Abigail never saw her face, so why would he go out of his way to make it up and take a chance that she would catch him in a lie? She frowned. No, he wouldn't do that.

She focused back on Al and saw him shredding a napkin. She narrowed her eyes. "All right, tell me what's going on. This doesn't have anything to do with Logan, does it?"

"Brian called me last night and I slept with him." He said it really fast and then slapped his hands over his mouth wide eyed.

Her mouth dropped open. "Whoa! Was it good?"

He stared at her incredulously. "Didn't you hear what I said?" His voice rose an octave.

"Yes," she said slowly. "Was it good?"

He threw his hands up. "Was it good?! That's what you ask?"

She stared at him wondering what else he expected her to ask. "I'm confused."

"Abi! I have never had a one-night stand." He raised his hands in the air as if he were expecting her to congratulate him, but she just stared.

"What about Roberto?"

If you could crush a person's spirit with a few simple words, she definitely did. His hands dropped and his face fell, but then lifted into a small smile. "Roberto," he whispered.

They both laughed. "You are such a weirdo. You can't even remember you all ready had a one-night stand which was apparently the best sex you ever had."

"No, no. I *thought* it was the best sex I ever had... until I met Brian." He waggled his eyebrows. Apparently after he had dropped her off, he received a call from Brian saying his shift was over. Al decided to go back to the restaurant and have drinks with him, and it went from there.

Abigail and Al went back and forth laughing about his sex life until Margi popped her head in reminding them about their patients.

WHEN LUNCH ROLLED AROUND, Al pulled Abigail into the waiting room knowing it would be empty. He held up her sunset painting against the main wall that led toward the back rooms.

"I'm thinking I'm going to hang it here," he said.

She blushed and looked around at the other art. It would technically match the rest of the room since Al had chosen a beach theme for the waiting room. But this painting was subpar to the rest of the art in the room.

She shrugged. "Are you sure it should go there?"

Al rolled his eyes. "It's the best piece in the place!"

Margi walked out from the kitchen in the back and settled at her desk in the front, leaning over to look at the art Al was holding.

"Oh my gosh," she said. She stood back up and walked around to where they were standing, taking the piece from Al. Holding it at arm's-length, she admired it. "Wow! This is a beauty. I think it would be perfect right there."

"Oh, you like it, huh?" Al asked, giving Abigail a pointed look.

"What's not to like? The way the artist captured the colors. Oh, it's just perfect!"

"I was thinking about commissioning this artist to paint more for our office."

Margi looked over at Al. "Oh! You know the artist? I would love their name! Maybe I can find some pieces for my house too."

"Did Al put you up to this?" Abigail finally asked, throwing an accusatory glance at both of them.

"Put me up to what?"

Al laughed. "Is it so hard to believe that people love your work, Abi?"

Margi's mouth fell open. "You painted this?"

Abigail blushed. "Yes, it's a hobby."

"I would love to see more of your work. I was serious when I said I would like to find some pieces for my house."

Al gave her an *I told you so* look before turning around and hanging the painting on the wall.

LOGAN SAT in his office and tapped his pen on the desk. Biting his thumbnail, he stared at his computer screen. He had a huge decision to make. He could either continue working for this firm, or branch out on his own and start from scratch. The current pressures and treatment at his work were starting to wear on him, and he wondered if the stress of starting his own practice would be as nerve-wracking or if it would alleviate some of the pressure he was currently feeling.

On one hand, he needed to worry about being able to afford his daily expenses, but on the other hand, it could end up paying out tenfold if he stuck with it. He couldn't take any of his current clients with him since he had signed a non-compete, but he wondered if some of them would transfer their assets over once the non-compete expired.

Glancing at the clock, he quickly grabbed his things and shut the light off in his office. The last thing he wanted to do was be late picking Abigail up for their date. Lately she was the only thing keeping him afloat. He had never known happiness like he had since meeting her and wondered if he would eventually screw it all up as he usually did. Trying to open up to a woman was a challenge for him, but she already knew more about him than any other woman he had ever dated.

He got home quickly and gathered up everything he would need for their date. Prepping the food, he carefully put everything into a picnic basket and carried it all to his backyard where he laid out a blanket and set the picnic basket on top. Looking at it, he tilted his head.

No, no. This is all wrong.

He picked them up and glanced around. *Where would Abigail like this the most?*

Biting the inside of his cheek, he walked closer to the stream and laid everything down again. *This is much better. She will love this.*

He hopped into his car and planned to make one more stop before heading to her apartment.

WITH HIS ERRANDS all taken care of, Logan pulled up to her apartment and stood outside the door. He straightened his shirt the best he could while also holding a single red rose for her. This date needed to be perfect. He needed her to know how special she was to him.

He raised his hand to knock, then glanced down at his clothes again. His khaki pants were pressed to perfection and his white button up shirt was buttoned all the way to the top. He quickly unbuttoned the top button. That would do. He knocked before he changed his mind about the button again.

She pulled the door open and he wanted to let out a low whistle, but refrained. A respectable man didn't whistle at his date. Her flowered sundress was fitted to her waist and then flowed down to her knees. White wedges graced her feet and her hair flowed down around her in soft curls. A timid smile presented itself.

He pulled his hand from around his back, presenting the flower to her. "You look absolutely stunning."

A blush filled her face as she took the rose from him and smelled it. "Thank you."

He stepped closer to her and briefly kissed her lips. Motioning him in, she went to the kitchen and pulled out a vase, putting the flower in water. When she turned around, she dropped her gaze. He reached for her hand and pulled her to him. "Are you ready to go?"

She nodded.

He led her to his car and opened her door for her. Going around to the other side, he slid into the driver's seat. Their conversation was brief as he drove. His mind drifted to work and he considered asking for her opinion on the matter, but didn't want to spend their evening discussing something that was beyond stressful for him. Tonight, he wanted to enjoy himself and forget everything weighing on him.

"Where are we going?"

He looked at her quickly and smiled. "You'll see."

A few minutes later, he parked in his driveway. She continued to stare out the window and didn't make a single move.

Logan slipped his hand into hers, startling her. She looked over at him, and a frown on her face quickly shifted to a slight smile. He caressed her cheek and she leaned into his warmth, a small move he loved.

"Are you all right?"

"Yes." She smiled and looked around. "What are we doing at your place?"

He hopped out of the car and came around to her side, opening her door for her. "I thought it might be fun to do dinner here."

Taking her arm, he led her around the house to the backyard where the blanket and picnic basket sat. They sat down and she looked around at his backyard from that angle. The deck coming off of the back of the house was large enough for a patio set. A set of stairs led off of the deck to the grass. One reason he had chosen that particular spot was that the lawn was thick and soft. He pulled various dishes out of the picnic basket as the birds whistled in the trees and the creek babbled next to them.

Producing two wine glasses, he pulled out a bottle of wine they had picked up in Napa Valley. They enjoyed sandwiches and potato salad, along with fruit salad and green beans. After they were done eating, Logan put everything back into the basket and set it off to the side, scooting next to her and stretching his legs out alongside hers. They leaned back on their arms and looked out over the stream and his yard at the setting sun.

He studied her as she seemed to be lost in her thoughts again. A sigh escaped her lips as she laid down on the blanket, staring up at the sky.

Logan propped himself on one arm next to her, his other hand skirting along her stomach. "What are you thinking?"

She continued to stare up at the sky as the sun started to disappear, making way for the stars to peek through the orange glow. He continued his path with his hand and rested it just under her breasts, feeling the warmth of her skin through her dress.

"Abi," he whispered, wiggling his fingers a bit to get her attention.

Making eye contact, her eyes looked a shade darker against the setting sun. She flushed and shifted her eyes past his.

He tilted his head and studied her. He knew something was going through her head, and he also knew that if he didn't find out, he would worry needlessly until she told him. Running different ideas through his head, he wondered how he could coax it out of her while being a gentleman at the same time. He had an idea.

"Truth," he whispered. "I was worried I had lost you yesterday." Hoping his attempt at being honest would coax her into telling him what was going on, he waited.

Her eyes focused back on his, and she propped herself on her elbows, pressing a kiss to his lips. Electricity shot through him. He sighed against her mouth as his hand left her stomach to slide behind her neck. He pulled back but stayed only a few inches from her face as his fingers played with the hair at the nape of her neck. The feel of her against him, even if it was only a small amount of contact, was all he needed tonight. She kept her eyes closed and licked her lips, making it difficult for him not to kiss her again, but he refrained, waiting for her response. She opened her eyes to meet his gaze head-on. His eyes questioned hers.

"Truth," she whispered. She dropped her head and took a deep breath. "I'm scared I'm going to get hurt."

His heart broke a little for her in that moment. He had no intention of ever hurting her and hoped the day never came where either of them would leave. His fingers found her chin and lifted her face back up to his.

"I'm going to try my hardest not to hurt you. Okay?"

She nodded and his lips met hers in a tender kiss.

They watched the sun drop below the horizon as she lay wrapped in his arms. This was the perfect end to a perfect evening. She shivered, so he pulled her closer to his chest, also signaling the evening was coming to an end. He placed a kiss on her temple. "Let's go inside."

Pulling her to her feet, they gathered the blanket and picnic basket and walked in through the back door to the kitchen. He deposited everything on the counter, then pulled her to him, rubbing his hands up and down her arms to warm her up. "I should probably get you home. It's getting late."

He wanted nothing more than for her to stay the night, but he really wanted to show her he could be a gentleman and it was serious for him too. The last thing he wanted was for her to believe she was a booty call.

She glanced at the clock and nodded. Logan drove her back to her apartment and walked her to her door, waiting as she opened it, then he kissed her goodnight. It took all of his willpower not to follow her inside, but he knew it was for the best. She deserved to be treated like a princess and this was going to be the start.

ABIGAIL'S NIGHT was restless as she thought through the evening over and over again. Her brain kept going back to her conversation with Al, and she wondered if Logan was meeting up with another woman after dropping her off. She tried to put her mind at ease, but it was difficult. Why didn't he ask her to stay the night? Why didn't he want to come inside? None of it made any sense.

Eventually she fell asleep a few hours before her alarm was set to go off. When it blared, she dragged herself out of bed and to the shower, still analyzing the previous evening. He had told her he would try not to hurt her. Maybe his way of avoiding hurting her was by slowly cutting things off. But it didn't make sense since he said he was worried he had lost her.

She was confused.

Showing up at work was difficult as her brain was foggy and her body felt like a deadweight. Al talked all morning about Brian, and she listened the best she could without interrupting him to tell him about Logan. She really wanted his opinion, but he had listened to her talk about Logan so much lately, the least she could do was listen to him talk about Brian. She went through the day on autopilot, working through her patient list and then leaving. She waved to Al and sighed in relief for her three-day weekend when she stepped out of the building.

Leaning against her car was Logan. She frowned involuntarily. Unsure of what to say, she tentatively walked toward him.

"Don't be so excited to see me, sweetheart," he said and flashed his pearly white smile at her.

"Hi," was all she could muster as her brain seemed to cloud over with fog again, her exhaustion only increasing tenfold after working a full day.

He caught her hand and pulled her to him, placing a kiss on her forehead. "Hi yourself. Do you want to grab dinner?"

After throwing her things on the passenger seat, she leaned against her car. "Sure." Her brain whirled wondering why he could possibly be there. He didn't seem too interested in her based on his actions the previous night, yet there he was.

She followed him to a local restaurant and they sat at a booth across from each other. She picked up the menu and skimmed it, not knowing what to say to him or how to act. She felt his eyes watching her, but pretended not to notice. The silence passed between them until the waitress came by to take their orders. Taking their menus away, she no longer had anything to hide behind. She stared at the table, shredding her napkin.

Logan's hands reached across the table and grabbed her hands in his. "How was your day?"

The warmth spread through her body at his touch, and she stared at their hands intertwined. "It was okay. How was yours?"

His thumbs glided over the backs of her hands. "Good. Pretty productive. I got an early start."

She nodded, keeping her eyes on their hands. She knew she should just come out and ask him if he was seeing someone else, but she wasn't sure this was the right time or place for that conversation. Silence enveloped them for a few minutes. She tried her hardest to keep her eyes off of his. He could read her too well, and she didn't want to get into a deep conversation at the restaurant.

"You look tired," he said.

She nodded.

"Didn't sleep well last night?"

She shrugged.

"Are you upset with me over something?" His fingers gave hers a squeeze, encouraging her to look up.

She gave pause to that. She wasn't technically upset. She was just confused. She shook her head.

"What's on your mind?"

"Nothing."

"Abi," he paused, "what aren't you telling me?"

Their food arrived which blissfully saved her from having to answer. She pulled her hands from his as the waitress set down their plates. She briefly looked up at Logan who was intensely watching her. Shifting her gaze to the waitress, she thanked her and tried to will her to stay to avoid the awkward conversation that was about to follow. The waitress, of course, left and Abigail was alone with Logan once again.

She was beginning to wonder why she agreed to come to dinner in the first place. Of course, it was because she was crazy about him and even though she was confused, she still wanted to be around him. She sighed and rubbed her eyes as he continued to watch her. He made no move to touch his food.

"Can we please talk about this later?" she asked. He nodded.

They both ate in silence. It wasn't intentional on her part. She just didn't have anything to say. When they finished, Logan walked her to her car, but caught her wrist before she could slide in to escape the conversation. She silently cursed and wished they had discussed it in the restaurant so it would be over with by now.

Damn my procrastination.

Putting his hands on either side of her body, he trapped her between him and the car. That was a moment when she wished her claustrophobia would kick in just so she could escape his arms, but the bastard stayed at bay. She shifted her gaze to his chest.

"Logan, I'm just really tired and want to go home."

"Okay, I will come over and we can talk there." He stood still, not moving his arms, waiting for her reply. He wasn't about to let it go.

"Okay," she agreed.

Hopping into their separate cars, they went back to her place and she kicked herself for not, once again, saying something sooner. Or *at least* being better at hiding her feelings until she could straighten things out in her head. Thinking of him with another woman was tearing her up. Logan followed her inside, and she attempted to busy herself in the kitchen, but he grabbed her hand and pulled her to the couch. There was no getting out of it now.

"Spill," he said.

They were both facing each other and she continually wrung her fingers in her lap and stared down. "Are you seeing someone?" She finally spit out. She dared a look up and fixed her eyes on his aston-ished expression. Apparently he wasn't expecting that.

"I'm seeing you..." he said slowly. "I think."

"I know," she shook her head. "Are you seeing anyone else?"

His eyes clouded over with confusion. "No. Should I be?"

Shifting her gaze back to her hands, she shook her head.

"Are you seeing someone else?"

She looked up and furrowed her eyebrows. "No, of course not."

He put his hands on hers. "Then why are you...?" Understanding dawned on his face. "This has to do with the woman at the restaurant, huh?"

She didn't answer. It did and it didn't. She may have been a client, but Abigail wondered what he had been doing all of those nights when he had been working late, or even the previous night when he dropped her off and left.

"I thought we were past this." He sighed and leaned his arms against his legs to drop his head in his hands, rubbing his face. "Abigail, you need to talk to me about these things. Stop bottling everything up."

The irritation in his voice was evident. She shrank back and chided herself for talking to him about it. She should have kept it to herself. Biting her lip and taking a deep breath, she shifted her gaze back to her hands which he was no longer holding. Tears sprang to her eyes as the last few days weighed on her. That was another reason she didn't like relationships—they made her emotional.

He sat back up and grabbed her hands. "You are the only person I'm seeing. Period. Do you believe me this time?"

The irritation was still there which didn't help her emotions. She let out a deep breath she didn't know she was holding and fought the pool of tears that threatened to fall. She wasn't sure what to say. If he was that annoyed with her, there was a good chance he was telling the truth, but she still didn't understand why he acted so weird the previous night.

His hand swiftly grabbed her chin and tilted her face to his before she had a chance to react. The annoyance written across his face quickly switched to concern when he looked into her eyes. The waiting dam of unshed tears glistened in her eyes. He scooped her up in his arms and set her on his lap, wrapping his arms around her.

"Abigail, please believe me when I say you are the only one I'm with and the only one I want to be with."

She leaned her forehead against his with her eyes closed. They stayed that way in silence for a few minutes before he spoke again. "Now what's this about? There has to be more to this than you have told me."

Opening her eyes, she looked into his face where he studied her. His arms were strong around her as he held her on his lap. Suddenly she felt silly over her overreaction. She blamed her lack of sleep. She moved to slide off him, but he kept a firm grip.

"You're not going anywhere until we have this settled."

She sighed, defeated. "Why didn't you ask me to stay last night?"

"What?"

She looked down at his shirt and played with a button. "Last night, you brought me home, kissed me, and left. Our normal pattern has been spending the night at each other's places or at least sleeping together."

She blushed as she realized how ridiculous she sounded. They weren't required to sleep together every night or spend the night with each other, and it was a little absurd she was insinuating that.

"Abi," he sighed. "I was trying to treat you to a real date since you seem to want more of a relationship. We haven't really been on a date before, so I was trying to be a gentleman. A gentleman doesn't ask his date to sleep over and have sex with her."

Oh. My. God.

Her face burned as she realized she was the pervert in the relationship. He was just trying to be a gentleman and here she was trying to get him in bed. She turned her face away from him and pressed her lips together.

Fuck. Fuckity fuck fuck fuck.

A shudder rocked his body and she rolled her eyes.

Here it comes.

It was quiet at first and then he didn't attempt to hold it in as he laughed loudly, clutching her to him. She tried to sit rigid and keep an annoyed look on her face, but she ended up laughing alongside him. Here she had been pondering over everything excessively and he was just trying to be a good, decent guy.

"Don't laugh at me." A giggle escaped her when she tried to sober up.

He hugged her to him tighter. "If you want to sleep with me, that's all you have to say."

Before she could respond, he picked her up and carried her to the bedroom. Her heart pounded in her chest with anticipation, and her body reacted in kind as she quivered. Dropping her on the bed, he quickly undressed and pulled her clothes off. Then, he was lying on top of her with his mouth pressed to hers. She sighed into his touch as his hand slid down to the heat between her legs. Slipping a finger into her, he pulled back and looked into her eyes. "For the record, I wanted to sleep with you last night."

She moaned as he teased her and pressed a finger deep within her. Her eyes rolled back as the heat spread into her neck. "Logan," she gasped and writhed below him. He watched her face as he aligned a second finger with his first.

Fuck yes.

She reached for him and circled her fingers around his girth. His length thickened in her hands as his eyelids drooped. Masterfully teasing, her back bowed off the bed as the rush ran through her body with her first orgasm. She breathed heavily, still gripping him between her fingers. Her hands slid up and down his length slowly, circling around the tip. He squeezed his eyes shut as she watched his face flush. She quickened her pace as his hips moved along with her hand. His eyes snapped open and he grabbed her hand to stop the movement.

Quickly, he aligned himself with her and pushed in. Her back arched and she moaned as he filled her. He didn't wait for her to stretch, he immediately moved quickly, pumping faster and faster until her moans turned into cries. Her body was still so sensitive from her first release that it was sweet torture. She gripped her head as he adjusted her leg to hitch over his hip. As he sank deep within her, she saw stars. Her release came quickly as did his, shuddering together and collapsing. Her body quivered around him as it attempted to relax.

She ran her hands up and down his back, catching her breath.

He pulled back and placed a kiss on her lips, running his fingers along her jawline. "It's only you. You are the only one I want to be with."

13

Logan woke up alone in bed with the smell of food hitting his nose. He slid off of the sheets and searched around for his boxers. They had been haphazardly tossed across the room. Smiling, he pulled them on as he remembered the night before. They had spent most of the night talking and having sex. It had been perfect.

Opening the bedroom door, he made his way to the kitchen and stopped short, watching Abigail pull french toast off the burner. Her nightgown hit just under her butt and when she moved, it pulled up slightly, teasing him.

This woman, he decided, *is so oblivious to how wild she can make me.*

She turned as if hearing his thoughts and smiled. "Good morning."

"Good morning, beautiful. It smells amazing." He walked over and placed a kiss to her neck, his hands tightening on her waist, trying to resist taking her back to the bedroom right that minute.

Food first, he decided.

Logan grabbed the various plates she had been filling and carried them to the table while she carried over two glasses of orange juice. He was amazed at how easily they could laugh together. They ate breakfast and made light conversation until it occurred to him that he never told her he saw her paintings.

"Hey, Abi..."

"Yes?" She looked up from her food and smiled.

"Remember the other morning when I left you that note?"

"Yes."

"I was looking for paper since I didn't want to wake you, and I went into your studio."

"Oh." Her smile dropped and her eyes shifted down.

"Abi, please look at me." When she did, he continued. "I'm so sorry I invaded your privacy, but when I stepped in there, I couldn't stop staring. You are so unbelievably talented. I don't think you realize how talented you are. Your painting of the view from our hike is absolutely stunning."

She shifted her gaze back down, clearly not believing him.

He stood up and pulled her up with him. "Come on."

"Where?"

"Just come with me," he said. He pulled her down the hallway by her hand and entered her studio. She started to shrink away and retreat, but he wrapped an arm around her shoulders and led her over to her easel where the painting from their hike still sat. "This," he motioned at the painting and then gestured at the entire room, "is perfection."

She started to shake her head, but he cut her off.

"No. You have so much talent. I don't know why you hide it."

She stood silent for a few minutes and he waited. Eventually she looked over at him, her eyebrows furrowed. "Are you just saying that?"

His eyes widened. "Are you crazy? No! I would never say that if I didn't believe it. I mean, look at this." He pointed at the painting from the hike. "This looks *exactly* like the view from the hike. It's exactly as I remember it. And I don't recall you taking a picture which means you did this from memory. It's unbelievable!"

A slight smile touched her lips.

His hand grazed her cheek and tilted her chin up to him so she was looking into his eyes. Her eyes darted away briefly but rested back on his. "I would never lie to you about this. I hope you believe me."

She stood on her tiptoes and kissed him. His fingers buried into her hair as he deepened the pressure. The sweet taste of syrup lingered on her lips and a slight hint of sweat hit his nose reminding him of their long, strenuous night. He groaned as he felt the blood draining from his head. He needed her.

Never breaking contact with her lips, he walked her backwards into her bedroom and pushed her onto the bed. Climbing on top of her, he ran a trail of kisses from her lips, down her chin to her chest, and nipped at her nipple through her nightgown. His fingers skirted up her thigh and found that she wasn't wearing any panties. As he ran a finger over her, she bucked against his hand.

"Still piqued from last night, huh?"

She only moaned in response as his finger slipped between her wet folds. Her wetness made him even harder making it difficult for him to refrain. His fingers gripped her nightgown and pulled it off swiftly, along with his boxers. Aligning himself with her and with her resounding 'yes,' he slid in and watched her eyes roll back as she arched her back beneath him. They moved in unison as her walls clenched beneath him, her sweet arousal hitting his nose as she milked him accompanied by her moan of pleasure.

His balls tingled as he came close to his release making it hard for him to hold on for too long. Before he knew it, he shuddered as he exploded into her, releasing all of his pent up sexual desires. They both collapsed, out of breath.

Dragging themselves out of bed, Abigail pulled him to the bathroom. They managed to get through the whole shower without having sex, but the sexual tension was high. He caught her watching him on multiple occasions and he had to refrain from taking her again.

Shutting the water off, he stepped out first and held a towel out for her. Beads of water dropped from her hair and ran down her chest. He followed one as it ran beneath the towel covering her up. He groaned and she flushed at his response.

She pushed him up against the wall as she yanked his towel off of his waist. He didn't need much convincing as he was pulling hers off as well. Grabbing below her butt, he lifted her up to him as her legs came around his waist to support her weight. He set her on the edge of the vanity and entered her hard. She gasped and dropped her head back as he continued the sweet assault, loving that he could be rough and she craved every ounce of it. They both shuddered, climaxing quickly. This had to be a new record. Sex had continued all night and now all morning, and there was no one else he would rather be with.

He dropped his head into the crook of her neck, catching his breath. Despite all of the orgasms they had had, he wasn't sure that he was quite satisfied yet, but didn't want to wear her out.

Her hips rocked against him and she wrapped her legs tighter around his waist, pulling him closer so he sank just a little deeper when his shaft hardened again. She quivered, her body gripped his deliciously.

She leaned forward and kissed along his jawline and down his neck to his collarbone. "Abi," he moaned. His mind flashed. He knew he was in Abigail's bathroom, but his brain was playing tricks on him as past emotions started to flood into his head. He wasn't quite sure what the trigger was, but it was somewhere in his neck.

She rocked her hips against his and continued to run kisses down his neck. He thickened in her, knowing it was her he was with, but his brain was still confused.

He breathed heavily trying to fight the flashback, trying to force his brain to remember he was with Abigail, the woman he wanted to be with. The woman he was falling head over heels in love with. His eyes clenched tightly shut and his hands balled into fists. Her movement stopped just in time for him to gather his wits again, thankful for the reprieve.

He didn't know what she was doing, but realized she was worried when she scooted back slowly to pull him out of her. He grabbed her hips to halt her movement, worried she'd trigger him again. He needed to clear his head before she could move or else risk being tossed back into his head of age old memories he'd rather not recall.

She sucked in a breath, knocking him back into reality. His eyes flew open and he studied her face, worried he'd hurt her. His hands stayed on her hips, but took care not to grip tightly.

"I'm okay," she reassured him, a small smile at her lips.

She's incredible.

He pulled her to him and sank deep. She moaned. Her legs were wrapped tightly around him and they were as close as they could be. He pulled her hips and slammed her back to him, wanting to make her scream in pleasure—needing her to know that she was his and that he was hers. And only hers.

He repeated his movement several times and then carried her to the bed and dropped her on it. She stared back at him, her eyes clouded with desire, and he knew he had her.

He crawled onto the bed and then flipped her over and entered her from behind. She inhaled as he entered her. Every time he pulled out, he thrust in just a little bit harder, trying to fill her like she had never been filled before. He plunged deeper and deeper until he felt her sex clenching around him. Her body gripped his as they both shuddered and dropped to the bed.

Now, he was satisfied.

~

ABIGAIL WOKE up in Logan's arms as they had slept most of the day away. He stirred when she tried to slide away quietly and pulled her back to him. "Where do you think you're going?"

Wrapping her arms around him, she laid her head on his chest. "Nowhere." She thought back on the last several hours and couldn't help the smile that seemed to be permanently fixed to her face. There was nowhere she would rather be. She hugged him tighter.

Lying against him, her fingers traced his abs. Then it occurred to her. "Did you not have to work today?"

Looking up at his face, he rubbed the sleep from his eyes and met her gaze. "I probably should have, but I've been working so much lately, I think I can afford to take a day off. I may have to go in for a few hours tomorrow or just work extra on Monday."

"I'm sorry."

He frowned down at her. "Sorry for what?"

"Keeping you from your job."

He laughed and rolled over so she was under him. "Because I've had such a horrible day," he said sarcastically. She blushed. "I would take this over work any day," he whispered. Their lips met but before it could turn into more, he pulled back and grabbed her hand, pulling her up with him. "Come on. Let's get cleaned up and eat some food."

They hauled themselves back in the shower, but kept their hands to themselves when they dried off. Hopping in Logan's car, they went out for dinner and decided to see a movie afterward. During the movie, Logan held her hand or kept a hand on her leg the entire time. She smiled inwardly at how far they had come. She hoped he felt the same way, because she was hopelessly in love.

They ended up at his house that night and crawled into his jetted tub together. They took turns massaging each other's back and fell asleep in his bed wrapped in each other's arms. The next morning, she went home so Logan could work for a few hours. He texted her later that night and said he had worked longer than expected and was going to go home to sleep, but would talk to her tomorrow. She frowned at that as she had been hoping to spend the night with him again. Her body longed to feel his next to hers as she lay in bed alone.

Sunday morning came and went without hearing from Logan. She anticipated they would go out when she heard from him, so she had showered and then sat on her couch watching TV while the minutes ticked by slowly. Finally her phone rang and she picked it up quickly, trying to not sound too eager.

"Hey," she said.

"Hi, sweetie. I won't be able to see you today."

Disappointment coursed through her as she looked down at the skirt and blouse she was wearing. Standing up, she went to her bedroom. "Okay. Are you all right?"

His voice sounded... different. "Yeah, I just want to get some work done on my house."

Her spirits lifted slightly. "Do you want me to come help you? Four hands are better than two." This was perfect. The two of them could spend all day together getting things done around his place. It was her hopeless attempt at seeing him.

"No, just stay home and relax."

Her face fell as she sat on her bed. "Okay."

"I'm sorry," he whispered. "Maybe we can get together tomorrow."

She nodded even though he couldn't see her. "Sure."

They said goodnight to each other and hung up. She stared at her phone, frowning. Something was off. She considered going to his house anyway, but didn't want him to get upset with her. Changing back into her sweatpants and t-shirt, she wandered into her art room and sat in front of the easel. She stared at the blank canvas before her and sighed, trying to decide what to paint. Raising her brush to the canvas, her arms seemed to have a will of their own as she let out all of her emotion.

The sun set and a darkness fell over her painting. She sat in the dark room staring at the finished product before her. Her normal cheery pastels had been replaced with dark colors and a nightmarish scene was on display before her. Black trees with curled branches surrounded a little girl in the forest, her one-eyed bear dragging behind her on the pine-needle bed beneath her feet. Faces with yellow eyes appeared in the dark woods watching the little girl as she stared wide-eyed into the distance.

Abigail's stomach growled and she tore herself away from the painting, shaking her head. This one was going to be listed online for sale as soon as possible.

∾

LOGAN STEPPED BACK from the walls and leaned to the side, stretching his back with his hands on his hips. Turning his head, a shallow pop echoed through the room from the temporary satisfaction of his neck releasing tension. The walls were now a deep maroon to accent the bookshelves, the floor nicely polished, everything cleaned spotless.

This room he was proud of. The fact that it was Abigail's favorite room made him enjoy it even more. He imagined her paintings hanging on the walls and decided he needed to ask her if he could have one. He had it bad. That woman was his kryptonite. She could make him weak at the knees and ask for anything from him and he'd give it to her. Furrowing his eyebrows a bit, he worried she would cost him his job. Not because she demanded his time, but because he wanted to spend so much time with her, time he didn't have.

He glanced out the window at the stars peeking through the scarce clouds. He was so engrossed in working on the room to drown his thoughts, he didn't even notice how much time had passed.

Shaking his head, he sighed. Work gnawed at his brain. His head played the words his boss said over and over again. "If you don't work sixty hours a week, you can kiss your job goodbye."

He wondered if he was going to be reamed separately because he had taken Friday off, but so far he hadn't been pulled aside. The office had been bustling Sunday morning when he went in. One of the partners had called a meeting that he hadn't heard about because he had been with Abigail. Thankfully he had dropped into work and stumbled across it otherwise he was sure he would have lost his job over it.

His teeth worried at his bottom lip as he realized he wouldn't be able to see Abigail much with that kind of work schedule. He used the house construction as his way to think things through while working with his hands. The question wasn't whether or not he was going to work the sixty hours... it was for whom.

He shook his head and flicked off the lights in the library. "I need to open my own firm," he mumbled.

14

M onday morning, Al's smile lit up the room as soon as Abigail walked in. It was contagious.

"Whoa. Good weekend?" she asked.

"The best! I spent the entire weekend with Brian. He even made me breakfast."

She listened to him recount his weekend, and she told him how happy she was for him despite the fact that she was worrying about Logan. Al never suspected anything was going on with her; he didn't stop glowing. She laughed at all of the stories he told her about things Brian had done. She was thrilled he had finally found someone who could make him so happy, even if they had only been dating a week.

Her day went by quickly despite her anxiety over Logan. She half expected to find him leaning against her car when she left work, but he was nowhere to be found. By the time she got home, she still hadn't heard from him and the dread built in her chest. When her phone signaled a text message from Logan had come through, her heart beat rapidly.

Working late tonight.

She sank onto the couch and sighed. She sent back a sad

emoticon and dropped her phone on the coffee table and prepared herself for the dread she knew was coming.

Her night was uneventful and she didn't hear from Logan again. She tried to be productive and took photos of her art for the online store she intended to create. It helped to distract her for a few hours, but it didn't last long enough.

After her lack of sleep, she decided it needed to end. She couldn't keep pining over Logan and needed to just not worry about it. Easier said than done, but she found new determination on Tuesday when she arrived at work. For the first time in the last few weeks, she put herself into her work—talking to her patients and carrying light conversation with her co-workers. Her heart twinged once in a while as she thought of Logan and that they may not see each other again, but she tried to force her brain not to worry. He had assured her numerous times that she was the only one he wanted to be with, but she had a gut feeling there was something else going on. A gut feeling she couldn't shake.

Tuesday skated by without hearing from him, but she spent Tuesday night keeping herself busy around her apartment, taking on projects she had kept putting off and researching various websites to sell her art.

She decided to call Kailynn when a text came through from her asking how everything was going.

"How many people have you shown your art to?" Kailynn asked.

Abigail smiled. "I've shown three people."

"And?"

"And they have all loved it so far."

"I knew it!"

Abigail laughed even though she knew Kailynn would rub her victory in Abigail's face. Then Kailynn put Abigail on speaker, so she and her boyfriend could talk to Abigail about the different art websites. He gave her pointers on dos and don'ts, and explained the different outlets for selling. By the end of the conversation, she felt like her head was spinning and she had several pages of notes. She thanked both of them for their time and ended the call. That was definitely something she was going to have to research more.

Wednesday and Thursday, she treated the day the same. She put herself into her work and tried to avoid the dread in her chest. To distract herself, she asked Margi what kind of artwork she liked and brought several pieces for her to consider when she got to work. She lined them up behind Margi's desk so she could look at them.

One of Abigail's patients checked in while they were looking and he peered over the counter.

"Did you paint those?" he asked.

Abigail threw a smile at him and nodded, hesitation gracing her face. She never intended on anyone else seeing these aside from Margi and Al. The familiar feeling of dread crept into her chest as she waited for his next words.

"Those are incredible. You should sign up for the craft fair next month. I bet you could make a killing."

Al happened to step out of the back just as he was saying that. "That is such a great idea, Roger! I'll help you in your booth, Abi."

Abigail looked between the two as they discussed the logistics of everything. "Wait. What?"

Al waved her off as Roger gave him the details of the fair. He apparently was the coordinator for it and was telling Al how to sign up for a booth and the costs. Margi joined in on the conversation, throwing out ideas on how to attract people. Al wrote down all of the information while Abigail stared dumbfounded at them.

"I'm not doing that!"

They all stopped talking and looked at her.

"Guys, seriously. I've never done anything like that."

A second patient entered the lobby at that moment and walked up to the desk, keeping a respectful distance away as she thought they were discussing Roger's chart. She then spotted Abigail's painting that Al had recently hung and walked over to it.

"Wow," she whispered.

"It's beautiful, isn't it?" Al asked.

"Very beautiful."

Al turned and lifted an eyebrow at Abigail.

She raised an eyebrow and pointed a finger at Al. "No."

"When's a better time to start?" Al asked and shrugged before turning back to Roger to discuss the fair.

Abigail looked between them, and then threw her hands up in the air and walked into the back. That was something she would have to talk him down on later. When Al had his mind set on something, it was generally hard to talk him down. But, now she had five people who had seen her work, and Kailynn was right, no bad reviews.

She sat in the chair in her patient room and dropped her chin in her hand. Thinking about the craft fair at this point all ready made her jittery. But would it be so bad to put her art out there? They all clearly enjoyed it. Her nerves were on edge at the thought of baring her soul to the world... or, more specifically, to the local crowd. What if she could have success? What if more people enjoyed her art? She needed to think this one through.

WHEN SHE ARRIVED home Thursday night, she dropped onto her couch and sighed. But a knock on her door pulled her from her thoughts and had her back on her feet quickly. Too quickly for her liking. Swinging it open, she found Logan on the other side with takeout, all smiles.

"Hey, beautiful!" he said.

She let him in and watched him lay everything out on the table, confused. Maybe he had just been working late and she was reading too much into it.

"Abi, come get food." He smiled and gestured to the table.

She sat down and watched him briefly. He was smiling and filling his plate with food from the takeout containers.

"How was your week?" she asked.

He met her eyes and his energy was contagious. "It was great! I've been working late every day this week schmoozing some huge clients, and they decided to transfer all of their funds to me to invest. This is huge, Abi. My boss is over the moon, and I *might* actually get to take a decent vacation for once."

Her worries instantly melted away when he took her hand in his, her chest finally feeling light.

"How was your week?"

She shrugged. "Uneventful."

He kissed the back of her hand and then let it go so she could dish up her plate. "I've been so stressed out about this. I'm glad it's finally over."

They ate the Mexican food he brought and then settled on her couch to watch a movie he rented. He hugged her to his side and kissed the top of her head. "I missed you."

She smiled. "I missed you too."

She leaned against his chest with his arm around her as they watched the movie. When it ended he pulled her face up to his and kissed her deeply. Her fingers tangled in his hair and pulled him closer as her body yearned for his. It had been five days since she had seen him and her body was letting her know. He laid her down on the couch and pulled her shirt up until her chest was exposed. He bit her nipple through her bra and she moaned. Shedding their clothes, he peppered kisses along her neck as her fingers dug into his shoulder. They skipped the foreplay as they were both too eager for each other. He entered her hard. They moved in unison until they quickly came together. Pulling back, he planted a kiss on her lips and got up.

"I really need to head home."

Her eyebrows furrowed as he pulled his clothes on. This was a new one. Normally they at least cuddled together for a few minutes, but here he just got up as soon as he finished.

"Do you want to spend the night?" she asked.

"Tempting, but I have an early day tomorrow and I'm afraid if I stay, we'll have a very... naughty Friday." He winked at her and she blushed, thinking about their last Friday together and the sex-capade that commenced.

She sat up on the couch, and he planted a kiss on her lips and left. She wasn't sure what to think. He was acting normal and explained why he had been busy all week and why he wasn't spending the night, but it still seemed off. There was something he wasn't telling her. She pushed it out of her mind and showered before crawling into bed.

LOGAN LEANED FORWARD on his desk with his chin resting on his fists. He had been staring at the computer for hours. The Voss family had decided to stay with the firm, a huge win for him. He had bent over backwards to keep them around and they finally agreed.

But, the win didn't go to Logan. It went to Paul. Of course, Paul was Logan's boss, so he was going to reap the benefits, but he took *all* of the credit. No thanks to Logan at all. None of the other partners even knew Logan had been working with the family. So when the whole company sat in a meeting earlier that day and every single employee was yelled at for their lack of effort to keep the major clients around, Logan was astounded.

Several of his co-workers glanced his way to gauge his reaction and he was certain he could have caught flies in his open mouth. The real kicker was when Paul reprimanded Logan specifically for his absence, even though the days had been cleared through both Paul and human resources. It was all Logan could do not to get up and walk out.

Maybe he should have walked out.

A knock on his door startled him and he looked up to find Kevin leaning against his doorframe.

"Hey, man," Logan said and rubbed at his eyes.

"Come grab a drink with me."

Logan didn't even think twice before nodding his head and following Kevin out the door. He wondered if he should go to Abigail's place to spend the night with her, but he was so wound up, he knew he wouldn't be good company. He really didn't want to stress her out or unload on her, and since Kevin already knew the situation, it would be better for him to discuss it with him.

They sat on barstools at a bar near their office and ordered drinks. Kevin ordered a beer, but Logan knew he needed more than that, so he ordered a scotch on the rocks. The bartender brought their drinks right away and walked off.

"Dude, you must be pissed," Kevin said.

Logan nodded his head slightly before taking a huge gulp of his drink, feeling the liquid burn down his throat. "That's one way to put it."

"Paul is a dick. He wouldn't be anywhere without the work we all put in, especially with all of the large clients you've been landing lately. Then he goes and takes the credit as if he's a one-man team. Unbelievable."

"I think what pissed me off the most was that he denied my vacation time."

Logan had everything planned out. He was going to try to take a week off and see if Abigail could swing the time off as well. He wanted to go away with her. The weekend in Napa had been so relaxing for him and the thought of doing it again with her by his side was a dream.

Kevin turned on his stool to face Logan. "You asked for vacation?"

"Yeah, I figured with all of the work I've done lately it wouldn't be an issue. Not to mention I have several weeks I haven't taken over the years that I want to use up."

"Huh."

Logan furrowed his eyebrows and looked over at Kevin. Kevin never was a man of few words, so when he all of a sudden had nothing to say, there was a reason for it.

"What?"

"I'm just surprised you asked after taking a few days off the last few weeks."

Logan shrugged. "I needed the time off and it was good to get away. I've worked my ass off for this company for seven years and have never asked for time off. I deserve it."

"Oh I'm not arguing, man. I agree. Everyone in the office needs to take time off before they all have nervous breakdowns from the pressure we are all under. I just meant that I'm surprised you asked for the vacation with how pissed off Paul was about you taking those two days off. That was ballsy."

Logan's ears perked. He knew Paul hadn't been happy with him, but he had never made any comments to Logan about it. He had approved the vacation time when Logan had called in. Granted it was last minute, but it was approved regardless.

"Why was it ballsy? I earned the vacation hours."

"You know Paul. He went around running his mouth about how if anyone gets any ideas about taking vacation time when we've lost large clients, then they'll be fired."

Logan nearly spit out his scotch. "He what?"

"You didn't know?"

"No!" Now it all made sense. When Logan had approached Paul about taking a week off, Paul rolled his eyes dramatically and yelled at him about how there was work to do and he needed to stop expecting special privileges. Logan brushed it off as Paul having a bad day and had planned on asking again later. Being publicly shamed at the meeting made more sense to him now.

"Yeah, dude. You need to be careful. All of the partners have noticed the time you've taken off, not just Paul. There's a lot of gossip going around."

"Such as?"

"Everyone thought you were going to be axed until you brought on that last deal. That saved your ass."

The hairs on the back of Logan's neck stood up. He was that close to being fired and didn't even know it. Here he thought he was a great employee with all of the work he had been doing, but they didn't see it that way. They only noticed when he *wasn't* working. It didn't matter what he did while he *was* working. The problem also was that the partners didn't know the clients he was bringing in and retaining. Only his team members and Paul knew.

His mind went to Abigail. He had always been a workhorse until he saw her at the reunion, then everything changed. He no longer wanted to spend his Friday nights, or any night, working when he could be with her.

And that brought back the age-old question: should he branch out and start his own company?

A resounding 'yes' echoed in his head, but he immediately dismissed the idea. It would take time and money, and he would lose all of the clients with which he had spent time building relationships. Everything would have been for nothing.

Kevin ordered them both another round. "This one's on me, man. I wasn't trying to bum you out. I thought you knew all of this."

Logan clinked his glass against Kevin's beer bottle. "Thanks for telling me."

ABIGAIL DIDN'T EXPECT to hear from Logan during the day on Friday since he was working, so she was able to keep her mind off of him for the most part, but Friday night came and went without hearing from him. She sighed and fell asleep with her phone clutched in her hand. Saturday morning, she woke to find no messages from him. She dragged herself out of her bed and decided to make a productive day for herself. She restocked her apartment with supplies and food. She did her laundry and cleaned the apartment. She even spent time researching the craft fair. The entry fee was a little steep, so she wasn't exactly jumping at the chance to enter. Mentally, she counted how many paintings she would have to sell in order to break even, but even that was a challenge since she wasn't sure what she would even charge for each painting.

Feeling overwhelmed, she shoved her laptop away from her. Chewing on her lip, she considered calling Kailynn, but decided against it when she saw it was already nearing 9 p.m. Suddenly frustrated she still hadn't heard from Logan, she grabbed her phone and opened up a text message.

Did you want to come over tonight?

His response didn't come for a half hour, but when it finally did, it was a sad face.

Schmoozing clients tonight.

She rolled her eyes and dropped her phone. "Yeah, right." When she finally settled down to sleep, a few tears slipped from her eyes. She knew when she wasn't wanted.

She managed to fall asleep, but it was fitful. She dragged herself into the shower first thing and pulled on her butt shorts and a tank top. Leaning into her refrigerator, she was debating on what to eat when a knock interrupted her. She sighed loudly and yanked the door open, her irritation at everything getting the best of her. Logan smiled and leaned in to kiss her. She turned her face just in time for him to kiss her cheek.

He gave her an odd look. "I would love to take you out to breakfast."

She wanted to tell him no, but she loved spending time with him so much that saying no was difficult.

"Okay. Let me change."

He caught her around the waist and pulled her into his chest. "I think you look great just like this."

She laughed, her mood immediately shifting, and stepped away from him, shaking her ass as she walked away. "Somehow I don't think the other patrons would."

He yelled out a few more protests while she changed but gave up when she came out wearing a pair of jean shorts and a tank top with a bra.

They drove over to a local breakfast establishment. After placing their orders, Logan went into detail about a business deal he landed with new clients. He was so excited that he gestured wildly and his eyes lit up at the work he was doing. It was something she could see that he was truly passionate about.

"I think this will really help me gain some footing with management," he said.

"Are they unhappy with you?"

He shrugged. "Honestly? I don't really know. It seems like they

don't really understand how much work I put in, but this will definitely help. They've been wanting us to land new clients, and I did
just that."

She wondered if she was crazy to think he didn't want to be
around her. He was so engrossed in his work that she decided it was
just her being crazy and not him.

Logan left shortly after breakfast, but promised to be back. He
was gone nearly the entire day and during the time, she painted a
picture of the view off of the deck at the resort. She had forgotten to
take a shot of it with her phone, so she tried her hardest to work on it
from memory. Any spot that was hazy, she just filled in with whatever
came to mind. It wasn't like it really mattered anyway. Anyone who
ended up with the art wouldn't know what the original scene was
that inspired this particular painting. She was always too hard on
herself.

When Logan got back to her apartment, he looked exhausted. His
smile didn't quite reach his eyes. He collapsed on the bed and fell
asleep immediately. She watched him as his face relaxed in his sleep.
Dark circles were beneath his eyes that she hadn't noticed at
breakfast.

Poor guy is exhausted.

She swiped some hair off of his forehead and he stirred a bit in
his sleep, but didn't wake up. He had been working so much lately,
that she wondered if he was getting enough sleep at night. Based on
the ragged look of his face, she suspected he wasn't. Then, she felt
guilty. She had wanted him to come over and when he suggested it,
she jumped at the chance since she hadn't seen him much. The
problem was that her apartment put him an additional fifteen
minutes away from work than he would be if he had gone straight
home. So not only was he losing sleep at night driving to her place,
he would lose even more in the morning to get to work.

She couldn't let him do that for her, not if it was making him this
exhausted. She vowed to talk to him about it later before snuggling
up against him and falling asleep.

Her alarm woke them both up and Logan kissed her before slipping out to get an early start on his day.

Her work day passed by quickly and soon she was back at home expecting Logan to call. He called shortly after she arrived and they spoke for an hour about their days before hanging up. She sighed, content, feeling like they were getting back into the swing of things.

The next day, Logan was leaning against her car again when she came outside. She smiled and walked up to him. He looked perplexed, but kissed her and asked if he could come over. While he followed her home, she glanced in the rearview mirror several times, gnawing at the inside of her cheek. She nearly rear-ended a car when she was trying to make out the expression on his face.

Focus Abi.

Parking, she walked to her door with him following close behind. She immediately moved to the couch as she watched his face change from several different emotions. Concerned, she reached for his hand which made him flinch.

"Are you all right?"

His eyes met hers as regret seemed to flash across his face which was quickly masked. "I've just got a lot on my mind."

"Anything you want to talk about?" She hoped he would talk to her. She felt like he had been keeping something from her, but was trying not to read into it too much since she thought she overreacted way too often.

He shook his head. "Can we just sit here a bit?"

She nodded and stayed where she was, watching him. Her heart hurt. He was battling with himself over something. He grabbed her hand and pulled her to his side where she leaned against him and rested her head on his shoulder.

"Abi, I..." He paused. He worried at the bottom of his lip while staring straight ahead.

She leaned up and touched his cheek. "What's wrong?"

His eyes closed as he took a deep breath. "I..." Frustrated, he ran his hands through his hair numerous times and sighed loudly.

She watched his face contort between several different emotions again. This wasn't good. Definitely wasn't good. "Logan, are you—"

He pulled her lips against his feverishly and cut her off. She tried to pull back to ask him what was wrong, but he just applied more pressure, so she gave up and sank into his arms. He pulled her onto his lap, and his lips softened as his feverish kisses turned into light kisses. His fingers ran through her hair as his lips were tender against hers. Slowly undressing while barely breaking contact, his hands gently ran over her body.

Gripping her waist, he picked her up and held her close to him as he walked to her bedroom. She circled her legs around his waist and ran her fingers through his hair.

Lying her gently on the bed, he crawled on top of her, aligning himself with her. He looked into her eyes and he slowly entered her. She sucked in a breath and stared straight back into his eyes. This gaze she could hold. His movements were slow and controlled, not rough and eager like they almost always were.

He brought his head down to hers and softly kissed her lips as they moved in rhythm with each other. His movements gradually picked up the pace, but he still managed to be gentle. He caressed her side with one of his hands while the other tangled in her hair.

"Abi, you are so beautiful," he breathed against her lips.

She ran her hands along his chest and tangled her fingers in his hair to try to increase the pressure on the kiss. He never gave in though. He softly kissed her, and then gazed into her eyes the whole time he pumped into her.

The feeling grew and she tried to place her fingers on it. It was love. This was what making love felt like. Every feeling she had been feeling was being poured back into him. His lips moved against her skin and he gazed into her eyes. He whispered words she couldn't make out, but she knew he felt the same way.

The momentum built as she arched her back. They both gasped as they shuddered together, his head dropping to her chest as they caught their breath.

Logan picked his head up and looked into her eyes as he laid down next to her. He pulled her against his chest and kissed the top of her head. Her arm circled around him as they lay in silence.

"Abi," he whispered.

"Hmm?"

He was silent, so she looked up at him. Lines etched across his face as it crinkled with confusion. She furrowed her brows and reached a hand up to his cheek. "What is it?"

He stared at her for a second longer before letting her go and sliding off of the bed. "I need to go."

Confusion crossed her face as he left the bedroom. She yanked the top sheet off of the bed and wrapped it around herself as she followed him. He was putting his clothes on quickly as if he was in a hurry.

"Logan..."

He ignored her as he pulled on his shorts and shoes.

"Logan, tell me what's wrong."

This time he turned to her. "I'm sorry. This wasn't supposed to happen. I can't do this anymore."

"Logan," she whispered. He couldn't do what anymore? Them? Panic flooded into her chest and she gripped it with her hand as she felt the walls closing in around her. He just made love to her and now he was leaving? It would be one thing if it was a one-night stand, but that was not one-night stand sex. After all of it. After everything they had been through the last several weeks and he was all of a sudden leaving without so much as an explanation.

"If this has to do with how tired you've been, you don't need to come over here. You don't need to see me as often if you need sleep. I'll understand. I can be patient."

He paused briefly as if he were thinking about it, but then continued with pulling on his clothes.

She promised she would be honest with him, so she took that as a last ditch effort. "Truth: I love you, Logan. You've meant so much to me the last several weeks. I love you."

Her only indication that he heard her was he faltered while buttoning his shirt. He took a deep breath, walked quickly over to her, and pecked her on the cheek. "I'm sorry, Abi." Then, he walked out of her apartment.

She expected him to walk back in and tell her he made a mistake, but nothing. She stood like a statue staring at the door, not sure what to think, her heart hammering in her chest.

He wasn't coming back. The weight of it settled on her shoulders.

She covered her mouth with her hand to stifle her cry and sagged to the floor as the tears poured from her eyes.

LOGAN SAT in his car in his driveway and beat his fists against the steering wheel. "Damn it!"

He vowed to never let his emotions get the best of him, but here he was, sitting in his driveway... alone. Breaking up with Abigail was by far the hardest thing he had ever done and it was a rash decision. One minute he was stressing over work, the next minute, he was having sex with his girlfriend, and the next, he was dumping her. He knew he cared about her, but trying to make her happy would be impossible at this point.

Earlier that day, Paul had threatened to fire him. For what? Logan didn't know. He assumed it had to do with asking for vacation after everything he heard from Kevin, but Paul didn't give a reason. He came into Logan's office yelling and threatened to fire him and everyone else on their team, and then stomped out.

Apparently all of the hard work and long hours they had been putting in didn't matter in Paul's eyes. All employees had been placed on a trial basis regardless of how long they had been loyal to the firm. Logan risked losing his job if he wasn't at work for the minimum sixty hours per week, and he had been pushing it ever since he met Abigail. Taking those few days off put him below the sixty hours. He had since made the time up working late nights and on the weekends, but it didn't matter. The damage had been done. The partners didn't see anything except the few days he was absent.

He almost walked out, but he didn't have enough money to fall back on if he couldn't get a new job right away, and opening his own firm was too daunting a challenge.

I should have quit. Would have, could have. While failure was high up on his list of greatest fears, why did he so easily give Abigail up since she was someone he had wanted for so long?

He pictured the look on her face when he had walked out and inwardly cringed. He had hurt her deeply, he knew that. She professed her love and he left. He was scum. He was less than scum. He didn't deserve her. He never had. While he wanted to spare her from being with someone who could only give her a partial relationship and with someone who would never be around due to his work, he never intended on hurting her. That was the last thing he wanted. But he managed to do it anyway.

"I'm a dick," he said out loud to himself.

He turned the key in the ignition and backed out of his driveway. Pulling into her apartment complex's parking lot, he immediately hopped out of his car and jogged to her front door, hand poised to knock. All of the lights in her apartment were off.

She must have gone to bed. He considered waking her up and apologizing, explaining everything that had been happening in his life to cause so much stress, to cause him to collapse, but he hesitated.

The last thing he wanted to do was hurt her even more. All of the stress in his life would burden her. He just knew it. That was something he couldn't put her through. The walls of his world were cracking, and he didn't want her to be there to witness the roof caving in and his inevitable failure. She deserved better. She deserved someone who could financially support her, so she could sell art and do what truly made her happy.

He dropped his hand and backed up.

"Whoa," he whispered. *Where did that come from?* Now he wanted to financially support Abigail? They hadn't even been together very long. He needed to take a step back. That was something he needed to think on.

She is better off without me. Sliding back into his car, he stared back toward her place. His hand hesitated on the gear shift, but then he put his car back into drive and headed toward his house.

She is certainly better off. He sighed.

15

Abigail tossed and turned all night as she tried to figure out what Logan had meant. This wasn't supposed to happen? Well, then why the hell did he come over to her apartment and have sex with her? After all of that time and he left after making love. If one thing was clear, it was that he didn't want a relationship. He just wanted sex. Period. It could never be more than that.

She had never felt so used in her life. Yes, she had consented to having sex with him and knew that a relationship probably wasn't going to grow from it, but she never expected it to feel like she was being ripped apart by wolves.

She felt like she was having panic attacks all night long, gasping for air. Reminding herself that she knew this was going to happen seemed to help relieve the attack, but didn't help the aching in her chest. She cried into her pillow and gripped the sheets, feeling like she was shredding apart from the inside out.

She couldn't believe she had fallen for him. After everything. She should have known better. That was exactly why she tried to avoid getting personal with a guy. No guy truly wants a relationship. And to think she loved him...

She texted Al in the morning, telling him she had the flu and wouldn't be making it in. Lying to her best friend wasn't ideal. Especially because he would find out sooner or later... and he was her boss. She knew she would probably get in trouble for it, but she didn't even care. She lay curled in bed all day as her last few weeks together with Logan played continuously in her head. Looking for some sort of sign on why he left, she never found one. Thinking about their trip to Napa Valley only made it more difficult. He had told her he was falling for her. And to think he had had feelings for her since high school, just like she had had feelings for him. How often did that happen? Was he lying the whole time? She thought they had a real connection that somehow brought them back together ten years later. She cried as her chest ached and felt empty.

Between all of the crying and fidgeting, she managed to fall asleep at some point during the day. Her dreams taunted her which didn't make things any better. All she could dream about was Logan. His face popped up everywhere. It felt like she had seen him every day for her whole life and to suddenly have him ripped out was excruciating.

She managed to sleep a little when night came, but the dreams appeared again and tortured her. Finally at 5 a.m. she decided she wasn't going to lie in bed anymore and got up to get ready for work. Dragging herself to the coffee stand, she ordered her normal latte but with a quad shot. She must have looked pretty awful because the barista gave her a sympathetic look. Pulling into her work parking lot, she sat in her car for a few minutes trying to decide what to say to Al. She worried that if she said anything at all, she would bawl nonstop. She took a few swigs of her coffee and steeled herself.

Walking into the break room, Al immediately stood up and gaped at her. "Abi, go home if you have the flu. I don't want you getting everyone sick."

She shook her head. "I don't have the flu."

"I know you're a workaholic sometimes, but seriously Abi, you look like shit."

"Al, I don't have the flu."

He stared at her for a few moments and took in her state of dress.

Her scrubs were wrinkled and her hair was thrown up haphazardly with fly aways all over the place. She had dark bags under her eyes which were slightly puffy from crying all night, and her eyes were bloodshot. "Honey, if you don't have the flu, then you better explain why you look like you do."

How was she supposed to talk about it? She stared at Al, her best friend, the concern radiating off of his face. She sagged into a chair covering her face with her hands.

"Oh no," she heard him whisper. His footsteps got closer until he was finally sitting next to her. He pulled her against his chest. "Abi, I'm so sorry."

That was all it took. She cried. Not just a few tears down the cheeks. She full-on bawled with ugly sobs and hiccups to follow. He smoothed her hair and said "shh" into her ear as he rocked back and forth. All the dignity she had left was gone in that one moment, and she really hated the feelings Logan brought about in her.

Margi came in at that moment telling them their patients were there, but stopped short. "Oh."

Al said he would be right out, whispered something to her, and then turned his attention back on Abigail. "Abi, what happened?"

She sat back and rubbed her face. "I don't know. He came over and we had sex. No, we made love. It was different... special. And then he just left and said it wasn't supposed to happen. Al, I told him I loved him before he walked out and he didn't even respond to it. He just said he was sorry and... left."

Al rubbed her back and sighed. "I'm so sorry, Abi."

She sat in silence for a few minutes. "You should get to your patient, and I need to see mine."

He shook his head. "You're going home. I told Margi to have a temp cover for you. I all ready had one coming in for you anyway since I thought you were still sick."

"But," she said.

He cut her off. "It's not a big deal. Take some time off. You have a ton of vacation anyway. Just let me know when you're ready to come back."

She blew her nose into a tissue he handed her and then nodded and stood up. There was no point arguing with him. He wouldn't budge. "Thank you, Al. I don't know what I'd do without you."

He pulled her in for a hug and they split ways. Walking by Margi's desk was incredibly awkward, but Margi threw Abigail a sympathetic smile and told her to feel better. Abigail thanked her and walked as quickly as she could to her car before any of her patients saw her have a meltdown.

When she pulled up to her apartment, she sighed. She couldn't spend another minute alone there or she would go crazy. At that moment, her phone rang. Part of her hoped it was Logan, but deep down she knew it wasn't. She pulled her phone from her purse and saw her mom was calling.

"Hi, Mom," she said as cheerily as she could.

"Oh, hi sweetie! I was going to leave you a voicemail since I figured you were at work."

Anita's voice was just what she needed to hear. She sighed into the phone as she felt her dam breaking. Next thing she knew, she was bawling into the phone and telling her mom all about Logan and how he left. Of course she left out all of the details that a mother didn't need to know.

"Oh sweetheart," she sighed. "It's all going to be okay."

Abigail clutched the phone tighter to her ear. "I miss you and Dad."

"Well, why don't you come down and visit us? You said Al wants you to take vacation, so take it. And we would love to see you. It's been so long." Even over the phone, Abigail could tell Anita's hopes were getting up. Despite her parents trying to come see her during the holidays, it still felt like she hadn't seen them in years.

A voice in the background could barely be heard, but she knew it was her dad, "Anita, who are you talking to?"

Anita's voice sounded faint briefly as she turned her head away from the phone. "It's Abigail!"

Soon George's voice was coming over the speaker to her. "Hi honey."

"Hi, Dad!" She always smiled at his voice. She usually only spoke to her mom on the phone, so it was a special occasion when she heard her dad's voice.

"George, I was just telling Abigail she should come visit us because Al wants her to take a vacation," Anita said.

"That's a great idea. Come see us," said George.

"You know, that actually sounds like a lot of fun. It would be nice to get away from here for a bit." Her heart stung, and she wanted to add it would be nice to guarantee she wouldn't run into Logan.

"Yeah? Well, you should come," Anita said. Abigail heard clicking on her parents' end of the phone. "All right. It's done!"

Anita squealed and Abigail couldn't help but laugh as she dabbed at her eyes. "What's done?"

"I just booked you a flight! It's at 11 a.m."

Abigail's eyes widened as she looked at the clock. It was already 8 a.m. "Mom! I still need to pack!"

Her parents just laughed on their end. "You better get moving! See you soon, honey! We love you!"

The phone went dead and she just stared at it. That was a quick change in events. She quickly texted Al.

My parents booked me a flight to see them. Will most likely be gone a week.

So glad to hear that. Have a blast!

She hopped out of her car and ran into her apartment. Quickly grabbing her suitcase, she threw a few different outfits together without thinking. She wasn't too concerned about the clothes since she figured it would be low-key as they would just hang out around the house or the beach. She knew her mom would take her shopping at some point though, so she would have new outfits to wear anyway which made it unnecessary to pack much.

After packing her suitcase, she pulled out a small bag she liked to use as her carry on and threw in a book along with some head-phones. When she saw her notebook which had her notes about the art websites she discussed with Kailynn's boyfriend, she grabbed it and tossed it into the bag. There would be no better time than while on a relaxing vacation to focus on her art. Zipping everything up, she double checked the airline reservation her mom emailed her and ran out the door with her bags. Her mom had booked her to fly out of Oakland International Airport which was about an hour and twenty minutes away. She watched the clock as she drove as quickly as she could to the airport without getting pulled over. She managed to get there at 9:45 a.m. and her flight was scheduled to board at 10:30 a.m. Luckily the airport wasn't horribly packed and she was able to get checked in and through security with enough time to stop into a little shop to grab a few magazines and snacks. When she finally boarded her plane and took her seat, she let out a deep breath and was finally able to relax. That was an intense two and a half hours, but it took her mind off of Logan which she was grateful for. Now that she was sitting on the plane heading to Florida, she had way too much time on her hands to think.

WHEN SHE FINALLY LANDED IN Cape Coral, Florida, she breathed a sigh of relief. Being claustrophobic on an airplane could be a little worrisome. She had never had any panic attacks on an airplane before, but she knew it could happen if she felt trapped enough. Turbulence also made it incredibly difficult for her to keep herself calm. Luckily, there wasn't much of it on her flight.

She made her way to baggage claim and stood off to the side while she waited for the carousel to begin spinning. She glanced around for her parents, but couldn't see them. Then, she heard her name being shouted.

When she turned around, Anita was excitedly waving alongside George. She ran up to them and gave them each a long hug and cried. George wrapped his large bear arms around her and pulled her against him. "It's so good to see you, kiddo."

"I've missed you so much," Abigail whispered. They stood as a group in a long family hug and she didn't even feel embarrassed in the slightest. It had been way too long since she had seen her parents.

Finally, they broke away and she wiped at her tears. George asked what her bag looked like and she described it for him as he went to wait at the carousel which was now moving.

Anita put her arm around Abigail and hugged her to her side. She was the same height as Abigail with the same brown hair; although, hers had some gray mixed in. She had a fairly small frame and wore a pair of light blue jeans and a purple short-sleeved button up shirt. Her hair was pulled up into a ponytail and she had a little bit of makeup on her face. The main reason Abigail didn't wear a lot of makeup had to do with the fact that her mom didn't. She was raised to look at herself being beautiful without the help of cosmetics. Although, cosmetics definitely made Abigail feel a little bit better at times.

Overall, Anita and Abigail looked incredibly similar.

George pulled her bag off of the carousel and came toward them. He was a larger man at around six feet tall. He was very muscular as he liked to exercise regularly, but also looked as if he had been enjoying the sweets a little too much lately. His hair was mostly gray, but had been brown when Abigail was growing up. He wore blue jeans and a blue button up shirt. He also had the bushiest eyebrows ever. Anita used to bug him about tweezing or waxing them, but he refused, saying it wasn't manly. They always rolled their eyes at him.

Her parents led her to their car as they chatted about their house and the updates they had done since they had moved there. She listened and smiled along, so happy to finally be away from California and with her family. Pulling up to her parents' house, she stared in awe. Their beach house was lit up as they left on the lights. Expansive windows covered the house completely. Palm trees surrounded the house which had a plush green lawn. A two-car garage was attached to the ranch-style home which was painted yellow with a red door. Inside, her parents gave her the grand tour which started in the living room. A wrap-around couch filled the center of the room and a see-through fireplace on the wall looked into the master bedroom behind it. The kitchen off to the left had a double oven and granite countertops with a large island in the middle. A dining table sat off to the right and large glass sliding doors led out into their backyard which had a pool and access to the Gulf. The master bedroom was exactly like the rooms you would see in a home show. The fireplace off to the left looked into the living room, and off to the right was their bed and a large walk-in closet. A master bath was attached which had granite countertops with a large jetted tub and makeup vanity. They walked by the laundry room and a spare bathroom near the entrance to the garage. Her parents then lead her into the only other room in the house, the guest room. It was just as large as the master, with its own bathroom attached and its own walk-in closet. Abigail's mouth gaped. The pictures her parents had shown her in the past never did it justice.

"Mom, Dad, your house is so beautiful."

Anita smiled. "We're glad you like it. And of course you know we always have this room available for you any time you'd like to visit."

She felt like Anita should have added "hint, hint" onto the end of that sentence. Abigail smiled. "I know. I'll try to make more of an effort to get out here in the future."

Anita looked at her watch. "We should all get to sleep if we want to be somewhat productive tomorrow."

It was 2 a.m., and Abigail could tell her parents were exhausted. They said goodnight and parted ways. As she lay in bed, she picked up her phone and saw that there were no new messages. She sighed and powered it off. She wasn't going to use it again until she went home, she vowed, and slipped it into the nightstand next to the bed.

16

The next morning, Anita, George, and Abigail enjoyed breakfast on their back patio and watched the waves come into the Gulf. It was so relaxing being outside and watching the water, it almost made Abigail forget all of her troubles. Almost.

They made small talk but mainly just enjoyed each other's company. Being an only child, Abigail had always been very close to her parents. They had taken her traveling with them all while she was growing up, so she got to experience much of the world at a young age. She wished most of it had happened when she was older as she would remember more of it and appreciate it more now, but she wouldn't take away the memories of spending the time with them.

They spent the day lying around the house watching movies and playing games. After the late night, none of them cared to exert too much energy, but there wasn't any rush anyway. Logan popped into Abigail's head frequently throughout the day, but she tried her hardest to push him out. He didn't deserve her energy.

At the end of the night, she crawled into bed and stared at the ceiling. She had kept her promise to herself of not looking at her phone, but she was very aware of it in the drawer next to her and was tempted to see if she had any messages. She scolded herself for hoping he would call and shoved the thought aside as she rolled away from the nightstand. A few tears slipped from her eyes as she thought about their last night together. The worst part was, she knew he wasn't thinking of her and wasn't in agony like her. It was unfair. She fell into a fitful sleep and woke up the next morning to her parents banging around in the kitchen.

She stumbled out of bed and into the living room, dropping herself onto the couch. Her parents laughed together as they made breakfast, not yet realizing she was in the room. She watched them as they giggled and her dad put his arms around her mom. He gazed lovingly at her as she mixed up pancake batter. Feeling like she was intruding on their moment, Abigail laid down on the couch and just listened to them.

Tears sprang to her eyes almost instantly. That was what she wanted. She wanted someone to look at her the way her dad looked at her mom. She wanted someone to help her make breakfast for her child. She wanted her own family to wake up to every morning. She wanted a relationship.

She put her hands up to her eyes and wiped at her tears. She had thought Logan could be that person for her. He was the only person she had ever considered as someone she could be with the rest of her life, and now he was gone. The only man she ever loved. And he didn't love her back.

Taking a deep breath, she closed her eyes and tried to take her mind off of Logan as she listened to her parents laughing. Their voices drowned out her thoughts as she focused on them, wishing she had taken the time to come see them during the past few years. She had missed this.

"Abigail?"

She opened her eyes to Anita standing over her.

"How long have you been out here?"

She stood up. "Only a few minutes."

"We made breakfast," she said.

Abigail smiled and joined them on the patio again. She picked at her food, but tried to eat more than she had the day before so they wouldn't question her eating habits. Her appetite was gone and forcing herself to eat was incredibly difficult. She wasn't sure if she had lost weight, but with the looks Anita was giving her, maybe she had. It had only been four days though, so how much weight could she have lost?

After breakfast, Anita asked her if she wanted to go shopping with her, which Abigail said yes to. It wasn't a vacation unless she went shopping with her mom. Anita took Abigail to a nearby mall and they spent hours going into every store and trying everything on. They had a tradition of picking out an outfit for each other in every store. The person was then required to try it on. Sometimes they picked out outfits that they both loved, and sometimes they would pick something crazy just for the laughs. In just about every store Abigail managed to grab the wrong sizes for herself. Normally she was so good at gauging her size that she was beginning to think she had lost weight.

She sighed and looked at herself in the mirror of her dressing room. Her hip bones seemed to jut out a little more, so she had definitely lost some fat around her middle, and she didn't have much to lose as it was. Anita threw some more outfits over the dressing room door for her to try on, which distracted her from scrutinizing herself. Several stores later, Abigail had five shopping bags which Anita matched with her own.

They eventually stopped at a restaurant in the mall to have lunch together. Abigail pored over the menu, but nothing sounded good to her. She ordered a side salad and ignored the look Anita gave her.

"Abigail," she said as soon as the waiter walked away.

Here we go. Abigail sighed.

"You really need to eat more than a side salad. You barely touched your breakfast and have barely touched any of your meals for that matter."

"I'm not hungry, Mom."

Anita put a hand on hers and paused. "You really love him, don't you?"

Tears sprang to her eyes instantly and she took a deep breath to keep them at bay. Grabbing her napkin, she dabbed at her eyes. She nodded as she didn't trust herself to speak.

"I've come to realize that if things are meant to be, they will happen. Just give it time. If you two were meant to be together, you will be."

Abigail smiled through her tears. Her mom, always the optimist. The problem was that even if Logan were to come back, which she didn't expect him to, she didn't know if she could forgive him.

The waiter brought their food over at that time and they changed the subject. Anita kept handing Abigail french fries off of her plate in an attempt to get her to eat. She ate a few to make her mom happy, but food just didn't have the same effect on her anymore.

They continued their shopping trip and ended up in an athletic store. Abigail stared at the shoe section.

Anita came up beside her and looked where she was staring. "Do you need shoes?"

Abigail bit her lip, thinking back to Napa Valley. "Yes, I threw my tennis shoes away recently since they were in bad shape."

Anita started walking in that direction and turned back toward Abigail. "Well, come on then."

They pulled out several different pairs for her to try on and Anita insisted on Abigail getting a pair of bright purple or bright pink shoes. She laughed and settled on a pair of the brightest purple shoes she had ever seen in her life. They were running shoes which she decided were good enough. She wasn't much of an athlete and neither was Anita, so they didn't really know anything about brands. She didn't see any hiking in her future, so running shoes were good enough for her. As she purchased them she wondered how she was going to get all of her new stuff home. Her bags had already doubled since lunch, and despite not packing a full suitcase, she was worried she wouldn't make everything fit.

They called it a day shortly after they left the athletic store and got home just as George was starting dinner. Abigail helped cut up some broccoli to steam as George prepared steaks and Anita made mashed potatoes. They laughed while telling George about some of the outfits they made each other try on in the stores, and after dinner they did a fashion show for him. They knew he didn't care to see the clothes, but they enjoyed having fun with it, and it was a way for him to spend time with the women. Anita had found a few new outfits for him as well, so after they were done parading their clothes, they made him do the same with his new outfits. Abigail laughed until her stomach hurt, something that had been lost on her recently.

When she settled down to sleep, she finally had a smile on her face. She sighed into her pillow as she prayed for a good night's rest.

GOD APPARENTLY DIDN'T HEAR Abigail's prayers as she tossed and turned all night. When she stumbled into the kitchen the next morning her parents immediately stopped talking and stared at her.

"What?" she croaked. She cleared her throat and tried again. "What?"

"Did you sleep, honey?" George asked.

She shook her head and went straight for the coffee pot. There was complete silence behind her as she filled a mug with the black coffee. She opened the fridge and pulled out the milk to dilute it a bit and then turned back around. They both gave her concerned looks. "I'm fine."

She sat at the kitchen table and busied herself looking at the newspaper. The local news didn't particularly interest her, but she didn't want to have to deal with their prying looks. After a few minutes of total silence she sighed and turned back around. They were still standing where she had left them, watching her.

"I think you should go see a doctor, honey," Anita said.

She rolled her eyes. "I don't need a doctor, Mom."

"You're really starting to worry us," George chimed in. "You've barely eaten, you look like you haven't slept in days, and you're becoming thinner right before our eyes. At first I assumed it was jet lag, but this was your third night here. You should be sleeping better by now."

Turning back toward the table, she took a swig from her cup. "I'll be fine. Stop worrying."

She knew they were having a silent conversation behind her. It was like they used to do when she was growing up and they didn't want her to know what they were saying. They would have a whole conversation just by looking at each other. It was insanely freaky. A few minutes passed before she heard them moving around again which meant they decided on something, which also made her slightly nervous. But she was an adult, it's not like they could force her to do something.

They ate breakfast and she made every effort to eat more than she had lately just to put their minds at ease. They watched her plate with those judgmental eyes of theirs.

She rolled her eyes at them. "Stop it."

They just shrugged and pretended to look around while eating, but somehow their eyes always managed to come back to her plate. When they finally finished their breakfast, she told them she would clean up, but they insisted on doing it and told her to go relax. Being forced out of the kitchen made her go to her bathroom to take a shower. Her reflection stared back at her in the mirror. She had dark bags under her eyes and she could swear her face looked thinner. Her brown eyes looked hollow and sunken into her face while they were a shade of red from the lack of sleep. If it was possible, she had wrinkles around her eyes that looked sad.

And now she knew why her parents were so concerned.

The shower took every ounce of energy out of her body, so she fell straight onto her bed afterward to relax for a few minutes before joining her parents. Her eyes slowly drifted shut and, blissfully, she fell into a slumber.

She woke up a short few hours later, but a few hours were better than nothing. She felt infinitely better and walked out into the living room where her parents were reading on the couch.

Anita smiled up at her. "Did you sleep okay?"

She nodded. "Actually, yes. I feel a lot better."

"You look a lot better," George said.

They sat on the couch in silence as her parents continued to read, and then suddenly, Anita looked up.

"Abigail, how has your painting been going? Are you doing much of it lately?"

George set his newspaper down, focusing on Abigail.

She shrugged. "Yes, sometimes. You know me, I get in my moments."

"Have you thought about doing any fairs or websites?" George asked.

She narrowed her eyes. "Who put you up to this? Did Kailynn call you? Or Al?"

They looked at each other and then back at her in confusion.

"Kailynn? I thought you weren't speaking to her," Anita said.

"We saw each other at the reunion and have recently started speaking again."

"Oh that's wonderful, honey. I always liked Kailynn."

"So she didn't call?"

Anita shook her head. "Al didn't either."

"We just thought that maybe you should try selling some of your art. And there's a craft fair coming up in a few weeks. Maybe if you're still here, you could get a booth," George said.

What were the chances that both her parents and Al would suggest she enter a craft fair within a few days of each other? There was something in the water, she decided.

"There's no way I would be able to paint enough material for a fair in a few weeks. Plus, I don't have any of my supplies, and I have a job I need to go home to."

Her parents looked at each other and shrugged before her dad jumped in. "It was just an idea."

Then they went back to their reading materials. Abigail wasn't in the mood for reading, so after a few minutes, she went back into her room to change into her swimsuit. If she was going to be lying around, she figured it might as well be in the sun. Grabbing a towel, she walked out onto her parents' lawn and laid it on the grass over-looking the gulf. Lying on the towel, she stared up at the sky and watched the clouds, making out different shapes like she did as a kid.

A giraffe. A lion. A seahorse. Logan.

Logan.

She took a deep breath and stared at his face she made out in the cloud. Even in cloud form, he was perfect. A single tear slipped from her eye and trailed down her face. She couldn't recall a time in her life when she felt more devastated and broken hearted than she did now. The weight of her grief crushed her chest, but she couldn't tear her eyes away. She reached her hand up in an effort to stroke his cheek and ask what happened, but shook herself back to reality. She let out a shaky breath and dropped her arm, watching as the cloud shifted into another form.

Closing her eyes, she took several deep breaths and concentrated on clearing her head. When she opened her eyes again she thought about what her mom said: if it's meant to be, it will happen.

She laid outside in the sun for an hour before her parents called her in for lunch. Shaking off her towel, she dropped it on a lounge chair by the pool and put a smile on her face to ease their worries. They made sandwiches for lunch. She forced herself to eat the whole thing even though she suspected they added extra meat, cheese, and vegetables to hers to get more calories in her. She was completely stuffed afterward, but at least they weren't watching her every move anymore.

After lunch, she went back out in the sun and her parents joined her. They spoke easily and laughed together by the pool. The distrac-tion was welcome. She avoided watching the clouds in fear she would see Logan's face again and have a meltdown, giving her parents another reason to be concerned about her. The afternoon turned into the evening and eventually they went to sleep. She rolled around rest-lessly again and only managed to get a few hours of real rest.

17

Lying awake when the sun came up, Abigail stared at the ceiling. Her head lolled to the side as she stared at her nightstand where her phone was located. She never told Al when she was coming back for sure and wondered if she should power it on just to make sure she didn't have any messages from him. Telling herself it was necessary, she grabbed her phone eagerly. Holding her breath, she waited to see if any messages would come up from Logan. No messages came through and she was surprised at the blow she felt. She clutched her chest at the rejection she felt all over again. It really was over. The little bit of hope her heart still held was crushed in that instant. Powering her phone off, she dropped it back into the nightstand and rolled over to try to sleep despite hearing her parents making breakfast in the kitchen.

Anita knocked on her door a while later, but she didn't answer. She lay still hoping her mom would think she was sleeping, but it didn't work. Anita crawled on top of her bed and sat next to Abigail, her back to her. Anita's hand pulled Abigail's hair back. "Are you hungry?"

She shook her head.

"Do you want to talk about it?"

She sighed and rolled over to face her mom. "Mom, I want what you and dad have. And I thought..." Breaking off, she choked back a sob, the grief gripping at her chest.

"You thought you found it with Logan," she finished.

Abigail nodded, unable to speak.

Anita wiped Abigail's tears away. "I know I already said this, but if it's meant to be, it'll happen. Unfortunately that doesn't help your current situation."

Abigail took a deep breath. "I don't know, Mom. Even if he came back, I don't know that I would forgive him."

Anita nodded. "Sometimes your heart won't give you a choice."

She sighed. "I wish I wasn't being controlled by my feelings. I want my appetite to come back and I want to sleep at night."

"You will get out of the slump. Exercise might help with that. Maybe you should take your new shoes on a run. The fresh air might do you some good."

She was right. Abigail needed to exercise and getting out of the house might help as well. She sat up as a burst of energy hit her. "That's a good idea. I think I will do that."

Anita left the room so she could change. Pulling on her new tennis shoes was painless, her blisters had deflated, and new skin had already grown in their place. Tying her hair up, she went out into her parents' neighborhood and started jogging.

Boy was she out of shape. She couldn't have run for more than a quarter mile before she was huffing and puffing. She slowed down to a walk and told herself it was okay to walk during her first day of exercise.

Keeping her mind off of Logan, she looked around at the different houses lining the streets. The roads wound around the canals, and houses lined every free space. She stared in wonder at the beautiful architecture in the area. Coming across a small house at the end of a street, she saw a for sale sign sitting in the front yard. She walked up to it and grabbed a flyer out of curiosity.

Surprisingly, the house was something she could afford. It was small at only 1,500 square feet, but plenty big enough for her, and bigger than her current place. She turned the thought of moving to Florida over in her head. She really had no reason to stay in Modesto aside from Al and her job. Nothing else was keeping her there. Certainly no relationships were. However, her only draw to Florida was her parents. She didn't have any friends there or a job.

She folded the flyer and tucked it into the strap of her sports bra and started jogging back toward her parents' house. The idea of moving to Florida seemed better with each step she took. She breathed in the fresh ocean air and could taste the salt on her lips when she reached their house. Breathing heavily, she made her way inside and walked straight to her bedroom. She pulled the flyer out of her shirt and tucked it into her suitcase. She didn't want to mention her idea to her parents and get their hopes up in case she decided against the move. That wouldn't be fair to them.

When she emerged refreshed, Anita had a plate of food waiting for her at the kitchen table. She surprisingly felt hungry and gulped it down quickly, along with a glass of orange juice. Her parents were lying out by the pool, so she joined them and slipped into the cool water.

"How was the run, sweetheart?" Anita asked.

"Surprisingly nice. Thanks for the suggestion." She dunked under the water real quick as she treaded water in the deep end. "Thanks for breakfast. It was really good."

Anita smiled. "I'm glad you liked it." What she was actually saying was, "I'm glad you ate it."

Abigail treaded water until her legs got too tired, and then swam to the edge, pulling herself out. Lying in the sun, she dried off. By the time she crawled into bed that night, she had a smile on her face and felt like her depression from the morning was a distant memory. Sleeping like a rock, it was the first time she didn't have any dreams of Logan.

∼

Six days. It had been six days since Logan had seen Abigail. He hadn't slept much in those six days and it was apparent to his bosses at work he was basically a zombie in the office. He went through the motions and still managed to land large clients for his firm, but they still weren't satisfied. He was beginning to think it was impossible to please them.

Suddenly his job didn't seem so important, not without Abigail at his side. He couldn't blame his job for his decision to leave her, but he was under so much stress that he managed to convince himself that she was better off. And maybe he was selfish, but now he didn't want her to be with anyone else but him. His boss droned on to him about how he needed to apply himself more to the job despite all of the money he had made them, but Logan had tuned him out. Abigail was on his mind, and she was the only thing that mattered.

"Logan, are you listening to me?"

Logan looked up at Paul and could imagine the steam coming out of his ears based on how red he was in anger. And Logan didn't even care. Here he had pored so much time and effort into his work without so much as a "good job" for bringing on as many large clients as he had. And it drained him. Drained him to the point of leaving Abigail, the woman he was very much in love with. What kind of life was that?

"It's no life," he said softly.

"Excuse me?" Paul said.

Logan realized he wasn't happy. He hadn't been for a long time, and he certainly was not happy enough to stay with this company. "I quit."

Paul's eyes widened as Logan's words hit him. "What?"

Logan stood up and gathered the few personal items he kept at his desk and tossed them into his briefcase. His heart pounded at his rash decision, but he felt lighter. He even felt happier suddenly. "I quit."

"You can't quit!" Panic seized Paul's face.

Logan stopped at that and cracked a smile, which slowly turned into a loud laugh, drawing stares from his co-workers nearby.

Suddenly this was hilarious to him. Maybe it was the delirium from the lack of sleep, or maybe it was because a heavy weight had suddenly been lifted off of his chest. Whatever it was, it was hysterical. "Oh, I can, and I just did."

He snapped his briefcase shut and walked out of his office, passing by Kevin on his way, whose eyes were as wide as saucers. Everyone in the building seemed to be standing, watching the spectacle before them. Logan threw smiles at all of them, suddenly feeling sorry for them that they all still worked for this firm. Paul kept hot on his heels, and Logan had to refrain from skipping in glee.

"If you walk out that door, we will never take you back."

Logan stopped and turned around right at the exit to the building. Glancing around at all of his co-workers, surprise on most of their faces, he looked back at Paul. "I don't need this job." Then he spun on his heel and walked straight out. Abigail was the only thing on his mind.

LOGAN KNOCKED on the door in front of him and waited. There was no answer. He picked up his phone and dialed Abigail's number and it went straight to voicemail. He glanced around the parking lot and didn't see her car.

She was probably at work. He considered driving there, but the conversation they needed to have would be better in the confines of one of their houses. He sighed and sat on the ground in front of her door. Twirling his phone around in his hand, he knew it was likely that she wouldn't be home for a few hours. It was still early, but he couldn't imagine waiting around at his house for her to get off work.

He scrolled to Angie's name in his contacts and hit the call button. Listening to it ring, he wondered if she would answer or if she was in class. When it rang for the fourth time, he let out a sigh. He needed to talk to her or he would go crazy.

"Hey, bro!" She finally picked up on the fifth ring before it was about to hit voicemail.

"Hey, sis."

"Uh oh. What's wrong? What did I do? Or was it Trevor?"

He would have cracked a smile under different circumstances. "Can't a guy just call his sister?"

There was no humor in his voice. The line was silent for a few beats before she replied.

"Are you okay?"

He let out a deep breath. "I screwed up."

He could hear her moving on her end of the phone as things were shifted around. Then it went silent again.

"Tell me what happened."

He recounted the last few weeks of his time with Abigail and went into detail about his workload. Angie listened dutifully and only interrupted on occasion to clarify things.

"Now I'm sitting in front of her apartment door waiting for her to come home."

"Wow."

"I screwed up huge, didn't I?"

"Yes, you did, but there's still a chance you can fix it."

"You really think she might give me a chance?" That's what he was hoping for, but after everything that happened, he didn't expect it. He didn't deserve it, but he knew he had to try.

"Look, Logan. I don't know her. If I were her, it would really depend on the guy. If he had treated me poorly at any point in time, I would tell him to fuck off. That being said, if he were a good guy like you, yes, I probably would give him another chance."

Logan's hopes lifted slightly. "You aren't just saying that since I'm your brother, right?"

"Not at all. I'm being honest. You're a good guy who made a mistake. It happens. Even if it was a colossal mistake."

The corner of his mouth twitched slightly, but didn't quite reach a smile. "Thank you, Angie."

"You're welcome. Do you know what you're going to say?"

He shook his head even though she couldn't see him. "I think I'll start with groveling."

She laughed. "That might be a good place to start."

"Yeah."

"I hate to cut this short, but I need to get to class. Call me later if you want to talk."

"Thank you for listening."

"Anything for my big brother."

They said goodbye and he slipped his phone into his pocket, leaning his head back against her door. Now he only needed to figure out what he could do to prove how sorry he was and to make it up to her.

No pressure at all.

nita and Abigail went to a mall in a neighboring city the next day. Anita somehow managed to talk Abigail into buying a bunch of exercise clothes as she was convinced Abigail had fallen in love with running because she had gone on another run first thing that morning. The main reason she had gone running was to clear her head and look at that house again. She hadn't made any decisions on moving, but the fact that she hadn't tossed the idea completely out of her head had her a little intrigued. Normally she could make a decision fairly quick and not mull over it. Staring at the house again, she still hadn't made up her mind.

When they returned home from the mall, an easel with a large bow attached was set up on the patio. Setting her bags on the floor, Abigail immediately went outside and ran her fingers over the top of it before turning back to Anita and George who were both now standing next to her.

"We thought you might want to paint while you're here," George said.

"Is this because you want me to enter the craft fair?"

George shook his head. "No, we just thought you might like it. We will never push you to do something you don't want."

Tears welled in her eyes. They knew her so well and knew that just by picking up a paintbrush, she could usually make herself feel better. She walked up to them and wrapped her arms around their necks. "Thank you. It's perfect."

Their arms squeezed her quickly and let her go so she could go play with her new toy. She ran her fingers over the brushes and acrylics her dad had picked up. He knew exactly what kinds of tools she liked to use. Setting a canvas upon the easel, she twirled a brush between her fingers and stared at the water.

She knew exactly what she was going to paint.

LOGAN STEPPED out of his car and stared at Abigail's work, her car nowhere to be found. He had spent the day before waiting around her apartment complex until a neighbor came out and told him she hadn't seen Abigail for several days. After calling Abigail's cell several times and repeatedly getting her voicemail immediately, he decided he needed another course of action. Her work was the only other place he could think of that she might be, and if she wasn't there, maybe Al could be of service to him.

Logan paused with his hand on the office door, wondering if Al would even help him. Regardless, he knew he needed to try.

Pushing the door open, he smiled at Margi. "Hi, I was wondering if Abi is in, and if not, could I speak to Al?"

"Abi is on vacation this week. Are you here for an appointment, dear?"

Margi clearly didn't know who he was, which he was thankful for. He wasn't sure how Al would react and half expected to be tossed out, but if he didn't have to battle through her to get to Al, it would be a bit easier.

"No, I don't have an appointment. This is regarding a personal matter."

She told him to have a seat and that she would grab Al as soon as he was done with his patient. He nodded and sat down, looking around the room. There weren't any other people in the waiting room, so Logan was hoping there wouldn't be an issue with Al seeing him. That was assuming Al *would* see him. He wasn't sure what he would do if he refused. He waited about ten minutes and began to think Al was making him wait longer on purpose before Al popped his head into the waiting room.

"Hey..." Logan said and hesitated. Al clearly didn't look happy to see him, but Logan knew he deserved it. After the way he treated Abigail, he expected Al to ask him to leave.

But he didn't. Al only looked him up and down and then sighed. "Come on back."

Logan followed Al, but stopped short when he noticed Abigail's painting on the wall. It was breathtaking. Pressure pushed at the back of his eyes. How he let a woman go who could view something so beautiful, so special, was astonishing to him. She had an amazing talent to see the beauty around them and be able to put it on a canvas.

Al cleared his throat and Logan blinked rapidly looking over at him.

"She painted that," he said.

Logan nodded. "I know," he whispered.

Following Al again, he led him to an office off to the side of the break room that Logan didn't notice the last time he was there. Not that he would have anyway since his eyes were glued to Abigail the entire time. Al pointed for him to sit at a chair across from his desk.

"She's at her parents' house," Al said as soon as they both sat down.

Wow, this is easier than I thought it would be. "Thank you," Logan said. "Do you happen to know their phone number or address? I would like to talk to Abi, but her phone keeps going straight to voicemail."

"Yes, I can get their phone number to you, but that's it. After that, it's all you."

"Of course!"

Al rummaged through some papers and then wrote Abigail's

parents' phone number down on a sticky note and handed it to Logan.

"Thank you!" Logan probably said it a bit more enthusiastically than he should have, and he probably shouldn't have attempted to push his luck, but he was curious. "Why are you helping me?"

"Honestly?" Al said. "Because you look as terrible as Abi did the last time I saw her."

Logan's chest tightened knowing she was in pain because of him. He must have flinched because Al gave him a look saying, don't screw it up this time.

"I'm going to make this right."

Al nodded. "Don't make me regret this."

ABIGAIL SAT BACK and stared at the piece before her. She had painted her parents' backyard, overlooking the gulf. This was one of the easiest pieces she had ever painted and her shoulders all of a sudden felt lighter. She belonged here. She belonged in Florida. The sound of footsteps shook her from her thoughts as she saw Anita approaching.

"Is it okay if I see?"

She nodded.

Anita came around to her side and stared at the freshly painted piece.

"Wow," she whispered.

A rush of joy filled Abigail's chest at her mom's approval. Creating art wasn't an easy thing to do, especially for Abigail. She always second guessed her colors, her layout, everything. And when someone was impressed by her work, she couldn't help the happiness that came over her.

"George, you have to come see this," Anita shouted.

George came outside a minute later and was staring at her painting. "Abigail, you are so talented. I don't know where you get it because it certainly didn't come from us."

She smiled. "Thank you."

Anita put an arm around Abigail's waist. "Have you thought more about selling your paintings?"

Nodding, she looked over at her mom and dad. "Yes. Actually, the other day when you mentioned the craft fair, I was surprised because Al was trying to get me to do one back home. Kailynn also is encouraging me to create a website, and her boyfriend gave me pointers. I have been taking pictures of the paintings. I was thinking about setting up an online store soon to see if anyone has any interest."

"I can help you with that! We should work on that while you're here," George said.

Although retired, George used to work in the web design business. He learned to create websites at the last company he worked for and became exceedingly good at it. Abigail was surprised it had never occurred to her to ask him for help.

She nodded. "Yeah, actually, I'd really appreciate the help." And she knew that it would get her butt in gear. She was a procrastinator when it came to projects such as that. The painting she loved and didn't need the motivation to do, it was the work that goes into selling it that was the problem. She loathed that part.

Abigail snapped a picture of the painting and then cleaned up her paint brushes. Her parents carried the rest of the supplies into the house for the night. They spent the rest of the evening talking about the website and the goals for it. She got her parents' opinion on how much she should list the paintings for and did research on what other artists were doing, but hadn't made any decisions quite yet. They looked around at domains and eventually settled on a website specifically geared to help people sell their art—one that Kailynn's boyfriend suggested. George set the page up and found out she needed a business license, so they went through the process of getting her license in California. By the time they were done, she was overwhelmed and so much information was swirling around in her head. The thought of having to file taxes for everything was exhausting, and she was thankful Anita volunteered to read into it for her to find out exactly what she needed to do each year in regards to the sales.

By midnight, they were all tired and decided they would spend the next day uploading all of her art to her new account and place prices on everything. Dropping onto her bed, her head hit the pillow and her body immediately relaxed. Taking a deep breath, she fell asleep quickly.

19

The smell of french toast hitting Abigail's nose put her on her feet in a flash. She popped her head out of her room and saw her parents cooking away in the kitchen. Anita spotted her first and smiled. "French toast is on!"

"Yes!" Abigail shouted. Running back toward her bed, she jammed her feet into her slippers and pulled a robe on around her pajamas. Her appetite was back in full force. Running into the kitchen, she slid a piece of french toast off of the griddle and onto her plate just as it finished cooking. Nothing tasted better than her parents' breakfast foods. Sitting at the table, she plowed through two plates of food before slowing down to take a breath. It felt good to feel the warm buttery goodness sliding down her throat, followed by eggs, hashbrowns, and a glass of milk.

George leaned back in his chair, the newspaper laid out in front of him, a mug of coffee halfway to his mouth. "Slow down."

She raised an eyebrow and shoved another forkful of syrup-slathered french toast into her mouth. "First you're upset I'm not eating enough and now you're telling me to slow down?"

Anita's laughter echoed from the kitchen. "She has a point."

A smile cracked on George's lips. "Eat away."

"Thank you." She took another bite for emphasis although she was full and hadn't planned on eating anymore. Even though her stomach felt like it was extended several inches and weighed down by food, she felt incredibly lighter. She laughed along with her parents as they joked, her heart happy, and the thought of moving there sounding better with each minute.

She loaded the dishwasher while her parents relaxed and then sat at the table with George while he uploaded pictures of her art. Setting prices on each painting was difficult. Her art came from her soul. There was always a piece of her in every stroke whether it be based on her mood or based on how she viewed a particular scene. She didn't feel like the art was worth much, but after much coaxing from her parents, she agreed with their pricing. They made a deal that if any of her art didn't sell but she had hits on her page, then she would lower the prices until she had a fan base and could justify the increase in prices. Although, she didn't actually expect any of that to happen.

The page went live and they all stared in anticipation to see if the visitor counter would increase at all. After what felt like an eternity, she sighed and laughed. They were ridiculous. Obviously people weren't going to find her page *that* fast, despite her hoping they would.

She forced herself out of her chair and told her parents she was going on a run.

Walking back to her bedroom, she threw on a new pair of yoga capris and a tank top with her new tennis shoes. Looking in the mirror, she realized how much weight she had really lost during the last eight days since Logan had left. Her face and hips were thinner. She looked almost sickly, but her eyes didn't look nearly as sunken in as they had before. The bags were smaller since she had finally started sleeping again, but the dark circles weren't completely faded yet; although, she knew they would fade with time.

"This is ending. Now." She made the declaration out loud to make it more final.

She waved at her parents as she stepped out of their house and started a steady jog through the now-familiar streets. Running to where she found the house for sale seemed so appealing now. Not only did the ocean breeze hitting her face make her feel better, she felt better in general being near her parents and wondered if leaving everything else she'd ever known behind would be the right decision to make.

Standing in front of the house, she stared at it and pictured living there. Only a short distance from her parents, she knew she would always have a friendly face nearby. One of the neighbors stepped out of their house and she glanced over at them to gauge their age. She wasn't sure if it was a retirement-type of area or if there were younger families around there. Not that it really mattered in the end. As long as she got along with all of her neighbors, she didn't really care. The neighbor looked to be around her parents' age. In a neighborhood full of retired couples, she wouldn't have to worry about the noise from loud parties, and ideally, there would always be people keeping an eye out for each other since they would be home more often.

She bit her lip as she walked to the side of the house and peered into the back over the fence. A porch overlooked a small pool, similar to her parents' backyard without the gulf access. She pictured herself sitting with her easel on the back porch, painting and selling all of her art online, attending craft fairs with her parents, and gaining a fan base, all while never having to work a day in her life because painting didn't feel like work. It was her outlet. Being able to solely live off of her commissions and never having another care in the world would be the life. She leaned against the fence and sighed. If only she had someone to share it with.

Shaking her head against the thoughts, she jogged back toward her parents' house contemplating calling a realtor, but knew she should bring it up with her parents first. Their opinions always meant a lot to her and while she didn't want to get their hopes up, she knew that the fact that she hadn't made up her mind about the decision at this point meant she was seriously contemplating the move.

With their house in sight, she sprinted the last several hundred feet into their yard and bent over gasping for air. Her lungs wheezed, but she patted her back mentally at the progress she had made with exercising as she sucked in the salty air. Sticking with it for more than two days was progress. Smiling inwardly, she walked toward the front door and stopped dead in her tracks.

Logan was standing in front of her.

20

There she was. Every emotion Logan had been feeling seemed to slap him across the face. He wanted nothing more than to run to her and wrap his arms around her, but he knew he couldn't. She wouldn't be receptive to that, not after everything he had put her through. And he didn't blame her. He ended things pretty terribly. But, now, watching this sweaty, red-face woman, he knew he loved her. His love for her consumed his entire being. He needed to make things right with her.

She looked good. Despite how exhausted she looked from the exercise she just endured, she looked good. He watched as she took a deep breath and waited. Waited for the backlash of his showing up and wondering if her parents had told her he was coming.

She took a few steps back and then turned toward the street, walking away from the house. From *him*. She definitely wasn't expecting to see him, nor was she happy.

He ran after her. He knew he couldn't leave it like this. He had to make her understand that he was stupid. That he was a downright idiot who gave up on someone so amazing, so right for him for something so wrong for him. He needed to tell her. He needed *her*.

Coming around the front of her, he held his hands up. "Abi," he started.

She shook her head and tried to walk around him, but he stepped in her path.

"Abi, please."

She turned and walked back toward her parents' house.

He had to make her understand! He stepped in front of her again, half expecting her to slap him or run him over. She looked like a woman on a mission. That mission being to get away from him as fast as she could.

"Abi, I know you hate me. Just please hear me out."

She pshawed and stared at the ground, but she didn't move. That was progress as far as he was concerned.

He reached out, but she took a step back.

"Don't touch me." Her words came out strong and forceful. He didn't expect it to come out any other way. He was a cruel person. He deserved it.

He held his hands up to show her he wouldn't touch her, but her eyes were still downcast. Eventually he dropped his hands and clasped them in front of him. He needed to keep himself at bay or he knew he would reach out again. He longed to wrap his arms around her.

"Can we please talk?" he asked.

She shook her head and stepped around him, reaching for the door knob. "Leave me alone."

His heart hammered. *No. I can't lose her. Not like this!*

The pressure suddenly pressed against the back of his eyes and he wondered if he would be able to keep himself standing when all he wanted to do was fall at her feet.

"Abi," his voice broke, the emotion pressing against his throat. All the words he wanted to say were right there, but he wanted to make sure she was willing to listen. He needed her to listen.

She hesitated and he held his breath.

Please, please.

She sighed and turned around to look at him. She gave him a

once over, which he couldn't blame her. He looked pretty awful. His clothes were wrinkled and his hair disheveled from the red-eye he took. He hadn't had a chance to freshen up, but didn't plan on it. He wanted to see her as soon as possible. It had been far too long since he had laid eyes on her.

He had an awful layover that lasted five hours during the middle of the night. The entire airport was a ghost town and no shops were open, so he just sat and tried to think of what he'd say to Abigail. There was so much he needed to say, but was worried he could never put it into words. And whatever he said, it would never be enough. It could never express how deeply sorry he was.

She sighed again. "You have five minutes, nothing more."

Five minutes!

That was a godsend. Five minutes was an eternity for him. His body seemed to come alive as he scraped all of the cobwebs off of his brain. He was going to win her back if it was the last thing he did.

She nodded toward the front door and walked inside. He followed closely behind, still worried she'd slam the door in his face, which he wouldn't blame her for doing. He certainly deserved it.

Two older people were sitting in the living room reading the newspaper, presumably her parents. The woman stood up when they entered and walked over to him.

"You must be Logan," she said.

"Hi, Mrs. Green. It's nice to meet you in person." And it certainly was. If it wasn't for this woman, he wouldn't be standing there right now. He knew it must have put her in a tricky spot to allow Logan to come, and by the wide-eyed look on Abigail's face, it was tricky for her not to tell Abigail.

The man then walked up behind Anita and shook Logan's hand as well.

"Mr. Green, it's nice to meet you."

"What the hell is going on here?" Abigail loudly stated.

Everyone turned to look at her. Anita patted her arm, and he was thankful that she was about to explain what was going on because he didn't want to be under fire for this one, not when he already had so much he needed to apologize for.

"Logan called us to ask permission to come see you."

"And you said yes?" Abigail's voice raised an octave and was suddenly louder.

"Of course I did. If he wants to spend his money to come see you, then there must be a good reason for it."

Abigail blinked at them, still with the wide-eyed stare. And then she shook her head.

"Come on." She led Logan into a bedroom and shut the door behind them. "Your five minutes start now."

He took a step toward her, but she immediately increased the distance by taking a step back.

He sighed. "Abi, I'm so sorry about walking out that night. I know you probably don't believe me or that you hate me or whatever, and I totally deserve it. I was mean and insensitive, and I deserve anything and everything you throw my way."

She looked down. "Okay... I won't deny that. So what are you doing here?"

"I got home that night and I couldn't sleep. I felt like my world had collapsed without you there with me. I thought it would go away because I normally don't get attached to people, but as the days went on, I couldn't stop thinking about it. I picked up my phone so many times to call, but I kept getting your voicemail like your phone was off or something. I wasn't sure if you had blocked me or if you changed your number or what. But I took that as a sign that I needed to come see you to get you to talk to me." He took a deep breath. "I went to your apartment and waited around for you, but your neighbor came out and said she hadn't seen you in a while, so I went to your work. Al told me you had come here."

She sighed and rubbed her eyes. "How did you get my parents' number?"

"Al gave it to me."

She bit her lip, a few emotions crossing her face that he couldn't quite decipher. "So you came to apologize? I will have to think about whether or not I can forgive you. You hurt me badly, and I just can't forget that so easily."

He nodded. "I know. And I don't expect you to."

He tentatively took a step toward her again, hoping she wouldn't pull away. She folded her arms and took a step back, but it didn't discourage him. She averted her eyes and took a deep breath, but he caught it despite her not wanting him to see it. He caught the tears that sprang to her eyes, and it gutted him. She lowered her head.

"Abi, I have to make it up to you."

She blew out a shaky breath. "You don't have to make anything up to me. We weren't dating. We were just fuck buddies, nothing more."

Hearing her call them fuck buddies stung, and he wasn't sure if she believed it or was just saying it as a defense mechanism. But, based on the tears in her eyes, he would take a guess that it was the latter.

"I know you don't believe that," he whispered. He took another step toward her, and she took another one back. He continued until her back hit the wall behind her.

"It doesn't matter what I believe. You made your decision." If her arms hadn't cinched tighter across her chest in an effort not to reach toward him, he may have believed her.

She wanted him as bad as he wanted her. That much he knew, and it gave him the will to continue.

"Abi, that's what I'm trying to tell you. It was the wrong decision." His hand came to her cheek. She flinched, but he gently touched her anyway as he lifted her face up to him. Electricity shot through his body at the slight touch, warming him, piecing him back together.

She shook her head and tried to look away, but he held her face in his hands. "I can't do this again, Logan," she whispered. A few tears managed to slip from her eyes. "You have no idea what it felt like when you left."

"I know how you felt because I felt the same way." He wiped at her tears with his thumbs. She furrowed her eyebrows at him as he caressed her cheek. His other hand rested on her hip and pulled her to him. Her resolve was breaking. He was getting through to her.

"I felt you deserved better than me, but I've realized I want to be selfish and have you all to myself. I know it's not an excuse, but I've been so stressed out with work and all of the pressure they were putting on me. I collapsed. I couldn't take it and feeling like a failure with you made it so hard. I realize I should have told you what was going on, but I wasn't sure what to do as far as work went and I wanted to make the decision on my own. So... I quit."

Her eyebrows flew up. "You quit?"

He nodded. "I love you, Abigail Green. I always have. I was just scared and didn't know what to do because I've never loved someone before, so I made the worst decision possible and left you. It's a decision I will regret for the rest of my life." Her eyes searched his. "Being with you has been the scariest and most thrilling experience of my life, and I don't want it to end. And if you find it in your heart to forgive me, I will spend the rest of my life trying to make it up to you. All I know is how I've felt these last few days, and it has been agony. I know that if you felt a tenth of the pain that I felt, then I have to make it up to you because no one deserves that." His voice dropped to a whisper. "And you definitely don't deserve that."

As much as he tried to hide it, a few tears slid down his cheeks. He couldn't help it. He never wanted to lose her, not again. He needed to have her with him all the time. He would never feel complete without her in his arms. "Please give me another chance. I love you, and I don't want to lose you."

The tears poured down her cheeks. Her hands slid up to his face and wiped his tears away and pulled him down to her. As soon as their lips touched, his body came alive. He wrapped his arms around her as she wrapped hers around his neck. Their tongues mingled and then he placed a few soft kisses on her lips and pulled back. Putting his forehead against hers, he smiled.

"I think my five minutes are up, so I should probably go." He stepped back, but she grabbed his hand and pulled him back to her. He laughed. "I'm guessing my time has been extended."

She nodded and pulled him down into another kiss. His hands slid down to her butt and as he lifted her up, she wrapped her legs around his waist. He set her down on the edge of the bed and sighed against her lips and then pulled back, not intending on it going any further. He didn't want her to think he was there for the wrong reasons.

"I really need to shower," she whispered.

"Yes, you do," he laughed as he suddenly noticed the smell coming off of her.

She slugged his arm. "You aren't doing yourself any favors," she laughed. She stepped toward the bathroom and looked back at him, a questioning look on her face.

"I'm going to go chat with your parents," he said.

She nodded. He stepped toward the door, but quickly turned around and covered the small expanse of the room and kissed her. "I've missed you," he whispered.

"I've missed you," she said and pressed another kiss to his lips.

21

While towel drying her hair, Abigail pulled her phone out of the nightstand and powered it on. No new messages popped up, but she wasn't expecting one this time. She quickly dialed a number and waited for it to ring.

"Well hello, beautiful. It's nice to hear from you." Al's cheerful voice rang out on the other end.

"Al, did you give Logan my parents' phone number?"

Silence followed briefly. "That depends on how it went."

She did her best impression of sobs. "I won't be at work for a while." She sniffled for good measure.

"Rat bastard," he whispered.

She laughed. "No, it went okay. He got here a little bit ago and we talked. We are all right for now."

"Abi! Don't do that to me. You seriously just stressed me out. I just sprouted another gray hair."

"Oh please. And you deserve it for giving their number out like that. Where did you get it anyway? I don't recall ever giving it to you."

Silence followed again.

Her eyebrows raised. "You didn't."

"I may have," he whispered.

"You pulled it from my emergency contact list in my employee file!" It was the only thing that made sense. There was no reason for Al to have her parents' phone number otherwise.

"I may have."

She clicked her tongue against the roof of her mouth. "Shame on you."

They chatted about work for a few minutes and she told him she would most likely be back at work on Monday, but she'd let him know for sure later.

"And Al?" she asked before he could hang up.

"Yes, sweetie?"

"Thank you."

"It was my pleasure."

STEPPING OUT OF HER BEDROOM, Abigail found her parents and Logan huddled around a laptop on the dining room table. George looked up. "Honey, come here!"

She walked up behind them so she could see the screen and raised her eyebrows. There were notifications that she had sold two paintings.

"What? Seriously? How is that even possible?" The surprise in her voice was evident as three heads turned in her direction.

"You're incredibly talented. You shouldn't be so surprised," Logan said. His arm slinked around her waist, pulling her to his side.

She smiled at him briefly and then looked back at the screen. "How did people even find my page so quickly?"

George shrugged. "I may have spent a little money to advertise your page on the main page for this website."

"You did what? Dad! I need to pay you back!"

Anita interjected. "You will do no such thing. We are just happy you are finally realizing your talent and trying to sell your art."

Abigail's eyes welled as she hugged each of them. Then she

fanned her face with her hands trying to keep the tears at bay. "I'm going to need to go home soon to package those paintings up."

Her parents looked at each other and then looked at them. "How about we all go to dinner tonight to celebrate?" Anita suggested.

They all agreed on a time and place. Her parents told them they were going swimming so they could have the house to themselves for a bit. Logan had a rental car parked out front with his suitcase still in the trunk. He hadn't checked into a hotel yet and hadn't thought that far ahead. Her parents told him he could stay with them and in Abigail's room if it was okay with her. She hesitated, but only for a moment. She wanted to be near him, but at the same time, she worried he would leave again. And with him staying in her room, it made it feel like she was letting him off the hook too easy.

On the other hand, she knew she wanted to spend time with him and if he left to go to a hotel, she would be constantly waiting for him to come back. It made more sense for him to stay.

He carried his suitcase inside and dropped it on the bed to grab his swim trunks. She changed into her bikini quickly while he was outside.

"Your dad showed me the painting you did while you were here."

Pulling a sarong around her swimsuit, Abigail looked up at him briefly and hesitated. He hadn't exactly said anything about it, so she wasn't quite sure how to respond.

He caught her hand between his and pulled her to him. "It's so beautiful. You have a real eye for painting."

She blushed and tucked some hair behind her ear. "It's just a hobby."

"A hobby that could take you places."

Looking at him, she furrowed her eyebrows a bit and then shifted her gaze down. It wasn't that she didn't believe that he thought she had talent, she just found it a bit strange. Painting wasn't something she discussed with most people. Her paintings felt highly personal and showing people was like baring her soul. It didn't seem daunting for a stranger to see them on her new website, but it was difficult for someone she knew to see them. Her parents were the exception since they'd seen her paintings in all stages and had watched her develop her talent. They were the reason she was even painting as much as she was, from buying her her first children's easel as soon as she could hold a paintbrush to putting her in art classes once they realized she had a knack for it. She really owed everything to them. And now knowing that she could sell her art online didn't make her forget the fact that she could have what she wanted with that little house down the street. With the exception of Logan, who lived in California. She bit her lip.

Logan's fingers found her chin and tipped her face up to his. "What's wrong?"

"It's nothing. I just..." What did she want now? If she moved to Florida, she would give up her relationship with Logan. But he had left her. He could so easily do it again. And she certainly shouldn't base her decision off of being with him.

"It's just what?"

She sighed and pulled away from him. He immediately reached out to grab her hands, but she shook her head. "I want to show you something." She reached into her suitcase and pulled out the flyer for the house and handed it to him.

His eyes scanned over it. "It's a very nice house. Are your parents looking to buy another one?"

She shook her head.

"Oh," he said and sat on the edge of the bed, understanding dawning on him. "Are you going to buy it?"

She sat down next to him and stared at her fingers. "I'm not sure. I haven't made up my mind yet. I didn't think I'd see you again."

He set the flyer next to him and turned to face her, grabbing her hands. "Well, I'd be lying if I said I want you to move here. But, I don't want to hold you back from something you want. If you want this, I'll support you, and we can find a way to make it work. Maybe I could even start my own practice down here."

Her eyes welled suddenly against her will. He was actually considering moving to be near her and she hadn't even decided if she was going to. She wrapped her arms around him and buried her face in the crook of his neck. "Thank you. It means a lot for you to say that."

His arms pulled her tighter to him. "I want you to be happy. I need you to be happy. So if this is what you decide, we can make it work. But you need to make that decision for *you*."

She nodded against him and pulled back to see his face. "How did I get so lucky?"

He shook his head. "I'm the lucky one."

In that moment, she knew everything would be okay.

SNEAK PEEK!

Read on for a sneak peek of book 2 of the What If series titled The Meeting, featuring Kailynn and Chase.

THE MEETING
CHAPTER 1

K ailynn Winters brushed her auburn hair out of her eyes as she stared at the dress before her. It was already on a mannequin waiting for its close up to be posted on the website, but something was missing.

She chewed on her lower lip, a pin in her hand ready to pierce the fabric. But she needed to know what to pierce first. Doing a slow walk around the dress, she eyed it.

Drew, her boyfriend of nine years and her business partner, walked into the room. He noisily shuffled some papers on the table behind her, and she had to refrain from snapping at him. She was trying to concentrate! Couldn't he see that?

Several minutes went by with him being noisy and her circling the mannequin before she tossed her hands in the air.

"I give up! This dress is shit."

Drew walked over and looked at the dress. He peered down at it past his black-rimmed glasses. She used to find those glasses sexy on him, but right now, they made him look like a critic.

"It's good enough. Just take the picture so I can upload it."

She shot daggers at him through her eyes. "Good enough? I don't sell items that are good enough. I sell items that are great! Or fantastic!"

Her high school friend and marketer Jessica walked into the room. Jessica had come onto their team back in the beginning when they opened the company seven years ago. She used to give them suggestions for marketing Kailynn's work while Drew handled the business side and website. Eventually, he convinced Kailynn they needed more help. Jessica had another job, so she only helped them occasionally, or when they asked her to come by when Kailynn got a lot of items out in quick succession. It had been a long time since that had happened.

He rolled his eyes. "Seriously, Kailynn? We need to upload new stuff and you've been on a bit of a dry spell. Just call it good and move on."

"That's not who I am. You know that."

He shook his head and shoved his laptop into his bag. "Well, maybe you should think about changing."

She lifted an eyebrow. *Who the hell does he think he is?*

He rolled his eyes. Again.

"You know what I'm saying." And then he left.

Jessica watched Drew walk away before walking over to Kailynn. She looked over the dress.

"Kailynn, it's beautiful. I don't think there's much more that could be added to it unless you want more sparkle."

Kailynn didn't hear what she said, though. She still fumed as she stared at the door where he had just left. So much for support.

"He just told me to change. What the hell was that?"

Jessica leaned against the table. "I don't think he meant that."

"Yeah, he did." She sighed. "We haven't had the best go at our relationship lately."

"You guys will work it out. You always do." Jessica patted Kailynn's shoulder before walking toward the door. "I'm going to call it a night. Text me when you get out of here. I want to make sure you aren't up all night."

Kailynn waved and rolled her eyes. "Yeah, yeah. Night."

But she would text Jessica. She always did. It was nice having someone care about her wellbeing.

Finally, she looked back at the mannequin and snapped her fingers. "Bling! It needs bling!"

~

SEVERAL HOURS LATER, Kailynn drove home. It was already late, but she wouldn't hear the end of it if she didn't call Jessica.

Jessica picked up on the first ring and sounded out of breath.

"Did you finally leave?"

"Yes. It just needed a little bling. It's ready to go up on the site."

"That's great! I knew you'd finish."

A commotion sounded in the background and a muffled voice along with a door closing had Kailynn raising an eyebrow.

"Did I just interrupt some sexy time?"

"Um. Well... uh... no?"

"Are you sure? Because it sounds like you just asked me a question."

Jessica remained silent.

Kailynn laughed. "C'mon Jess! You can't leave me hanging! Where did you meet him?"

"At work."

"At work? I thought you said all of those guys are old. Oh my God! Is he robbing the cradle?"

Jessica laughed. "No. He's around my age."

"Do tell!" Kailynn said. If she wasn't getting any, at least she could live vicariously through Jessica.

"Not much to tell, really."

This gave Kailynn pause. "Why are you being so secretive? Are you embarrassed?'

Jessica and Kailynn usually told each other everything. Jessica knew all about the train wreck of a relationship Kailynn had with Drew. It hadn't occurred to her that Jessica would stop sharing. And if she thought about it, it had been a few years since Jessica had told her much of anything about her dating life.

"No. I just don't really want to talk about it."

"Oh. Okay." Kailynn paused as her apartment complex came into view. "I'm just getting home. I should let you go."

They said their goodbyes as she pulled into a parking spot.

Kailynn let herself into the small apartment she shared with Drew. He sat on the couch flipping through the channels on the TV and didn't acknowledge her. She set her purse on the table and immediately walked into the kitchen and pulled out a wine glass, pouring herself a hefty glass of Cabernet Sauvignon. Leaning her back against the counter, she sighed and took a long drink.

She had spent the rest of the evening in the office sewing on some bling to the waist of the dress. When she was finally satisfied, she took several photos to be uploaded to the website. Lately, things had been off. She still couldn't pinpoint exactly what it was, but she was not flowing as well as she usually did. Her mind seemed to be scattered, and she had a difficult time focusing on one project. Nothing ever felt good enough, so she would scrap the project and start on a new one, only to repeat the process. It was becoming ridiculous. And it was nothing like her.

A pile of clothes sat in the corner of her office, reminding her of all the projects she had decided weren't good enough. Maybe she *was* being too hard on herself.

Or maybe the items weren't good enough.

She sighed and picked up her phone, intending to call her friend Abi. After seeing the time, she set her phone back down. Tomorrow. She'd call her tomorrow. She didn't want to bother Jessica again since she hadn't seemed in the mood to talk.

A sudden sadness washed over her as she stared at Drew sitting on the couch in the other room. It wasn't like it used to be. When she used to spend late nights at the office, he would either hang out with her cheering her on until she was ready to leave or she would come home to find a hot bath drawn for her with a glass of wine waiting.

Now? Now, he didn't even acknowledge her. And she wasn't sure when things had changed.

Maybe things had gone stale and couldn't be fixed. But maybe not.

She walked over to the living room and sat down on the couch next to him. He didn't even look away from the screen.

"So," she said. "I finished the dress and took the pictures."

"Oh yeah? Finally. It'll be good to get something new up."

Finally? She rolled her eyes. Yes, it had been a while. Yes, she was a perfectionist. But she didn't want poor designs linked to her name floating around out there. It could be potential career suicide. Besides, there was nothing wrong with being particular.

She waited in silence. When he said nothing else, she prodded.

"Would you like to see the final product?"

He glanced at her briefly and gave her a strange look before turning back to the television. "No, I'm sure it's fine. It was fine before I left today, and I'll see it when I upload it."

"That's not why..." she drifted off. Was it too much to ask for support? To ask him to be interested in her work? To ask him to care and get excited about the designs she was creating?

"Never mind."

Silence passed between them. She took another sip of her wine, twirling the stem of the glass between her fingers.

"So, I've been thinking." She waited for him to look at her, but when he didn't, she continued anyway, "Maybe you're right about the other projects I've set aside. Maybe they are good enough."

"Told you so," was all he said.

She refrained from sighing. "Maybe you could look at them with me and see what you think."

He looked at her and rolled his eyes. "They're good enough."

"But you don't know what they look like."

"They're probably good enough. Just take pictures, and we'll upload them and see what happens." He turned back toward the TV, dismissing her.

THANK YOU

Thank you for purchasing and reading my book! I am so humbled you would choose mine to read. I really hope you enjoyed it!

One of the best things you can do for an author is leave a review. Please consider leaving one on Amazon and Goodreads. Thank you so much!

~K. M. Ryan

ALSO BY K. M. RYAN

ABOUT THE AUTHOR

K. M. Ryan was born in Spokane, Washington. She knew she wanted to publish a novel at the age of fourteen. Several (unpublished) books later, she finally decided to self-publish at the encouragement of her family and friends. She resides in Nine Mile Falls, Washington with her husband, two children, and one cat.

Find K. M. Ryan on social media!

www.authorkmryan.com
Twitter: @authorkmryan
Facebook: /authorkmryan
Instagram: @authorkmryan
TikTok: @authorkmryan